JUSTUS: THE LASH

Geoffrey Sadler

NEW ENGLISH LIBRARY

A New English Library Original Publication, 1982

First NEL Paperback Edition April 1982

NEL Books are published by
New English Library,
Barnard's Inn, Holborn,
London EC1N 2JR, a division of Hodder and Stoughton Ltd.

Photoset by Parker Typesetting Service, Leicester
Printed and bound in Great Britain by Cox & Wyman, Reading

British Library C.I.P.

Sadler, Geoff

The Lash (Justus: 1)
I. Title II. Series
823'.914[F]   PR6069.A3/

ISBN 0-450-05369-5

The Lash

BREATHING HARD in the dark, he ran.

Running, footsteps splashing ankle-deep where the ground gave way. Coarse swatchgrass standing man-high, feathering the lines of his body as he passed. Brackish water welling at every stride. In front a live-oak leaned, striking with a low bough for his face, and he reached to thrust it aside, ploughing on. Stumbling through the last shaky yards of land, water sheeting now to cover him in a fine clinging spray. Breath heaving harsh in his chest. Head and shoulders sunk. Reeling. Sweating.

Lone shape under the boughs. Running.

Night all around him. Dark and sweating heat. And behind him the noise of the hunters, closing in. He heard them smash through the canebrake back a ways, where his trail showed plain in the sodden earth; felt the ground shake under him to the pounding of their hooves. Cries and curses came after, and the full-throated baying of the hounds. Floundering to stand, he shuddered. They had the smell of him in their nostrils, he knew, live meat to be torn raw from the bone. Once their leashes were slipped, he could forget everything.

Up ahead moonlight struck bright through a tangle of willows, laying a sheen like a thin silver onion-skin on the flat surface of the bayou. Land ran out the same moment and he brought up short, sinking over his waist in water. The touch of it was warm to his body, dark and thick as molasses from the weeds and water-lilies on the surface. For a while he held there, waist-deep, his smooth

5

body gleaming with sweat as he looked about him. Darkness answered the look. Silvered water and the black outlines of trees. Canebrake and underbrush. Through it, the swelling clamour of the hounds as they closed. Fear shook him afresh where he stood, hearing the rasp of his own breath in the stillness, echoing. He swung round, and plunged forward into the bayou.

He trod water, going under. He felt the bayou close over his head, warm and thick and smothering. Filling his eyes, his ears, his mouth. He choked, limbs thrashing as he fought upward for the light of the moon. For a while it seemed that the water would fill him altogether, that his insides would swell and burst loose. . . . He broke surface halfway across the bayou, spewing the warm muck from his mouth, eyes staring wide in terror. Over by the near bank the cry of the hounds came again, louder and more urgent. He dived to the sound, going deep under water. Turning, swimming strongly now as he doubled back towards the shadow of the overhanging trees. Darkness again, and warmth of wetness pressing on him. He came up close by the far bank, where tall cypress trees clustered near to the water's edge. Their weathered knees jutted above his head, rising sharply from the mat of duckweed that covered the surface. Slimed himself, and dripping with the weed, he hauled on the nearest stump, sliding into shadow beyond. There, crouched in the dark, he waited.

Stillness. Foliage hung listless in humid night. Flat stretch of water, immense and shining under the moon. Above him the sky thick with cloud, a velvet black pierced only by moon and stars. Heavy scent of hibiscus and magnolia from the boughs ashore. Putrid reek of rotting cypress logs, and the scum that skinned the bayou top. No wind through the canebrakes. Somewhere distant a heron called, and the hounds gave tongue in answer. The sound of their onrush came to him, clear across the water. Splashing through soft ground where he had run only moments before. He heard, waist-deep in the bayou shallows, and hung to the gnarled stump, trembling.

They burst out from the last of the thickets and pulled in, grouped at the water's edge. The two trackers were first, each struggling to hold in his brace of leashed hounds. Pressed to the

6

cypress stump, the breath of his body heaving against the soaked wood, he watched them. Huge mastiffs, bred for size and strength, lean-bellied and heavy in the chest and shoulder. He saw how even now they fought the leash, snarling and heaving forward to plunge in the shallows where the swatchgrass ended. Slaver hung gleaming at their jaws. The baying sound they made shivered through the cypress trees, and he felt his stomach lurch up for his throat. He bit hard into his lip, fighting down the urge to scream.

Behind the dogs and the men who held them came the riders of the patrol. Horsemen, grouped close together with broad-brimmed hats hiding their faces, slack-limbed and easy in the saddle. Coatless all of them, shirt-sleeved in the evening heat. How many he couldn't rightly tell. More than a dozen, maybe twenty. A few wore belted handguns strapped down at the hip, others had clubs and sheathed knives. One man, riding out to the flank, held a sawn-down shotgun in the crook of his arm. They were laughing still as they reined in back of the hounds, and he watched the corn-jug go from one to the other.

Poor white trash, come along to tree the runaway. By now he guessed they were most of them drunk and out for sport. That in itself did nothing to calm his fear. He'd seen the mauled remains of men taken by the patrollers. Hung wry-necked from a live-oak bough with the flesh flayed off their bones, gouged and chewed over by the hounds. If one of those laughing horsemen sighted him now, he figured he'd take his chances with the dogs.

Lawrence was at the head of the column, riding his grey gelding. Even as the fugitive watched he swung the tall beast broadside-on, stepping lightly through the shallows at the bayou's edge. White starched shirt and cravat gleaming where they caught the moon-light, black broadcloth pants and dark broad-brimmed hat that outmatched the deep colour of night. His clothes and the sleek lines of the horse he rode made a strange contrast with the grimy homespun of his neighbours and the broken-down nags most of them straddled. Lawrence wore a handgun thonged down at the hip, resting his palm on the butt as he rode. It was not that weapon, though, that held the watcher's eye. His look was for the long coiled whip Lawrence had palmed in front of him on the

7

gelding's neck. A heavy blacksnake, two fingers thick at the butt, and tapering to a vicious lash at the tip. Uncoiled, it reached a good twelve feet and had power enough to break a man's back. That, or strip him down to the bone, piece by piece. He clenched his teeth at that, sinking his nails hard into the rotting cypress wood. He had felt the weight of that whip, and not long ago. Right now he wasn't likely to forget the man who owned it.

From its grip of the wood his hand stole down, reaching under water. There in the waistband of his ragged breeches it closed on the cold touch of metal. An eight-inch length of hoop iron, hammered and filed to a keen cutting edge, bound at the haft with thick twine. He'd stripped it from a broken barrel weeks ago, in readiness for this time. Close to, it made a formidable weapon, but right now it was like to be as useless as any busted twig. All the same he held to it, feeling the water lap at his wrist, his glaring eyes on the horseman across the bayou as the old scars itched along his back.

'You see him, Jared?' Lawrence's voice had a shrill edge to it, coming harsh over the water. He swung his fretting mount again, pulling rein as the gelding snorted and kicked, uneasy in the shallows. Air hissed as he shook out the long whip, flicking at the leafy bushes landside of him. At the sound of his voice the laughter stopped, and the bunch of swaying riders behind him came straight in their saddles, sensing trouble.

'Can't say as I see nothin'.' The nearest of the handlers hauled back the straining hounds on the leash, frowning as he spoke. 'Me, I figger we done lost him, Mister Lawrence . . .'

Lawrence struck viciously to clip leaves from a nearby bush, and the horse jerked sideways under him as he swung. The waiting riders, too, flinched at the sudden move. 'Like hell we lost him!' the plantation boss bellowed in anger, his long whip whistling back in the air. 'He's in this bayou someplace, an' I don't aim to leave without him, you hear me?' He half-turned in the saddle, rounding abruptly on the other horsemen, his voice rising afresh. 'You men, you hear me good?'

Muttering, they nodded hurriedly. One, unsteadier than the rest, chuckled loosely as he took a swallow of the corn. Lawrence drove at him with a smothered oath, bludgeoning the thick whip-stock to slam the jug from his hand. Pressed to the rotting stump, hand still clutching the knife-haft under water, the fugitive heard the muffled splashing as the jug went into the bayou, and bit down hard on his lower lip.

'Best do like I tell you, Munson.' Lawrence had control over his voice now, and it bit like iron. He dragged off his tall mount, the whip coiled back at his shoulder. 'We lose him 'cause o' you, and you got trouble. Just bear it in mind, is all.'

He turned again to the darkened bayou, setting his back to the chastened drunk. Around him the rest of the patrol lapsed to an uneasy silence. For a while only the frantic baying of the hounds could be heard.

'They kin still scent him, seems like,' Jared's partner put in. He lurched to stand, biting on his words as they came. From the look of it he had a harder task to keep a grip on the leash. 'Either he's into the water, or he doubled back somehow . . . could be acrost the other side by now, I guess.'

Lawrence grunted at that, lowering the whip. He nudged the gelding, backing from the shallows and alongside the two dis-mounted handlers. For a time he eyed the crying dogs, not speaking. Across the bayou the hidden man clutched at his hoop-iron knife, and shivered.

'Ain't got around us yet,' Lawrence decided. 'We was close on him, he didn't have no time. No, he'll be in the water someplace, an' I reckon he ain't none too far off . . .'

'We could try along the bank a ways,' Jared suggested. Fear was in his voice, as in all the others'. Crouched in shelter, the fugitive guessed that the patrollers knew Lawrence pretty well, at that. 'Maybe he's laired up in the underbrush yonder . . . dogs should bring him outa there in a coupla shakes, I reckon.'

'Uhuh.' It was Lawrence's turn to laugh, an ugly deep-throated sound. He lunged erect in his stirrups, signing with the coiled whip to the men about him. 'We gonna try that. Hooker, take your dogs down by the willows yonder, see if he's hid there. Sim, Clayt, you go with him, beat out them bushes till there ain't nothin' left to find, you hear?'

He chuckled softly stroking the whip-stock alongside his face, hidden still by the dark. Watching as Hooker's leashed mastiffs dashed into the first of the willow thickets by the water's side. Two or three horsemen followed, muttering yet as they rode.

'Jared, take a look at the far side, see if your team can run him down. . . . . Get after him, Burns, an' some of you others . . . take Munson along, he ain't no use to me, drunk as he is.'

'Sure thing, Mister Lawrence.' The handler's answering laugh was forced, uncertain. He hauled on the leash, dragging the clamouring hounds away, stumbling out through the reed-beds that lay far off to the left. Aiming for a shallow reach someplace, where he could get his dogs across. Jared had lived along the river all his life. He'd know where to find it. The man in the water trembled, sweating harder, and hunched himself low in the cypress shade.

'Reckon I'll wait on,' Lawrence was saying as the second group of riders took off after the dogs. He sat his horse solid as a rock, facing across the smooth surface of the bayou, the long whip resting once more on the animal's neck. 'I aim to set right where I am, an' once he comes up for air I'll blast the goddam haid off his shoulders. The dumb bastard!'

Under the water his grip on the knife had begun to pain him, the hard iron biting his palm through its sodden twine. Slowly, cautiously, he loosed hold of the useless weapon, his hand coming again to rest on the slimed wood of the cypress stump. Across the water the dark mounted figure of Lawrence reared tall as a statue against the night. All at once he was grateful for these cypress trees that overhung the bank and held him in shadow.

He heard them crashing a way through the thickets beyond him, the hounds and their snarling calls sounding above the voices of the men. When the noise dropped for an instant, he was aware of his own harsh breathing in the stillness. To his own ears it seemed to ring out over the bayou, louder than the trapped hammering of the heart against his ribs. For a while he got the feeling that Lawrence, too, could hear. That the lone horseman who faced him across the narrow stretch of water was holding back, biding his time, letting his victim sweat. The man who stood to his waist in the dark water stifled a groan. He leaned, resting his face on the rotting stump, fighting to quell the uncontrollable shuddering of his limbs.

Light struck sudden on a crusted log that lay some distance to the left of him. Caught in the moon-gleam the dark shape quivered, its gnarled surface sending back glints of silver fire. Almost as though it took on life, moving as the light fell across it. Alongside in the water ripples spread, fanning in towards his hiding-place. It was then, as the first uncertain twitch of fear went through him, that the log turned, shifting sideways, and he knew that he hadn't been wrong after all.

He pressed his face harder against the cypress stump, sinking his teeth into the rotting wood so as not to scream aloud. Sweat broke afresh from the pores of his body, covering him in a second clammy skin, blinding as it ran into his eyes. The limbs that had trembled now held like stone, paralysed by terror.

Ripples touched, lapping the stump and his own waist as the long shape passed. Peering in spite of himself through the sting of sweat in his eyes, he saw the huge bull gator as it bulked across his line of vision. A great greyish armoured shape, cutting the pattern of moonlight, water arrowing back to either side of its body as it swam. Above the half-sunk snout a pair of close-set eyes glowed red against the night. He heard water scatter to the lazy flick of its passing tail, and dug his teeth deeper in the foul-tasting rot. That tail, and those jaws, would break him apart surer than Lawrence's blacksnake whip. Worse even than the hungry mouths of the dogs. Gators pulled their prey under to drown, often as not, and the thought of being dragged deep in the bayou until his lungs burst was enough to turn him sick.

Up ahead the great shape swung, water churning as it eased halfway back for the place he was hidden. Even as it moved a baying clamour came from the bank, and an outburst of curses from the men in the thickets. Something broke forward against the light and plunged for the water. A heavy splash came back to him as it struck.

At the noise the gator came to life, turning again for the far bank. At once the red glare of eyes was gone, the huge tail lashing as it thrust away through the water. The spray of its wake

11

showered his bent head and he shuddered, looking up slowly. He saw the massive log-shape cleave the bayou towards the sound of struggling in the water, bubbles spitting to burst in the spot where he had lain a moment before. Smell of the gator reached back to him, a rich thick stink that mingled with the scum and the matted weed. He spat out the clinging punk, fighting down the foul taste in his mouth.

Along the bank rose a fresh uproar of voices, and the frantic yammering of hounds. Men and horses started back towards the sound. From close to the water a gun blasted, the sudden explosion throwing echoes that shivered over the bayou and in the fringing trees. Fresh shots followed, their noise swelling, racketing like thunder in the empty space. He saw again the gator's lashing wake as it swung in the water, heading away from the men on the bank. Pistol slugs sent up fountains from the surface close to its body, spatting in the scum and the weeds. The long grey shape outran them, sliding to cover in a reedbed further along the bank. Abruptly the echoes died, leaving only the voices.

'Gahd damn, some gator! Musta been fifteen foot, sure...'

'Where in hell is that dumb dog?'

From behind the cypress stump he caught a glimpse of them, moving back. The mounted figures first, then the dog handlers. They bunched together at the water's edge, looking out across the bayou that now lay still as it had done only moments before. Most of the horsemen were silent, sullen. The dogs no longer yelled, snarling deep in their throats. One handler, the one they called Hooker, held to a single mastiff now. A broken leash trailed from his hand.

Lawrence, as ever, was at their head. Smoke curled still from the gun he held. A shaft of moonlight fell across him and for an instant his face showed, pale and thin-lipped and merciless under the shading brim of the hat he wore. Around him the others glanced up uneasily.

'Figger you musta hit him, Mister Lawrence,' the man called Burns said after a while. From the way his eyes went, it was plain he was thinking about the alligator. The man in the water began to breathe again.

'Didn't look any too painful to me.' Lawrence's features twisted, vicious in anger. 'The hell with the gator! How come you let the hound clear, Hooker? I had you figured better than that.'

'Ain't no fault o' mine. Reckon he just busted loose....' Hooker scowled, glaring down at his feet. He held to the one remaining mastiff with both hands on the leash, grimly. 'One thing, Mister Lawrence, I don't aim to lose no more hounds over your man tonight....'

'Goes for me too,' Jared said.

Lawrence stiffened visibly as they spoke. For a time face and body alike seemed to harden to stone, his free hand clenching on the coiled whip. Slowly, he sheathed the gun.

'Is that right?' His look went over all of them as he spoke. Not a man answered. There was no need. Their faces said it all. Lawrence let go a harsh breath and bit on his lip, still scowling. The silence that followed was strained and hard to bear.

'Like as not the gator took him,' Jared was saying. He scanned the black stretch of water cautiously, gripping his own two dogs. 'He's loose right now, Mister Lawrence. Ain't no use riskin' another good hound for nothin' at all....'

'That's right,' Hooker said, and a number of riders murmured agreement. At the sound, the horseman who led them clenched tighter on his hold of the whip, his pale face contorted in rage.

'Ain't none of you about to change your minds, huh?' Lawrence asked. The same silence answered him.

He touched heels to his gelding, bringing the horse up out of the shallow water and on to the higher ground under the trees. There, half-hidden for the moment in shadow, he glanced back over the bayou.

'At first light, I aim to be back here,' Lawrence said, and his voice grated across the water to the man who crouched sweating in the cypress shade. 'When I find him, he'll sure as hell wish he hadn't run.'

He swung the whip overhead the same instant, the lash taking the crown from a nearby bush with a sharp snapping sound. Beneath him the horse sprang forward, cantering away under the

13

dark hanging boughs. The other horsemen followed, then the handlers, hauling their dogs. Hooker was last, pausing a while to look regretfully across the water. After a time, he too followed. Darkness closed on the vanishing men, and there was silence.

He waited after they had gone, crouching there for a long time, until the blood beat aloud in his ears and the stillness gave way to the hundred sounds of the bayou night. Slowly, breathing hard, he came upright on his feet in the water and stood, looking about him.

Moonlight touched over him as he stood there, slimy yet with the strands of weed that hung from his neck and shoulders. It caught the features of the upraised head, with its black curled fleece of hair. The eyes whose blackness glittered silver-bright under the wide forehead. The thick-lipped mouth and broad heavy jaw beneath the flat stub of nose. The strong powerful lines of the upright body. Deep-chested. Narrow in the flank. The muscles hard as corded wood. The smooth sheen of the skin itself, reflected.

A black skin, polished and midnight dark, sweat-smooth, gleaming under the moon.

Wing-beats above him, sudden and startling in quiet. He lifted his head, watching as the night-owl swooped low over the flat stretch of water, wheeling away to vanish into the dark stand of willows at the far side of the bayou. It called once, softly, as it went, and his dark face paled a shade at the sound. Night-birds was all of them spirits, he knew that. Could be some ghost was calling out to him. Throwing a spell, maybe. He shivered at that, crossing himself. Didn't have no time for no white man's god, but a man couldn't be too careful, not out here in this place.

Quiet again over the bayou. Bright moonlight, splintering pale on the black smooth surface of the water. Moonbeams glinting on the matted duckweed, the thick bubbles that burst with a plopping sound in the carpet of slime. Beyond, the dark standing trees, and the distant gleam of water farther off, along the Atchafalaya.

Downriver they's a big water, Nestor had told him. So big, ain't no land to see. You make it that far, could be you get loose altogether.

He breathed out slowly, shaking himself all over like a dog, as if to throw off the memory of what had been. Turning, he waded through the shallows, laying hold of the massive cypress roots to haul himself up on to the bank. Moonlight shafted over him as he moved, silvering the heavy muscles of his shoulders. It caught, too, the raised knotted weals of the whip-scars that made a paler crosswise pattern on his gleaming back.

Some hours later, blundering out from a canebrake, he collapsed on a reach of soft slushy ground, and slept facedown where he fell.

LAFAYETTE   MARCH 7th, 1865

WANTED: RUNAWAY. VALUABLE PROPERTY OF MR JOHN LAWRENCE OF SWEET RIVER PLANTATION. PRIME STUD BREEDING BUCK, ANSWERS TO NAME OF JUSTUS, SOME TWENTY-FOUR OR FIVE YEARS OF AGE. STANDS ABOVE SIX FOOT TALL, BUILT BROAD AND STRONG. VERY DARK COMPLEXION. HAS A SULLEN DISPOSITION, AND MAY BE ARMED. WHIP SCARS ON BACK, RUNNING CROSSWAYS, FRESH HEALED. HAS BEEN LOOSE FOR TWO DAYS IN THE BAYOU COUNTRY. REWARD OF FIFTY DOLLARS TO THE PERSON WHO SECURES HIM. FOR INFORMATION THAT PROVES GOOD, TWENTY DOLLARS.

MR LAWRENCE SAYS THIS IS ONE MEAN AND DANGEROUS NIGGER. TAKE HIM ALIVE IF YOU CAN. IF NOT, THE MONEY IS STILL YOURS.

E. T. WHITESIDE
SHERIFF, LAFAYETTE COUNTY, LOUISIANA.

TOWARDS MORNING as the sky greyed out, came noise of movement in the water.

It waked him where he lay shielded by the canebrake, flat on his face to the marshy ground. He had been dreaming of ghosts, thin and pale as smoke, growing out of the twisted live-oak trees and reaching for him with their long gnarled hands. Other ghosts, too, that flitted on fleshless wings above his head, hooting like night-owls. Hearing this fresh sound he came awake, rolling easily on to one side to draw the hoop-iron knife. For a while he held his breath, listening.

The sound came from back of him, beyond the canebrake where the bayou made a brackish green channel through stretches of tall grass, overhung here and there with clumps of palmetto and willow. He heard it plain from that first moment, though his mind fought against it. By the second time it reached him there was no doubt at all. The heavy brushing of a body through the canes by the water's edge, coming after him. Another sound backed it. A low throttled snarling, checked only by the close setting of teeth. At once his own body tensed, his grip tightening on the wet twine haft of the knife. He rose to his knees carefully, his look shifting over to the nearby stretch of water.

Had to be the same dog, he figured. Must have swum clear of the gator and picked up his trail during the night. Now it looked like it was coming in to get him.

With his left hand he reached out slowly, casting around for some other aid. Soon his touch was met by damp moss and scaly bark. Part of a fallen bough, rotting close to the water's rim. Reaching, he scrabbled fingers underneath it, careless of the way his touch sank in rotten filth. Careless too of the spiders and bugs that scuttled unseen over his hand. Cautious, he eased it from the ground, lifting steadily. Feeling it give to his hand, he nodded, his breath coming easier for the moment.

The noise of the coming dog drew closer. Thrust of a powerful body through the canes, steps that splashed in shallow water. That, and a low-throated snarl that set his gut trembling afresh. Crouching there, he could see the creature in his mind, as sure as it could smell his own fear through the brake. The bristling wolfish head above the massive chest and shoulders, the yellow glare of eyes. Those bared, slobbering jaws. . . .

He'd seen the dogs at work, back on Sweet River. One time a young kid in the plough gang had tried to make a run for it. Name of Alexander. Thin undersized boy—kind of strange. Never said too much. Must have been crazy, come to think. Plain daylight when he made his bolt, and all of them out in the field planting the seed cane. Just cut loose from the plough and ran like a jackrabbit for over the hill. All of them there, watching him. Himself, and Mede and Cato and Glory. The women with them, Ruby and Sheba and others, and Mede's young kid Lucas who brought up the water at noon. Even Jacob the driver. Every one standing like to struck dumb at what they seen.

Then they heard Lawrence call out back of them, and they loosed the dogs.

He recalled how they'd stood then, gripping to their hoes, sweating more than a little as the big hounds went by them fast as lightning, cutting across the furrows at a lick and baying as they went. Those mastiffs hadn't fed for a while, and wasn't often they was off the leash. Not a hope for Alexander. The four of them run him down before he crossed the hill. First one hit him at a jump someplace between his shoulders, and the others piled on as he hit the ground. They could hear the screams from where they was stood, and the snarling of the hounds as they went at him like to pull him apart. He saw them tug and come away with their mouths bloody, holding chunks of flesh. From the look if it, one of them tore an arm clear away at the root. For a while the screams got kind of hard to take.

Sheba had started screaming too, and that set all the women off to hollering with her. In front of him Lucas was on the floor trying to hide his face someplace, and Cato bent over like he was going to throw up any minute. He got a taste in his own mouth like biting a rotten fruit, and for a while he thought he might throw up himself.

Pretty soon it got quiet up on the hill but for the noise of the dogs chewing him over, then Lawrence rode his big horse up and whipped them away. Wasn't much of Alexander left by then, just a mess of blood, and skin shreds with the bone showing through clean. Hard to think he'd been there running and alive scarce a moment gone.

All of them stood like stone statues as Lawrence came riding back with his whip at his shoulder. The hounds behind him, bloody but back on the leash with their handlers. Lucas crying and the women moaning. Glory saying *Oh my Lawd, my Lawd*, over and over. Off to the side, Jacob's face looked kind of grey. And when Lawrence went by them, they all looked down.

'Dumb nigger,' he heard Lawrence say as the horse took him by. 'Cost me five hundred dollars. Sonofabitch wasn't good for nothin' but to feed the dogs.'

And he himself saying nothing. His head down, watching the hounds as they went by growling, the bloody slobber in ropes at their mouths. Eyeing each bristling mastiff in turn. Hating them.

Them dogs gets treated better'n us plain folks. We only good to feed them.

First chance I get, I'm gonna rip out their bellies.

His teeth clenched, sweat running sudden into his eyes. Through the tall canes he saw something that moved like a black shadow, below him in the water. Easing about on his heels, right hand clasped on the haft of the knife, he felt a sick tremor in his gut and fought against it. Too late, for fear now. He missed first time—there wouldn't be no second chance.

Bringing his left arm back behind him, he pitched the wood hunk out for the water.

He heard the thick splash as it struck, caught sight of the long bristling shape as the dog swung around sideways towards it. He launched his own body forward in the same moment, knife-arm lifted, left hand out and grabbing as he went. One fleeting glimpse of that head turned towards him, baring its teeth in a snarl, the busted leash hanging at its neck, sunk shoulder-deep in water. Then he was in, lying half-across the animal's back, gripping for a hold in the thick hair as he struck out with the knife. He sank it fiercely, all but blind in the sudden killing rage. The blade went into the mastiff back of the right shoulder, biting through hair and flesh to thud haft-deep against the bone. He heard the dog yell, flinging up its shaggy head, and snarled himself in answer. With his left hand he got a hold on the leash, heaving back with all his strength as he stood to his knees in scummy water. In his right hand the knife came free, bloodied to the hilt. Against him the dog's cry choked. Fingers twisted in the ragged leather, he hauled again, a fearsome wrenching movement that tore at the sinews of his back. The hound's neck cracked sickeningly with the force of it, the animal swung off it's feet and over bodily on to its back. He went down with it, muck and slobber spattering him as he floundered on his knees in the water, not letting go the leash though the animal's head already hung wry to the side. Then the knife-arm came over again, striking clean for the space under the left forelimb where the heart beat. With the blow, the mastiff shuddered all over and went limp.

He made for the bank, dragging the wet heavy carcase behind him, his rage subsiding. He slung the mastiff clear, letting it thud against the marshy ground, and sank to the ground after it. His breath came harsh and heavy, and his heart beat at his ribs with thunderous hammer-blows. After a while his vision cleared, and the place was like it had been, the brackish water lying green and quiet in the half-light beyond the canes. Still breathing hard, he got to his feet, looking to where the big hound lay asprawl the earth with its head flung back. The wide yellow eyes glared at him still in death, the teeth bared. His own face hardened into cold, bitter lines. Bending, he gripped the sodden throat, his knife shearing through the stomach wall to lay the animal open.

Eat the heart, Nestor had told him once. Puts all they poison into you, boy. Make you strong. Make you mean.

When he had cut the heart loose, he chewed on the raw bloody meat until he was filled. He couldn't eat all of it, and after a while flies began to gather about the blood on his face and hands. He washed off the sticky filth in the water as best he could, and turned back for the hound. Dragging it by the leash, he swung it into the middle of the bayou. The lolling gutted shape floated for so long, then its slit belly filled and he watched as it sank, slowly, the worst of his rage dying to a grim satisfaction.

That one dog you ain't goin' see no more, Mistah Lawrence, sah.

An hour or so later his stomach cramped, and he threw up all he'd eaten.

Afterwards, deep in bayou country, as the sun spread through the live-oak boughs above him, he heard again the noise of dogs and horsemen, and knew he was still hunted.

REMEMBERING.

Harsh sunlight hammering the open ground. Lean bent backs, black and gleaming with sweat against the red blaze of Louisiana earth. Heaving forward, his shovel biting deep, flinging the red dirt over his shoulder above the ditch. He stands an instant, drawing breath. Blinking at the sweat that stings his eyes, tasting it as it trickles in at his mouth. On either side of him the walls of the ditch, rising chest-high, the sun blinding him where it strikes the bright red clay. Back of them, the big house and the quarters, and the fields of standing cane. Right of him, the willow-shaded drive where the dirt road follows the hill's shoulder over towards Palmetto and Lafayette. Up ahead, the bared backs of the ditch gang, the line of men with their shovels and picks, standing as one to draw breath. And beyond them, below the canefields, the bayou country lying quiet in the heat, glinting where light catches the flat water between the live-oak trees.

Smell of earth and cane, and sunstruck water. Reek of the sweating men in the ditch coming back into his nostrils. His eye takes them in as the gang lifts tools together. Not a man of them alike. Mede, the leader, long and thin, his skin a dark reddish-brown, his face and shoulders muddy with freckle-spots. His hair is dark, but it has red lights and grows long and wavy. Unlike his own thick, tight-curled fleece, Cato behind him, short and squat, blacker than Justus himself, his shoulders thick with bunching muscle. William then, and his brother Glory. Both of them big and powerful, looking like kin. Only the colour of them is different, Glory a deep brown while William's skin is a kind of greyish-black. Strange, that grey colour in a young fellow like him. He's seen some of the older men grey out that way, late on, when they ain't got long to go. One thing sure, it ain't lucky to be that way. The thought passes. He lifts the shovel, following Mede like the rest, and the line of them strikes in again. Up ahead, Mede starts to singing.

> *'Take this hammo' – uh!*
> *Care it to the capten – hah!*
> *Take this hammo' – uh!*
> *Care it to the capten – hah!*
> *Take this hammooooo . . .'*

He grins, hearing the high wavering voice as it holds the note, giving the bunch of them a chance to rest before they all join in with him, striking down. Good boy, Mede. Knows his job.

> *'Say to him ah'm gone*
> *Say to him ah'm gone. . . .'*

Digging, he hears movement above him on the rim of the ditch. He tenses, feeling the stare of the driver hit like an auger between his shoulder.

'Quicken it up, boy, you hear?' Jacob says.

He stands at the edge of the ditch, straddle-legged, the heavy whip coiled in his hand. A massive barrel-chested black, his curled hair greying at the temples, his broad-set body gleaming smooth and hard as hickory-wood. Huge shoulders on him like an ox, and big scarred hands. Jacob wears a red bandana at the neck, and a pair of kersey breeches with a brass-buckled belt. His face is hard and seamed like dark wood, only the eyes alive. Yellow-green eyes, like a dog's. Justus sees him with the tail of his eye, and looks down. The driver's back is a mass of whip-scars from the beatings he had as a youngster, beatings that would have killed most other men. Jacob once hit an overseer and lived through the flogging they gave him. In his time, he was the meanest nigger on Sweet River. Now he's the best watch-dog Lawrence could hope to find. Big as he is, Justus wouldn't care to tackle Jacob.

Mede looks back, raking a quick glance over his shoulder. The stare of those eyes is enough. The song quickens, and with it the pace of the men.

'Ef he asks you, was I runnin'...'

He works on faster, driving his shovel hard, pitching the dirt, as the voice of Mede whips them on. Breath coming harder now, the red walls and the man above him seen through a blur of sweat. As through a stinging veil he sees Jacob straddled there, the whip coiled against his thigh. Squatting by him is the kid, Lucas, with his water-bucket.

'Ef he asks you – uh!
Was I runnin' – hah!'

One other figure, away from the others. An old man in nearby tree-shade, squatting on his heels, balancing a hoe in his palms. Thin, frail old man in ragged calico shirt and pants, a wide-brimmed straw hat shadowing his face. Just sitting there, saying nothing.

Old man, name of Nestor.

'Tell him ah was flying'...'

Digging. The breath hissing through his teeth, whistling harsh as he strikes with the shovel. Muscles straining in the back and shoulders, twinges at his wrists as the blade goes hard into the ground. Blind now with sweat that flies off him, spattering the red earth underfoot. Feeling already the tightness across his chest, the tripped thudding of the heart against his ribs. In front the others, too, work on blindly. Their own joined breaths sounding in the enclosed space. The overpowering smell of sweat fills the ditch.

Back of him, Jacob is grinning. Some bitter thing in Jacob never did get free. Once, maybe, thought he might get loose from Sweet River. Never did. Now, only time he smiles is when he lays on with that whip, or watches his own kind suffer. Like now....

They're the only ones left him to hurt. If he struck a white man again, they'd hang him.

'Step it up, Mede!' Jacob calls out. He grins wider, letting the whip fall loose. Flicks in practice at a big blowfly, hovering past. 'C'mon, y'all lazy buck nigras.... Faster!'

Under the twisted trees Nestor looks up slow, pushes the hat back from his face. 'Leave'm be, Jacob,' he says. 'They earnt a rest, I reckon.'

At that everything stops. Mede's voice cuts out sudden and the whole gang turn, lowering tools, looking towards the two men above them. Justus brushes the sweat from his eyes, letting the blade of his shovel thud against the ground. For a while there's nothing to be heard but the noise of the five men breathing hard in the ditch. That, and the buzz of flies. And towering over them the huge figure of Jacob, the whiplash trailing dust in his grip. The hard face working, trying for something to say. The look of him angry and puzzled at the same time. Like somebody just hit him between the eyes with a rock.

He sees Mede start to grin, turns aside himself to smother a chuckle with his hand. Cato and Glory are both having trouble not smiling. Up along the road beyond, a dust-cloud lifts like smoke through the line of willows.

Lucas, scanning their faces from where he sits by the water-bucket, sees the twitching marks of laughter they're struggling to hide. Lucas is a bright young kid. Mede's boy all right, long and thin as a pole, but black and smooth-skinned like his mother Chloe. Now his own face puckers and he breaks into open laughter. With that, the whole gang laughs, and Jacob swells up like he's fixing to bust a gut.

'You talkin' to me, old man?' Jacob says. He swings round on the bent figure under the tree, pushing out his chest and squaring his shoulders. His yellow-green eyes are hard, slitted like a snake's. Right now, no one in the ditch would care to face him. 'Nestor, ain't your place to be out here a-tall. You head on back to the quarters, you hear me?'

Nestor looks up and smiles, turning the hoe in his hands. He's been out here fitting the broken shank since early morning, a job that shouldn't have lasted him a half-hour. Nothing to him, at first look. Bent, frail little man, the skin greying and beginning to hang loose on his bones. Face as pouched and gullied as worn leather, the hair tight-curled and salty grey atop his head. Still, he doesn't make a move.

'Ain't no use to handle 'em that way,' the old man says. 'You

24

wear 'em out too fast, they no good to Mister Lawrence, an' he ain't gonna thank you for it. Ain't that right, Jacob?'

For a while it looks like Jacob is about to explode. His whole face darkens and twists, and he leans forward, the thick-stemmed whip starting to lift in his hand.

'Nestor, you shut up your mouth, you hear me? Dumb sonofa-bitch. . . .'

Nestor doesn't answer. Just sits there, looking up at Jacob as the big driver swings up with the whip. The old man's eyes are watery, faded under their red-rimmed lids. Somehow, though Jacob can't stare them down. The huge frame of the driver shudders in rage, throat swelling so the bandanna threatens to choke him. Then the whip cuts down, popping a geyser of dust, and Jacob glowers at the ground like a beaten dog.

'You always was dumb, Jacob,' Nestor says.

His speech is different from theirs. When he talks, Nestor sounds like he says the words through a mouthful of pebbles, turning them over thick and kind of awkward on his tongue. Like this wasn't always the kind of talk he used. Now he leans forward a ways, cupping a hand to the rabbit's foot that hangs from a thong at his neck. As he does so, Jacob turns a mite paler than before.

'First off, my name ain't Nestor,' the old man says. 'I got my own name, an' I don't need no call for Nestor off no white folks. I ain't like you, or them boys in the ditch – I know what I am, you hear? An' next off, don' you mess with me no more, Jacob, or you goin' to be real sorry.'

In the ditch Justus and the gang stay quiet. Nestor scares them too.

'You don't scare me none, old man,' Jacob says. His voice sounds strange, kind of shaky. And he's breathing hard, like he just stopped running.

Nestor looks at him sly, his head to one side, and Jacob goes quiet. 'Ain't me scares you, Jacob,' the old man says. He touches the rabbit's foot softly. 'They's things about here you cain't lay a whip to . . . ghosts and spirits, blood-suckers, soul-eaters. . . . They ever'where hereabouts. Could be I even got me one in this tree back of me. You scared of ghosts, Jacob, an' you know it.'

He halts a moment, his look going past Jacob to the men in the ditch. Struck by that penetrating gaze, Justus feels his skin prickle as the sweat dries, and shivers.

'They's some kin talk with spirits,' Nestor is saying as he looks them over, one by one. 'If you got the power, ain't nothin' you cain't do. Man lays a finger on you, spirits come on him in the night an' claw out his insides piece by piece. . . .' His glance shifts back to the sullen figure of the driver, standing like he was rooted to the spot. 'Jacob here ain't as dumb as he looks. He heard about men like me, ain't that right, Jacob?'

'Yeah, I heard,' Jacob scowls, still looking at the ground by his feet. 'You keep away from me, old man, you hear?'

Watching, Justus finds admiration mingling with his fear. Himself, he wouldn't ever dare look Jacob in the eye. Yet here's this thin stick of an oldster that the driver could break across his knee, and he scares the hell out of them all.

But then, he knows like all of the others that Nestor has magic in him. And it don't pay to cross a man who talks with the spirits.

Up above him the old man nods, his hand shifting away from the rabbit's foot. 'Just do like I tell you, Jacob,' he says. 'You treat them boys right, I aim to see you don' get hurt none.'

Jacob spits in helpless anger, turning away. Nestor sits watching his massive back for a while, still smiling, and looks again to the hoe in his hands.

'Let's get back to work,' Jacob tells them. His voice is gruff still, and he holds his head low, not looking them in the face. Slowly the bunch of them pick up their tools, still grinning a little behind their hands. As long as Nestor chooses to stay here, they know they're safe.

Up on the road the dust-cloud spreads, thinning. Through it, and the line of willows at its verge, a glint of steel caught by the light of the sun.

'Soljers,' Glory says. By now they're back to digging. Wouldn't do for Lawrence to get too suspicious and ride on over. Still, the gang works easily, no one fixing to kill himself. Above them Jacob walks up and down the rim of the ditch, his whip coiled, doing his best to look in command. All the time in the world for a man to look back over his shoulder and down the road.

'It's our boys,' Cato tells him.

He watches as they come into sight. A small cluster of riders first, and after them, ranks of marching infantry, their worn uniforms showing grey through the red dust. Over at the tail of the column come guns on their limbers, and heavy supply waggons. Distant tramp of feet. Rumbling wheels in the road. Above them the banner, hanging limp in the heat. The blood-red flag with its Southern Cross of stars. Jacob's look follows them without love as the column winds along the crest of the hill beyond.

White men. Like Lawrence.

His hand grips on the handle of the shovel, twisting.

'Our boys, hell,' Mede says. 'Ain't done nothin' for us. . . .'

Jacob scowls at that, but says nothing for the moment. His silence lets the others in.

'Way I hear it, them Nawtheners ain't far off,' Cato puts in. His dark features hold a mean look. Vicious streak in Cato someplace. Mostly it lies hidden, but not always. Justus has seen him at hog-killing time, grinning wide as the hung animals squeal and the blood sprays out with the blows of the knife.

'They done burned Atlanta a while back. Them butternut boys of ours is due a beatin', I reckon.'

'You hush your mouth, you hear?' Jacob says.

Cato looks up at that, hard-eyed. For a while it looks like he might argue. Then he sees Jacob looming over him and looking meaner than ever. The stocky man mutters, his stare going down.

'Hey, Nestor!' Glory is suddenly brave. 'What you figger of these a-bolitionists? I hear tell they about to set us free, ain't that right?'

At that the whole gang pauses, looking to the old man under the tree. Justus with them, listening. Jacob, too, is quiet.

Nestor, looking up, doesn't even smile. He eyes Glory like he's sore at being asked. 'They-all white, boy,' Nestor says. 'White folks is all the same. Ain't you thought about that? Any reason they should treat us blacks different, Glory?'

'I reckon not.' Glory, too, looks sullen. He'd hoped for a better answer.

'That's right, boy,' Nestor smiles again, crookedly. 'You learnin'.'

Justus, following the marching column as it moves away beyond the crest, is suddenly aware of the old man's eyes on him. He turns, uncertain, and Nestor nods, still smiling.

'How 'bout you, boy? You figger them Yankees is any better?'

Justus frowns, conscious of those eyes and their mocking light. Ignoring the mean, scowling look of the driver standing over him, he meets the old man's stare. 'You right,' he says, and the bite of harshness in his voice sets Jacob looking twice. 'They all white folks. They ain't never goin' give us nothin', less we take it ourselves.'

For a minute the quiet that follows has him scared. Jacob glares, opens his mouth like he's going to speak, then shuts it again. Out beyond him Nestor ducks his salty head. 'Yeah,' Nestor has done smiling. He studies the big black youth in the trench as if seeing him for the first time. His lips are puckered in thought, the eyes gone narrow and shrewd. 'Yeah, boy. You smart, I kin see that. Just be sure you stay that way, is all.'

Justus breathes out hard, looking down at his shovel. He doesn't answer.

Over by the big house they've turned out to watch the soldiers on the road. Old man Lawrence and his son riding out by the edge of the canefield. The plough and hoe gangs ducking heads and pulling off their hats as they pass. The two white horsemen going by without a look, eyes on that grey disappearing line on the crest with its willow trees. Old man Lawrence, white-haired and thinning out with age. But hard as leather, sure and firm in the saddle. And his son, dark, thin-featured and mean. A taller, stronger version of his old man. He eyes them, scowling hard over the line of the ditch. Young Lawrence, he knows, has a fancy for Sheba. And Justus wants Sheba for himself. He clenches teeth, gripping again on the shovel-haft.

White Massa Boss!

In the ditch beside him they're getting restless, even Mede beginning to look uneasy. He sees Glory and William swapping glances, both of them grinning and chuckling like a couple of kids, and guesses what might be coming. If Nestor's in the right mood, he can stand a little teasing at times. Sure enough, it's Glory who sets it off. William at least has sense enough to keep his mouth shut.

'Hey, Nestor!' Glory has a hard time keeping down the grin on his face. 'You done tole us once you come from Africa – that right?'

'Same place your kin come from.' The old man's face stays impassive. 'Only difference is I was born there, I reckon.'

'Uhuh,' Glory can't even pretend to be serious. The grin threatens to split his face. 'You got your own name there, huh? What they call you back in A-frica, Nestor?'

Leaning on the shovel, Justus sees the flicker of change in those weathered features, and frowns. After Jacob, they oughta know better than to fool with the old man. Still, he answers.

'They called me Kofi,' Nestor says. His eyes are already slitted.

Glory laughs. 'Y'all hear that? They called him Cawfee!' He turns about to the others, the grin showing white in the deep brown of his face. William and Cato laughing with him as Mede stays quiet. 'Cawfee – sure is one hell of a name for a nigra, ain't it?'

Glory sees Justus eye him unsmiling. Turns to the burly figure of Jacob, frowning in silence. Abruptly the laughter stills. Awkward now, Glory meets the narrowed gaze of the old man under the tree.

'I ain't no nigra,' Nestor tells the men in the ditch. On Glory his faded eyes are hard, unforgiving. 'I a man. And you, boy, you a fool! You hear me good?'

Glory eyes the rabbit's foot at the old man's neck and licks his lips nervously. 'I hear you, Nestor,' Glory says. He looks down as he speaks.

'Good 'nough,' he old man says.

In the ditch the laughter stops, Glory and William crushed for the moment. Cato, though, decides to cut in on them.

'Way I hear, them Africans is dumb,' Cato says. He meets Nestor's stare without looking away. 'Hear tell they swing around in the trees all day, like they was monkeys or somethin'. You ever hear that, Nestor?'

Nestor smiles his crooked smile. 'Your kinfolks, maybe,' he says. 'Not mine.'

At that they all break up laughing, Cato with them. Even Jacob grins. The bunch of men turn back to work in the ditch, young Lucas chuckling still by the water-bucket. Over in the distance, the grey-clad column has all but disappeared. Old Lawrence and his son turn, and head back for the house.

Justus, setting himself to follow the rest, finds that he is held by the old man's level gaze. He looks to Nestor, questioning.

'You hear me, boy,' Nestor tells him. 'Difference between you an' me is – I know who I am.' He pauses, his look taking in the tall big-shouldered youth in front of him. 'You oughta know it too.'

Justus tries for something to say, can't find it. When he looks again, Nestor is no longer watching him. The old man picks up his hoe and gets to his feet, setting off at a slow shuffling walk towards the quarters. Justus turns, lifting the weight of the shovel in his hands. Above him, Jacob smiles.

'Could be we get to work now,' the driver says.

Justus doesn't answer him, turning his back. In front of him the other men of the gang fall into line, striking as one as Mede takes up the song again.

> *'Take this hammo – hah!*
> *Care it to the capten – hah!'*

Harsh breathing. Sweat, and the red glare of earth. Around them the canefields and the bayous, lying quiet.

The whole land shimmering in the steaming heat.

He strikes with the shovel, blood-coloured dirt flying over his shoulder and out of the ditch.

THAT THIRD day, they ran him hard. He could hear them at his back, for all the distance between. The hounds again, baying as they looked for the scent. The men yelling. The ground shaking under the horses' hooves. Whiles, he'd catch sigh of them through the trees as he ran. Dark, uncertain shapes on foot or horseback, spreading to take in the landscape of creeks and canebrakes that led back to the Lawrence plantation. They were all of them a way behind him, but closing. And sight and noise of them were enough to keep him running.

By now he was deep into the wilderness, and close to giving out.

About him the woodland was closing in, massive tree-boles looming up on every side. Boughs arched overhead, shutting off the light. He ran on through a world of green shadows, feet snagging and sliding free of the roots that stretched out across his path. Breath rasping from deep in his chest as his body reeled from side to side and his bare feet slammed down in the roots and mould. Trying not to think of the spiders and snakes. Fighting when bushes shook at a distance to forget the wild hog and bear. The neck-cloth that served now as a head-tie over his fleece of hair, and the spread boughs of the trees combined to keep off the glare of the sun. Such light as broke in was tamed and shaded by the green of their leaves. All the same he sweated, near to collapse. He hadn't eaten for two days, and drunk only once – and that sparingly – from a hole by the cypress swamp, after his pursuers had turned back that first time.

In front of him the ground blurred, swinging crazily somewhere near to his head. He lurched, hitting against a live-oak trunk, gasping at sudden pain as the bark raked at his ribs. For a while a red blinding glare thudded back of his eyes, redder than the dirt in the ditch. Slithering down by the side of the tree-bole, he figured he was finished. He had all but fallen, when thought of Lawrence came back to him, and the handlers with those unfed hounds. The sudden burst of terror cleared his vision, set him staggering forward again. Running blind and fierce as a hunted hare, though the earth reeled with him and the trees to either side tilted askew above and below. Running until the heart threatened to burst clear out from his chest. Behind him the voices of men and hounds grew fainter with distance. Putting out hands to steady himself against the swaying trunks as he went, he kept on running.

He ran until the sound of their voices died utterly. Until the one sound was the beat of blood, its hammer-blows thundering against the walls of his skull. He sagged against the nearest live-oak trunk, his body shaking to the force of his breathing, letting himself sink gradually to earth. Slowly the blood-beat ebbed, and with it the threshing of his heart against his ribs. Slumped with his back to the rooted base of the oak, heedless of the rough bark against his skin, he stared out ahead of him.

He had come to the point where woodland petered out into another swamp. Smaller than the first, tall trees leaning to surround the black water. Cypresses, gaunt and twisted by their years at the bayou's rim, hung with Spanish moss in their upper boughs. The greyish-white clusters gleaming eerily, ghostlike where the light broke through the leaves. Recalling his dreams of a coupla nights before, he shuddered.

In the foliage at the bayou's edge, birds called one to another. Close to the bank, he saw the water rippled, arrowlike, by a swimming shape. Beever, maybe. From here he couldn't be sure. He listened awhile to the noise of the birds. The liquid chanting of warblers in the tree boughs, deeper boom of the bittern closer to the reedbeds on the ground. No sign of gators, as yet, nor snakes. A shadowed stillness lay over the water.

Water.

Thirst woke in him afresh, clawing his parched throat. He went forward on his belly through the standing reeds, dragging himself over the soft yielding ground to where the water began. Reaching in, he cupped his hands and drank. The bayou top was thick and dank with moss and weed and rotting leaves, its surface black in tree-shade. Still, the water beneath was pure, fed as it was by fresh springs. He drank sparingly, like a miser, savouring the clean, sharp taste on his tongue. A slightly acid tang to it, that only gave an edge to his thirst. When he had drunk enough he lay, trailing face and hands in the water, letting moisture soak up against his body through the reeds, to take off the heat of his flesh. About him, in the trees and the reedbeds, the birds sang on. . . .

Cries woke him, and the yammer of hounds. Must have drowsed off a while, figuring he was safe and all. Crouched on all fours among the reeds, he fought a sudden flare of panic as he listened. Still some distance off, by the sound of them, but getting nearer all the time. For a moment he looked about him, seeking out some place to hide. None offered itself. After a while his look came back to the dark, shadowed water of the bayou. Frowning still, he nodded.

32

Hereabouts the reeds grew thick and strong, their stems almost the breadth of a man's wrist at the base. He drew the knife from the strip of hide that held up his ragged breeches and sawed through the nearest of them to cut himself a length. Sheathing it once more, he glanced at the wooded stretch around him. Here and there small birds flew upward as the noise of pursuit grew louder.

Still holding to the cut length of reed, he waded out into the shadowed water.

He let it take him, lapping warm and thick with its covering of weed. Up to his shoulders. Up to his chin. When his feet no longer trod the muddy floor he fitted the hollow reed into his mouth, and kicked back to where rushes overhung the bank. Dark water closed over his head as he moved, and in his ears the cries of men and beasts blurred and grew more distant than before.

He lay as close in to the bank as he dared, the bayou with its matted surface hiding him, breathing through the hollow tube.

An age passed before hoofbeats shook the soft ground and the first of the horsemen rode by. The man came so close that spray from the animal's hooves spattered the surface above him. Eyes open against the water, he saw as through a distorting mirror the great looming shape of the rider, as man and horse lurched by and then vanished. From where he was, he couldn't make out anything higher than the horseman's waist. All the same, when the second man followed, he had no trouble knowing him. The grey gelding and the hand that hung low by the horse's flank holding a coiled whip were proof enough. Fear at the sudden sight made him breathe faster, and he found himself praying that the passing hooves would drown whatever noise he made. Meantime the water had begun to press heavy on his ears and eyes, and he knew he couldn't hope to stay hid here for too long.

Lawrence had reined in his mount, as though looking about him. Long hours seemed to pass as he lingered there, the massive flank of his gelding all but shutting out the light. The man in the water stayed where he was, frozen like stone below the level of the reeds. At last, when it seemed his lungs could bear no more, the big horse swung, splashing away through the reedy shallows of the swamp. Abruptly, the horsemen were gone.

No dogs with them. His luck was in. They must have long since lost the scent.

He waited until long after they had gone before he ventured to lift his head above water. Once he'd got his breath back, he listened. In the distance the cries and yelps went on, further off than they had been before. Standing to his neck in the hot, slimy water, he grinned.

Looked like they'd lost him after all.

All the same, he stayed there until well through the afternoon, neck-deep in the bayou and listening, watching the light as it faded. The noises didn't come back. Still he didn't move. Dusk was coming on, and the swamp was all but velvet-black in the shadow of the trees when he finally waded back through the shallows and heaved himself ashore. His slimed body stank and he was a while cleaning off the scum and weeds. At the moment, that didn't worry him overmuch.

Frogs were croaking in the mud at the water's edge, their song taking over from that of the birds. From somewhere high in the boughs overhead he heard the first night owl call. Another ghost, maybe? He shrugged off the thought, too far gone in weariness to care. He made it back to the live-oak, set himself down by its spreading roots. For a time he stayed like that, open-eyed to the gathering dark. Thinking.

Must have slipped Lawrence by now, he figured. Not a sound anyplace. They were turned back for Sweet River, long gone. And now he was clear into the bayou country.

The big heavy-muscled black lying under the tree laughed to himself, softly, his bared teeth agleam against the deep ebony skin.

Mistah Lawrence. Looks like I fooled you, sure 'nough.

He stretched out beneath the oak, flexing arms and legs like a lazy cat. Before long, his eyes had closed.

His dreams, though, when they came, were of Sweet River. And of the woman he had left there when he ran.

SHEBA.

Dark in the quarters, pressing on him black and heavy as smooth broadcloth. In the cabin he shares with Glory and William, all the candles are doused with the coming of night. So dark, he can barely make out the shape of the low cabin roof above his head. He lies close up by the wall in his makeshift crib, covered by the one ragged blanket. Even now, with darkness fallen, the atmosphere in the cramped cabin is hot and stifling. He throws off the blanket, sprawling naked, sweating in the clammy heat.

Restless. Waiting for her to come to him.

No stars through the unglazed gap of window above his head, nor any breath of air. A sudden burst of white moonlight floods the room, splintering on the sill above him. The pale gleam falls over the body stretched out on the crib, glistens on the black smooth tones of the skin, marking the outline of his body. The head, broad-featured and strong, with its alert, questioning eyes. Deep chest and heavy shoulders, tapering down to the flat belly and narrow flanks, thickening again with muscle at the loins and thighs. He watches the same light as it falls beyond, to where Glory and his brother lie together under the one blanket. The two of them sleeping, their arms about each other, William's head rested on the chest of his brother. Glory and William, always was too close to pull them apart. If Massa Lawrence got to know how close, he might get to do something about it. Then again, maybe he does know. Maybe Jacob told him sometime. He shrugs, scowling, angered at his own restlessness. Ain't about Glory and William he's thinking right now.

Why don't she come?

Outside, in the trees bordering the canefields, he hears the nightbirds call. And as he listens, comes a scratching at the door. Like a cat had got loose somewhere. Only this ain't no cat. Starting to grin, he swings out of the crib and crosses to the door. In his grasp the wooden bar lifts easily, without a sound. He steps back, letting the door slide open a crack against the night, and a dark, lithe shadow flits by him into the cabin as the door closes.

'Justus.' Her voice, whispering against him. Her slender arms about him as he turns to bar the door. Feeling the warm flutter of her breath at his back, he chuckles, laying the wooden bolt in place. He swings round suddenly, catching her slim body up in his arms, lifting her from the ground. Grinning still, he carries her towards the crib by the wall.

Warmth of her unclothed limbs against him, cradled in the grip of his arms. The feel of her skin, smooth where his hands touch. Warmth of her breathing at his chest. Crossing, he feels the need for her surge up within him.

Sheba looks up into his face, and smiles. 'You feelin' strong tonight, is you, Justus?' Under the moon her eyes hold a glint of slyness. She slips one hand downward, touching him lightly where his manhood rises.

He sucks in his breath a moment, gasping. 'You take it easy, you hear?' he says.

Laying her down on the makeshift crib, standing back as the moonlight washes over her, he finds himself frowning. 'Jacob see you, girl?' he asks.

Sheba smiles again. Slyer, more catlike than before. Moonlight follows the lithe, slim lines of her body. Touching the small face with its narrow jaw, the smoothness of the throat beneath. White light shivers, slanting over her small breasts with their erect nipples, moving on to lose itself in furred shadow beyond. In daylight he knows her to be lighter than himself, a pale bronze colour. Almost a high yellow. Here, with only the moon to light them, their skins are one darkness together.

'Don' rightly know, boy. Didn't see him.' She reaches again for him, her eyes narrow and gleaming in moonlight. 'Jacob got a woman, now, you know that. 'Sides, he knows we ain't gonna run away, don't he?'

He laughs with her, softly. Nights, they're supposed to be shut into their quarters, and Jacob is watchman. Somehow, it never works out that way. Since Jacob settled for Leah to be his wench, none of the field hands have been watched too close.

Kneeling by the crib, he forgets Jacob. Forgets everything. Sheba shivers as he touches her breasts, fondling the taut nipples until her body begins to writhe. She moans, lifting herself to accommodate his urgent hand between her thighs. Her own hands on him, stroking and insistent. In his head the blood roars suddenly. He leans forward as if to lie over her, and the frail crib shudders.

'This ain't gonna work,' he says.

He can hear her giggling laughter as he lifts her from the bed and lies down beside her on the dirt floor of the cabin. At the sound, he glances back over his shoulder to where the other two figures lie together under the blanket. But Glory and William sleep on, undisturbed.

Sheba catches his wary look and grins.

'Why you lookin' at them, boy?' She chuckles softly, low in her throat. Her fingers on him, teasing. 'You figger you like a man to pleasure you?'

'You hush, girl,' Justus tells her. He leans, smothering her mouth with his own. Sheba responds, her mouth opening warm as their tongues probe and touch. Yet when he makes to move across her, she draws her lips from his.

'Not that way, big boy. You like to bust my back.'

Justus grins, rolling over to settle on his back. She knows more than one way, and they all as good. He feels his breath come sharper as she kneels above him, straddling his body. Aware of his own upright member, throbbing as it touches against her flesh. Sheba laughs again, stroking the rigid column with the underslope of her breast as she leans forward. He groans, feeling her cup him in her hand. She opens again to him, his own fingers sinking into moisture at the dark place between her thighs. Justus sets his teeth together, his eyes widening.

'Hurry it up, girl,' he croaks.

Sheba grins in answer. Lifts her body, arching her back. She comes down on to him real slow, settling. He feels his man go into her inch by inch. Slow circles of pleasure, rising upward, beating their wings inside his head. He grasps at her breast, reaches to take

37

the nipple in his mouth. Falls back, breathing harder. Slowly their joined bodies begin to move. 'Reckon young Massa might like it this way,' Sheba murmurs. She closes her eyes, shivers at the first foretaste of pleasure. Her hands on his shoulders, pressing. 'You reckon them white folks does it like us, honey?'

By now he's too far gone to answer. Any other time he might turn salty on her for talking about the white folks at all. But not now. Gripped by her spread thighs as she rides him harder, the only sounds he makes now are gasps or moans. Already he senses the fierce onrush of that tide in which he seeks to drown.

Sheba runs out of words, bucking as she rides his risen rod in a frenzy. Clawing at him. Calling out. He thrusts against her, shutting his eyes to the pleasure that swells almost unbearably at his root, roaring to be loosed.

Justus heaves up beneath her with a harsh inarticulate cry. Coming. Feeling the sudden savage joy as he shoots his jissom into her in shuddering spasms. A moment after, and Sheba arches, screaming like a cat.

'Ohh, Justus . . . That so good, so good. . . .'

He lies, spent, his body agleam with sweat. Letting her sink down across him as the pleasure ebbs. Juice of her own ecstasy running warm over his belly and from him to the ground. Her lips murmuring at his chest. He lies, stroking the tight curls of her hair, his big hands gentle in the aftermath of love.

'Sure was good, honey,' he tells her.

For a while they lie that way, kissing and touching.

'Hear tell that Hagar sick, over the big house,' Sheba says at last. She turns her face up to him as she speaks. 'Massa be needin' a new housemaid real soon, they reckon.'

She sees his sudden frown, the hard stare of his eyes, and looks down. At once his grip tightens on the curled locks of her hair.

'Sheba,' he tells her. 'You *my* wench, you hear? Don' want you over no big house with young Massa or nobody else. You for me, like I for you. Ain't that right?'

'Yeah, Justus honey, that right. You know it.' She glances up at him warily, her face showing pain from the grip of his hand on her hair. 'Let me loose, now, you hurtin' me. . . .'

He looses his hold, and Sheba breathes again, flinching still at the pain. Looking to his hardened face, she senses the remains of anger there, does her best to smooth it out of him.

'Sure, Justus. You know I don't need for nobody else.' She moves over him, kissing his sullen mouth, her hands stroking softly at his cheeks. 'Ain't nobody pleasures me the way you do, big boy. Sheba here thinkin' if we ask him, we might get to jump the broom for Massa. What you think, Justus?'

He nods, smiling, his anger already forgotten. Sweet Jesus, Sheba, for you I do anything. 'Start us a kid, maybe.' His hands forage lazily down the smooth curve of her back, savouring the soft moist touch of skin. He lets them come to rest at her round tight little buttocks, cupping them in his palms.

Sheba smiles, her own hands wandering. 'More'n one chile, sure 'nough. I got the shape for a good breeding woman.'

'If the sap takes . . .' he begins.

She reaches to touch him, and he knows that he wants her again.

'Ain't nothin' wrong with your sap, honey,' she says.

Into the small hours she leaves at last, with the dark already starting to grey out. Sinking on to the crib, eyes closing in pleasurable weariness, he figures he can only count on a few hours' sleep before daybreak. And once the day begins, he'll know how much steam that girl took out of him. Still, he smiles, rolling over to shut off the world. No better way for a man to spend his strength. A whole lot more pleasure in it than digging ditches.

He smiles again, closing his eyes to the greying light.

Ahhh, that Sheba.

A BIG man, lying in the roots of a live-oak close by the water. Eyes closed under moonlight, sleeping. Great sprawled limbs, black and smooth as the night itself. Somewhere in sleep he trembles, breath escaping with a sobbing sound. Beneath the closed eyelids, two spots of moisture gather, glistening under the moon.

Shouldn't have been that way. There was no need. No need.

'Sheba!'

Dreaming, he calls her name aloud. Only the night-owl

answers, its hooting cry a mocking sound as it crosses the swamp for the far line of trees. A ghost-voice, answering a man already dead.

A man alone, in a country of ghosts.

SEEMS LIKE his eyes open suddenly. Green boughs interlacing high overhead. Their leaves trembling as a faint breeze catches them, forty feet or more up into the treetops. Between the spread branches the sky pales. Getting on towards morning. He shifts position awkwardly where he lies, conscious of the chill droplets of moisture on his skin. Dew? Sweat? He can't be sure which, not yet. Somewhere in the watery distance he hears the noise of a fish jumping. He yawns, rubbing the sore place in his back where the live-oak roots dug in as he slept.

Back of him in the undergrowth comes a hint of movement. Abrupt crunching of a booted foot in the mould. A twig spans, the sound jarring through him. He springs up to his feet, half-turning, palms flat to balance his heavy body against the oak trunk. At first he hopes it's still a dream. Then comes the solid click of the gun-hammer levering back.

No dream, after all.

'Back up there, nigra,' the voice says. 'Stay right where you stood, an' don't try nothin'.'

He doesn't answer. Back on Sweet River a black man keeps his mouth shut until he's asked. And this one is a white man for sure. From the corner of his eye he sees him. A thin, undersized man, his threadbare shirt open to the belly in the morning heat. Worn denim pants tucked into high horseman's boots. Thin features, too, pinched and haggard under the broad-brimmed hat, a greyish stubble of whiskers coating the jaws. It's the eyes he watches, mean and glinting, narrowed almost to slits against the coming threat of the sun. That, and the long-barrelled revolver whose muzzle holds level with his own belly.

Seen him once before, the time the dog broke loose in the

cypress swamp. He was there then, riding with Lawrence and the patrol. Poor-white patroller, name of Burns.

Silent, faced by that levelled gun, the first flare of rage is quick to die. A sense of helplessness comes after, leaving him spent and drained, sick at his own foolishness. For a while there, he thought he had won clear at last. And now, to be caught like this. . . . The black mood engulfs him. His shoulders sag, letting his head sink forward to hit the rough bark of the oak. The breath comes from him in a hollow groaning sigh.

Out beyond him the white man laughs, a dry, mirthless sound.

'Yeah, black boy. . . You been played fer a sucker all right. . . .' Suddenly the voices acquires a harder edge.'Pull that knife, an' toss it over. An' remember, that reward says I don't need to bring you in alive.'

So they got a reward out for him? The thought falls heavy, thudding lifeless inside the walls of his skull. Reaching for the belted knife, his eye measures the space between himself and the threat of that levelled gun. Not a hope. Snarling under his breath, he tugs the hoop-iron free, pitches it to land by the booted feet beyond him. Again, that harsh mirthless laugh answers him.

'Now stand away from the tree, an' keep them hands lifted.'

He turns, his hands raised, facing the man with the gun. Feeling the impotent rage well up inside him, seething, clenching his teeth. Hand to hand, he could break this one on the point of his knee like a dead stick. Would do, too. Only the gun makes all the difference.

No sign of any other riders. Rest of them must've turned home. Can't see the horse either. Must be yonder someplace in the bushes.

The grey-whiskered man catches his glance and bares his teeth in a yellow grin. 'Seems like I got lucky, boy. . . . Horse run lame, an' I quit early. Lawrence an' the others went on home. Good thing I turned on back, huh?'

He stays motionless, not answering. Abruptly the mean eyes narrow to slits.

'You answer me, boy, you heah?'

'Yassuh,' he says through his teeth. 'Sure is a good thing, suh.'

Down by the booted feet, fresh movement flickers, catching his eye. A thin, coiling shape edges out from the shadow of the bush, gliding silently towards the boots that have roused it from its sleep. Burns, his back to the moving wraith, sees nothing.

'Name's Mister Burns, boy.' His eyes glinting in triumph now, seeing the caught look on the face of the black as proof of his fear and despair. 'You figger you kin say that?'

'Yassuh, Mistah Burns, suh.' His eyes still marking the coiled shape as it moves.

'That's right, boy,' Burns grins. With his left hand he reaches a thong of hide, brings it forward. Contempt is in those thin features as he gestures with the gun. 'You comin' with me, Mister Prime Field Hand, answers to name of Justus. . . . Hold out your hands, boy!'

Stretching out his clasped hands, he sees the snake rear suddenly.

Burns grins again, taking a step forward. 'You one smart nigra, ain't you?' he says.

And the uncoiled shape strikes, suddenly.

Burns yells out and the gun blasts a shot into the soft ground by his feet. Watching, Justus sees the snake with its head clamped tight to the patroller's thigh, fangs sunk in the flesh. Burns drops the gun, grabbing to tear the snake loose and fling it away to the side. He sinks to his knees howling, clutching at the wound, his face twisted in a mixture of fear and pain. Justus leans in quickly, picking up the gun where it lies.

'Gahd! Oh, my Gahd!' Burns is screaming, flailing about on the ground.

Close by the roots of the tree the snake reappears, sways to rear upward. Gun in hand, he watches it, fascinated into stillness. As in a dream his eyes take in the black lift of the belly, the pattern of brown crossbands at the back, the dark wedge of the head. The gaping jaws, the open throat showing white. Cottonmouth. For a while it seems to hang there, black lidless eyes measuring him. Behind him Burns is still calling out.

'Kill it, you dumb nigger bastard! Kill it!'

He stands stonelike, holding to the gun.

Snakes is all gods, Nestor said. Powerful strong spirit in a snake. He don't like for you to move. You do that, you dead. Stand quiet, like you know he the boss, an' most times you won't take no harm.

Course, even Gods get their mean days. We all of us get mean, once in a while.

Still standing immobile as the snake rears. Hoping the sweat don't show too plain on his face and in the palms of his hands.

The snake sinks, dropping back to earth. The thin brown-banded shape slithers away from sight, into the bushes. He breathes out, slowly.

Across from him Burns reaches, stretching out an arm for the fallen knife. The spell broken, he goes in fast, treading the iron underfoot. The revolver holds level on a point between the white man's eyes. Pale blue eyes, he notes. Wide now, all but crazy in terror.

'For Godsakes do somethin'!' Burns screams.

His look goes down to where the leg of the breeches is torn open against the wound. He sees the twin puncture-marks of the fangs, driven deep in the flesh. About them, a puffy, discoloured swelling with livid stripes of red running upward along the white skin.

Cottonmouth bite. Not a hope. Burns, too, must know it.

'Nothin' I kin do,' he says. He bends to pick up the knife. At the bitter look in his eyes Burns lifts a hand, begging.

'*Please.*' A hoarse sound, close to weeping. Tears welling in the pale, mean eyes, running out over the whiskered cheeks. 'You cain't leave me like this . . . not now. . . .'

Along his back the old whip-scars are beginning to itch. The memories they bring back are crueller than the salt they rubbed into the raw flesh afterwards. Awkwardly, he checks the loads in the revolver. A belly-gun, no shell-belt. But four shots. Man can't afford to waste one here.

The hell with you white folks. You took too much from me.

'You finished, Mistah Burns,' he says. His voice comes dry and level as grit. For a moment the white man stares into his grim, merciless face, shocked to silence.

Burns throws back his head and screams. The noise startles birds from the live-oak boughs overhead. A harsh, tearing, fearful sound. For a moment he feels his own gut flutter.

But only for a moment.

'Ain't nobody gonna hear you,' he mutters, his voice going unheard, drowned by the screams of the man who rolls in front of him, clawing the ground. 'You go ahead an' holler, Mistah Burns. You gonna be daid, real soon!'

He turns, sheathing the hoop-iron knife. Still holding the gun, he takes Burns' fallen hat and fills it with water from the bayou. Should do to tide him over for a spell. The screaming follows him as he leaves the open ground, making for the next stretch of woodland. He can still hear it long after he's in among the trees, but he pays it no mind, moving on swiftly as the first light comes spearing in through the branches. Careful, as he treads, not to step down on a sleeping snake.

Each step taking him further, deeper into the wilderness.

HE HEARS the low moan of the cowhorn Jacob carries at his waist, signalling noon. Lets go the hoe from a slippery hand, chafed raw in places where the coarse wood catches the skin. Justus stands a while in the bed of the ditch and draws an arm across his streaming face. Reek of his sweat and that of the gang, close and overpowering in the trapped space. And with it that older, fainter scent of the red Louisiana dirt, telling its own tale of deaths and burials in past years. Flies drone, settling on him here and there. Justus swats at them half-heartedly as he clambers out from the ditch. The gang with him as he makes for the shade: Mede and Cato, Glory and William. Lucas already there, squatted by his water-bucket. And further off he kin see the women layin' out for their midday rest. Ruby there, an' Chloe, Cora an' Lucy. . . . Yeah, an' Sheba too. . . . Smiles a moment, drawing his breath. Sun like to a hammer on his sweat-sluiced back. Up here in the open the stink of the bayou comes stronger, rolling up from the live-oak and cypress groves. Place as low-laid as this, ain't no wonder they forever diggin' ditches. . . .

Halfway to shelter, he finds his look drawn to that lone twisted tree atop the rise. Fixes on that frail, slumped figure lying in the shadow of the boughs. From under the brim of the old straw hat them dark eyes come searching to him.

'Over heah, boy,' Nestor says.

Stands an instant, uncertain, looking to the rest. Right now, none of 'em troublin' over him, he reckons. They all settled in shade with their backs to him, startin' on what food they got. He studies them a while, before that sharp stare draws him back. Nestor smiles, one hand stroking the rabbit's foot at his neck.

Justus heads over to him, halting at last in the shade of the tree. His huge upright shape throws a longer shadow across the seated oldster, blocking him from the sun. Nestor glances up into his puzzled face, and his own leathery features pucker as he smiles again.

'No call fer you to stand over me that way,' the old man tells him. Taps with a greying, fleshless hand on the ground beside him. 'Set down, boy. They's room, I reckon. . . .'

Awkward in the face of those glinting dark eyes, he ducks his head. Squats on his haunches alongside, laying both great hands flat to his knees. For a moment neither one of them speaks.

'Been lookin' at you, Justus,' Nestor says at last. His narrowed gaze rests on the younger man. Careful. Studying. 'You kind of bright, I reckon. . . . Way I see it, boy, you an' me kin git along jes' fine. . . .'

'Sure do 'preciate that, Nestor.' But Nestor doesn't look up. Eyes on the sunstruck ground before him. Somehow, the old man still makes him wary. Careful he don't make no fool of hisself.

Alongside of him, Nestor chuckles. A hoarse, throaty sound, kin to the way he talks. Like a bunch of pebbles in his mouth. The old man eases up a little, his back to the gnarled bole of the tree. At the move Justus looks up. Catches his eye. At once the oldster grins.

'Food heah, boy.' He lifts a packed bandanna from the shade and unwraps it as he hands it over. 'Go 'haid, take it. That good vittals there – sowbelly, cornbread. You eat up, boy. . . .'

'Thanks, Nestor.' He takes the offered parcel of food, uncertain still as he meets the gaze of those half-mocking eyes. 'How 'bout you?'

'Don't trouble over me, young feller. Nestor don't eat no more'n enough to keep a bird alive.' The toothless smile spreads, furrowing the grey, leathery creases of his face. 'Jes' eat up like I tell you, y'hear me?'

'Sure, Nestor. Thanks.' By now he's hungered more than a little. He sinks his teeth into the hunk of fat pigmeat. Chewing, swallowing, as runnels of grease slither down at the corners of his mouth. Nestor watches him a while as he eats. Smiles slyly, half amused. He leans back into the trunk, letting his eyes close. But the young man knows he ain't sleepin'.

'Yeah,' Nestor says, like he's talkin' to hisself. 'Been watchin' you, boy. An' I sure likes what I seen.'

'How that, Nestor?' He speaks thickly, his mouth full of pork and cornbread. For a moment the withered features harshen in annoyance, and he wishes he hadn't said a word.

'Jes' hush up a minute, huh?' the old man tells him. 'Let ole Nestor heah do the talkin', an' you find out soon 'nough. Ain't that right?'

'Anythin' you say, Nestor,' Justus says. At once the leathern smile returns.

'Yeah, boy. That better. That a way better.' He lies back easy, bony hands crossed on his chest. 'Now, you listen good, Justus. I like you a whole lot, an' I'm gonna tell you why... It's this way, feller. Trouble with folk around heah is, they don't know who they *is*—you take my meanin'?'

'I guess so,' Justus still don't sound too sure. Sound of his voice brings the old man's eyes open a crack, and Nestor chuckles. Shaking his salty grey head.

'You heard me tell this bunch before now. They got no idea who they is a-tall. Now you, boy,' he looks up, his hooded glance shrewd and calculating, 'I figure you somethin' like halfway there.'

'You recollect your folks, Justus?' He watches as the younger man shakes his head. Nods slowly, his eyes half-shut. He expected that anyhow. 'Naw, guess you wouldn't – you bein' jes' a little bitty baby an all.'

'Raised me up in the quarters with the rest,' Justus' voice comes dull, heavy to his ears. Across from him he sees the others turn a

46

moment, looking his way. Uncertainty in the set of their faces. Like they ain't too sure whether he one of them or not, while he here with Nestor. Cato's look holds longest. Kind of a mean glint to his eye. Like with *him* there somethin' more. . . . He bears the look, uneasily.

'Was Judith brung me up, Laban's woman, 'fore she died. . . .'

'Hell, I know that!' Nestor sits up all of a sudden, flapping a gaunt hand in impatience. 'I been here a while, boy. Remember?' Then he sighs, the brief gust of anger blowing itself out. Looks again to where the big wide-shouldered man sits quiet by his side. Nestor's harsh features turn a shade gentler. The voice, too, softens as he speaks.

'Judith wasn't yo' mama,' Nestor says. 'Reckon you knowed that from way back, huh?'

'Guess so.' His answer comes back muffled as he bites into the hunk of cornbread.

'Yeah.' The old man's look goes thoughtful, like he rememberin' how it was. 'I kin recall yo' mama sure 'nough, like it was only a couple days back. 'Stead of twenty years, mebbe. . . . Ole Lawrence bought you 'long of her when you was a chile. That was from up north a ways—Ole Man Benford's place by Gator Creek. Yeah, I kin remember her, right 'nough. . . .'

Nestor falls quiet a moment as big Justus sets down the food from his lips. Turning to the older man with a questioning look in his eyes.

'You knowed my mama, huh?' The youngster's voice is eager. Pleading, almost. 'What her name, Nestor?'

For a while the old man don't answer. His narrow-eyed glance shifting on a ways to where Jacob hulks in the shade of the levee wall, sunlight a dull gleam on his dark sweating, flesh. The glare of the driver comes back at him, harsh and unforgiving. Meeting it, Nestor shrugs his skinny shoulders. Lets his gaze ease on back to the man beside him.

'Rachel, that was her name,' Nestor tells him. For a moment, a faint smile appears in the dark worn leather of his face. Shakes his grey head, recollecting. 'Pretty, sweet-natured li'l wench. Light-skinned too. Don't take from her none, I reckon. . . .'

47

'Guess not,' Justus has all but finished the food. Now he licks the pork grease from his fingers, his look still curious. 'How 'bout my pa?'

'Yeah.' Nestor strokes his withered neck in thought. 'Could be you took from him, at that. . . .' Looks out over the sun-blasted canefields a while, his dark, glinting eyes narrowed. 'Marcus, he called. Never did see him, though. When Ole Man Lawrence bought her, Marcus was sold off downriver—someplace in Mississippi, is what I heard. Did hear tell, though, he was a prime powerful hand in the field while he was at Gator Creek. Good man with the wenches, too. . . .'

'How come you git to know 'bout him so good?' Justus asks. 'Thought you ain't never seen him. . . .'

The old man meets his eye. The same secret smile at his lips. 'Lot of things I know 'bout, boy,' Nestor says. His hooded eyes glittering like crumbs of glass in the sunlight. 'It my business to know, understand? I got my ways, an' reckon they ain't no concern of yours. . . . Jes' know I tellin' you like it is, you hear?'

'I hear you, Nestor', he says.

'Good 'nough.' The old man nods, still gazing out over the tall fields of cane. 'Now, Rachel, she long daid. Took fever bearin' a stillborn chile. . . . You wouldn't be no more'n two or three years old yo'self at the time. . . .'

Pauses. Nestor feeling the harshness of the big man's eyes upon him.

'Jes' hold on there, Nestor.' Justus' broad features show harder than a moment back. His keen stare questioning, like he wants the answer real bad. 'You tellin' me when my mama died, that time . . . it warn't my papa's chile she bearin'? That what you sayin', Nestor?'

The old man stays quiet. His closed sober face is answer enough.

'Whose?' The big man's voice grown suddenly cold. Merciless.

Still Nestor don't speak. Instead he lets his glance ease on round past Justus and the other seated slaves. On to the massive figure of Jacob, slumped against the levee wall. At the touch of those eyes on him, the driver looks up again, glaring.

'His chile,' Nestor says.

48

For a while Justus holds at that. Like the words struck him to stone.

'God damn!' His fists clenching hard as the words leave him. Look of his eyes murderous as he too turns towards Jacob. '*His* chile? You sure?'

'I recall it,' Nestor says.

'You tellin' me—that bastard kill my mama?'

His voice shakes, anger all but choking him. He grits hard on his teeth, still trembling with rage as the old man reaches to lay a long-fingered hand at his arm.

'Ease off, boy. You hear?' Those hooded eyes are rheumed and watery, but there's a hardness to them he can't look down. Justus lets the breath from him in a long shuddering sound and goes sullenly quiet. Nestor lets the hand slip from his arm, slowly.

'Jes' hold on to all that piss an' vinegar, chile.' The oldster tells him. 'Come the time, you gonna need it, sure 'nough.'

Justus don't say nothing, looking still to Jacob, hatred in every line of his clenched face. The splayed features of the driver meet him. The harsh yellow glare of the eyes. Jacob is out of earshot, but he kin read faces, sure 'nough, Justus chokes back a snarl in his throat. Fists still bunched at his sides.

One more count agin you, Jacob, the young man thinks.

'Come on, boy,' Nestor's voice comes at him as from a distance, low and compelling. 'You know that kinda thing happen all the time. . . .'

He turns, feeling the worst poison of the rage ebb from him. Leans back, brushing the sudden wash of sweat from his face. Seems like Nestor don't see him. Looking to the canefield as the sound of his voice goes on.

'Ain't only niggers, either,' Nestor says. 'Ole Man Lawrence, he been down the quarters more'n once, back in them times. Sheba, for one—she come from a bed-wench he had, back then. . . .'

'Don't want to know 'bout that!' The words slip from him sudden. Come out soundin' harsher'n he meant. In the heavy silence that drops down after, Justus swallows. Uneasy as that keen shuttered glance shifts back toward him.

'You don't want to know 'bout that?' Nester shakes his head

pityingly, his grey face puckering in leathery lines. 'What kinda fool talk is that, huh? Listen, boy. Nestor tellin' you the way it is. Best you should know it, 'cause you sure as hell gonna find out someday, whether it suit yo' pleasure or not. You hear me good?'

'I reckon.' Lowers his head at the words, feelin' kind of dumb in front of this old man who knows so much he don't. After a while he risks an upward glance. Finds that weathered face set like a mask into sober, thoughtful lines.

'Say, Nestor . . . how 'bout you? Ain't you gonna tell me 'bout yo'self? 'Bout A-frica an' all?'

He watches as the slow smile creases those features once again. Deep-set in the puckered flesh, Nestor's eyes glint more warmly at their depths.

'Sometime I tell you, maybe,' Nestor says. 'Right now, jes' remember one thing. Sweet River all you know, sure. But it ain't all. You hear me talkin'?'

'I hear you, Nestor,' Justus says.

'Hey, y'all nigra sonsabitches!'

Jacob's sudden yell brings the gang jolting to its feet, the driver up and straddle-legged in the dirt, that mad-dog look in his eye as he picks up the whip an' sets it to poppin' in the dust.

'C'mon now, it a way past noon. Move yo' lazy black asses, you heah me?'

His look coming back for Justus as the rest of them head for the ditch. The tall man meets it. The hate showin' plain in his face. His big hard hands bunched to fists at his sides.

God damn you to hell, Jacob. You kill my mama.

One day I sure as hell kill you.

Justus leaves the shade of the tree and the bent, frail figure still lying there, and heads back for the ditch at a run, the fierce sun hitting him as he moves. Keeping a hold on the hate and rage inside.

Nestor right. Come the time, he gonna need it all.

OLD MAN Lawrence sits quiet in the carved mahogany rocker, holding the julep in its long-stemmed glass, looking out from the open door to where the blue of the clear sky deepens, dusk settling on the line of willows in the drive. Out by the canefields the last horn sounds, signalling the end of another day. The nigras gone back to their quarters with first dark. Hearing it, the old man frowns, his pouched yellow face puckering in a network of furrowed wrinkles. Ain't got too many days left hisself, he figures. And right now he don't care to be reminded of it.

Old Man Lawrence shrugs at last. Lifts the chilled glass slow to his lizard lips. One thing to the good. John ain't gonna be home yet awhile. Come night, he be gone huntin' down the quarters for some black wench or other. Leaves him the place to hisself, an' he's given Hagar the evening free. Better that way for what he got in mind.

He drinks, the julep with its minty tang cooling him in the close warmth of the night. Lawrence chuckles, brushing at the gathering sweat on his face. What John gits up to nowadays ain't nothin' new. Once on a time, he used to be pretty hot that way hisself. Still ain't entirely lost the taste for it, even now. . . .

He smiles, the withered skin of his face creasing like parchment. A wistful look comes to the black hooded eyes. Things was a whole lot different when he first brought Effie down here, after they was married. Miss Euphemia Louise Decatur Williams. Yes, sir. For a while he studies on it, calling back her image to his mind: slim and straight, with her waist cinched tight and her bosom firm and high. Graceful way of walkin' she had—kind of *flowed* along the ground. Her face, too, with those wide blue eyes and hair like fine gold that he liked to run his fingers through 'most every chance he got. Yeah, Miss Effie. Real pretty smile she had. Kind of lit up her face. Even now, he ain't forgotten. . . .

Met her at a ball upriver in Alexandria. Took to each other so strong they was married inside a month. Tell truth, her daddy was a mite eager to git her off his hands. She was risin' twenty-seven and hadn't had too many offers. At the time he couldn't rightly understand why. But then, he was so struck with her, figures he wouldn't have seen it anyhow. . . .

He sighs, setting down the glass in his lap, fingers linking at the stem. Yeah, one thing wrong with Miss Effie. She got no use for bodily lovin'. Payin' court to her, compliments an' conversation an' all, that was just fine. But once between those sheets—that was sure as hell another story. Pretty as a china doll to the eye. But to touch. . . . Shakes his white grizzled head, a weary set to his features. Wasn't no way he could break her to it. She must have been raised to look on that kind of thing as sinful, brung up like a lady an' all. When he thinks on it, must have come as a shock to her, seein' a man naked for the first time in her life. Maybe she never did git used to it, neither. . . .

Not that she ever fought him off. Nothin' like that. Was more that when he got to touchin' her, that sweet body of hers sort of clenched up on him—turned all to icy stone. Sure, after a while they did manage to make love, after a fashion. But there was never no pleasure in it. More like somethin' he had to git from him, an' hurt her in the doin' of it. Once she bore John to him, they didn't do that kind of thing no more. . . .

The old man in the rocker lets out a long breath. Shifts the glass to his lips and drinks again. Poor Effie. She never did git used to life here on Sweet River. Always did feel kind of sorry for her, but then, a man has his needs. It's the way we made. An' once she gave up on me, wasn't nothin' I could do but go someplace else to take my pleasure. . . .

Some pleasure, too, down at the quarters.

Sips at the cool liquid. Starting to sweat again. Memory comes to him of the sweet black flesh of the nigra wenches he knowed. That heavy musky smell they had—different from Effie, more exciting, somehow. And the way they could love a man—that sure was somethin' to remember. Eyes half-closed, he nods, smiling faintly at thought of remembered cries, at the clawing touch of frenzied hands on his flesh, those times he spent hisself in a black wench. Those many wenches, too: Hannah, Hagar, Judith, Velvet. . . .

Come to think, they's more'n one on these quarters now he done sired hisself.

Chuckles throatily. Eyeing the glass, painted by the last of the sunset with its rich golds and greens, the colours seeming to swim together in the liquor. Sheba, now, for one.... No doubt about her, she took from Hannah after he been with her more'n once. Didn't let none of the other bucks near her, that time. Couldn't have been no-one else but him, no sir. Lately he got the feelin' that John took a shine to the brownskin gal. Kind of strange when you think about it, them bein' almost brother an' sister an' all....

Not that he ever tole him. Nor her, come to that. No reason. Anyhow, can't say as he blamed John for takin' after that wench. Given a chance, he wouldn't mind her hisself. Pity, though, that she an' that Justus are so close. Man has a right to his pleasure, sure, but he don't want no trouble among the nigras if it can be helped. Could be he'll have to talk to the boy 'bout that, sometime.

Nobody else to tell, 'less you count Nestor. An' he always was a tight-mouthed sonofabitch. Good blacksmith, though. Credit where credit's due....

Looks out again to the deepening night, dark eyes hooded in reflection. Effie's long dead now, God rest her. Died when John was still a boy, an' seems like he been a mean young feller ever since. At the time, doctor told him it was consumption, but he don't believe it. He reckons once she saw how it was, she just up and pined away. Year after that come the influenza, took seven of his best nigras in a couple of weeks. Hannah was one of them, Sheba's mother. It took Judith too, an' Velvet. Seems like the wenches was harder hit than the bucks that time....

Sound of a soft footfall breaks into his thoughts. Old Man Lawrence half-turns, glass in hand. Grins as he catches sight of the outlined shadow in the doorway beyond.

'Come on in, Beth,' the old man says. He smiles slyly, his black gaze hooding. 'Been waitin' for you, I reckon.'

Watches as she steps into the room, her bare feet making hardly a sound on the board floor. Slim and upright in the shadowed room, like the long-stemmed glass he holds. The deep brown skin has a dusky bloom, smooth as satin. The eyes dark and gentle as a faun's. Now they look down as she stands in front of him, hands low to her sides. Waiting.

Been with them a while now, he recollects. Hagar brung her up in the house after he sold her mother downriver when she was still but a child. Now, at fifteen goin' on sixteen, she still got that sweet-assed half-ripe look to her. Lately, it's begun to appeal to him. Lawrence looks a while at his own twisted hands, fingers knotted round the stem of the glass. Glances upward slowly, the lizard smile at his lips.

'Anythin' I kin do, Massa Lawrence?' Her voice light, girlish, eyes held down as she speaks.

Scanning that lissom shape, he nods, feeling the faint, remote stirring in his withered loins. Like somethin' happenin' a world away.

'Yes, child,' Lawrence tells her, a sudden hoarseness gripping his voice, making him pause and lick at his lips. 'You surely can. . . .'

Smiles again, holding out the half-drunk julep in its glass. Hoping his unsteady hands don't shake too much and spill what liquid is left.

'You jes' take this from me, Beth, and set it down on the table yonder.' Eyes her carefully as she takes the drink from his hand, studying. 'Times, cain't seem to hold nothin' in my hands no more.'

Beth smiles in answer, shyly. Soft and flowing as a deer through trees, she turns. Leans away from him to set down the drink on the nearby table. Watching the move, he sees the old calico dress lift a little, giving him a glimpse of her smooth bare legs to the thigh.

Lawrence licks again at his lips, edging forward. Leans in his turn, one dry-fleshed hand slithering up beneath her skirt, following the smooth slope of her thigh to where a furred moistness awaits him, out of sight. No drawers, like always. Lawrence breathes out slow, eyes hooding in anticipation, his scaly fingers exploring the moist firm lips that as yet he cannot see.

'Mercy, Massa Lawrence!' Beth's voice slips up a notch. 'What y' all thinkin' of. . . .'

She turns her head toward him, the dark, doe-eyed look of

54

surprise still on her face. Old Man Lawrence grins back at her, unconcerned. She called out this way last time he touched her, but neither time so loud that anyone could hear. The two of them done played this game before.

'Nothin' to trouble over, honey,' he tells her. His gnarled fingers still busy under her dress. 'Now you come here to me. . . .'

Scent of her hidden sex rises in his nostrils. Gits him goin'. Lawrence draws a breath. Lays hold with his free hand on her supple haunch to draw her to him.

'Like this, Massa Lawrence?' Beth smiles, perches lightly on the arm of the chair beside him. Below her the white-haired man eases back, the chair rocking gently as he shifts position. One hand with its twisted finger-joints slides upward to touch her breasts.

'Let me see those sweet titties, child,' Lawrence says.

He watches as she lifts them out from the loose-necked dress, feeling his sap rise again, gathering in force. Wouldn't have reckoned he had that much left in him at his age, but that's the way it is. With Beth, anyhow. He grabs the nearer overhanging breast. Sucks the nipple into his mouth, greedy as a hungered child. Beth bears the hard pressure of his lips, her face unaltered. Catching sight of the slow-forming bulge in his breeches, she reaches over lazily with a slim-fingered hand. Starts to unfasten his buttons, one by one. . . .

'Yes, my honey. Yes, child. . . .' His voice hoarsens again, and he catches his breath.

He lies back as she leaves the arm of the chair and slips down on her knees before him. Lawrence feels that gentle touch of her hand on his stiffening flesh. Then the softer, sweeter feel of her mouth as it closes about him. Flicker of her tongue as she strums at the head. She's young still, and inexperienced. No skill to her. Right now though, as that sweet, wet warmth moves back and forth over his straining organ, it don't matter a-tall. Lawrence moans out, a low, whimpering cry. Through half-closed eyes he catches a glimpse of her bowed head with its tight black curls, working on him. Then the pleasure lashes upward, and he comes in a single jerking spasm, slumping into the chair as her mouth takes the spurt of his semen.

Time passes, the sky outside darkening. Pretty soon John gonna be back, he figures. Lawrence licks at his dry mouth, black eyes slitted, cunning. Yeah, he reckons. The two of them still got time.

He looks up to her again. Meeting his eye, the young girl smiles.

'Reckon I know what you want from me, Massa Lawrence,' Beth says.

The sound of her light, childish voice rouses him. He nods hurriedly, eager to begin. Beth moves a step closer so her body almost touches his face. From here he kin smell the overpowering scent of where his fingers have been inside her. Above him, Beth smiles.

'Gonna have to git on yo' knees an' beg, Massa.'

Lawrence eases out of the chair, awkward, stiff-limbed, groaning a little as he gets to his knees in front of her. Pain rakes in his chest as he glances upward, and his breath comes short. One day, he figures, he gonna kill hisself doin' this. But seems like he cain't stop it nohow. . . .

'Beth, child.' The floor hard against his swollen knees, he pleads with her. 'Jes' a taste of your pussy, my honey . . . that's all I'm askin'. Please . . .'

Overhead he hears her girlish chuckle. She enjoys it as much as he does, the little bitch, he thinks.

'That what you want, huh?' she asks.

'Please, honey. . . .'

'That sure 'nough what you gonna git,' Beth tells him.

Hoists her skirt up to her belly, straddling over him. His taste still sharp and salty in her mouth, Beth watches the white-haired old man lay his mouth to the place between her legs, her face puckering a moment at the dry, leathery touch of his flesh. Hearing the sound of him as he slobbers and licks at her like a demented beast. Revulsion fighting in her with the sharp excitement of forbidden pleasure.

This the Massa on his knees to her now. An' he gonna make her come off any time. . . .

Beth murmurs softly. Touches herself with an eager hand. Watching his white head moving on her as the slow pleasure begins to pulse through her at the loins, she allows herself a smile.

Yeah. This sure as hell what Massa like doin' best of all.

56

A CHILL morning. The early greyish light pale and eerie over the outbuildings and the dead fields beyond. A strange ghostly time. The time for dyin', he reckons. Under the coarse linsey shirt, Justus shivers, standing with bare feet spread in the frosted mud. Penned inside the rail fence, the trapped hogs squeal, milling in terror as they try vainly to get out. Already they too catch the stink of death in the air. Poised by the shuddering gate, Cato and Mede look to him, waiting.

'Open it up!' Jacob calls out.

First through the gate is a half-growed shoat. Head lifted, and squealing high and loud as it dashes clear, ducking and twisting, it seeks a way through. He goes for it same instant the gate slams back. Glory and William alongside him, he flings on the hog. The force of his body slows it to a halt, Justus grabbing at its legs to take it off balance. Shoat goes over, thudding in the dirt, squealing as the bunch of them pin it down. Cato lunges over with the hook-bladed knife in his hand.

'Jes' keep a hold on him,' Cato says.

That look on his face agin. Like he got Lawrence trapped inside the shoat's body and cain't wait to lay the knife to him.

William hauls back on the critter's head, baring the throat. Under the three of them the long flank heaves, the squeals rising to a shrill peak. Cato snarls, leaning in, brings the knife in a swift movement across the animal's throat. Squealing gives way to a thick gurgle. The half-growed body bucks and heaves a while, then stretches outward. Thick blood fountains from the slit throat and Glory kneels, holding the tub beneath to catch the pulsing flow. No sense in wastin' blood. Come in useful for sausage later on. Justus grunts as the hog's blood spatters his face and chest, flinching at the taste of salt on his tongue. Abruptly the creature under him stiffens, the legs splaying outward.

'Yeah, by God,' Cato says. Holds to the dripping knife, getting up. That same savage killing look on his ebony face. Hog-killin'

57

the one time Cato gits to take out the hate an' poison inside him. Hate for white folks, mostly, but maybe for everbody 'cept hisself. He sure as hell gonna make it count when the chance was there.

Justus gets to his feet as the hog shivers its last. Stands, hands bloody at his sides, looking again to the gate. Far side of him Glory takes up the reeking tub, the hot blood smoking as he hauls it away for the storehouse beyond. Beside him in the dirt, the shoat lies quiet, the last of its blood draining from it into the ground. Even as he watches, Cora leads the wenches in, Ruby with her, an' Chloe. Lucy an' Sheba too. Sheba looks to him, smiling some, an' he grins back. Eager for the night again.

Justus turns away as they gather at the fallen hog, gutting it with their knives, shearing the flesh, hauling out the guts and tripes. He already got work to do.

Back of him Jacob yells out, and Mede draws on the gate. Next one out is a full-growed sow, huge and wide in the body. Head down, she bullets out from the opened gate. Justus dives for her first, and the weight of the hog slams into him, lifting him clear offen his feet. Hangs to her as she screams, driving him at the rail fence. Back of him William comes in fast, whacks for the skull with his knotted hickory club. Critter grunts and sags. Trembling, the heavy bulk sinks to its knees. Justus gets a hold on the neck and hauls. Glory and William diving in to pull with him. The three of them jumping back in a hurry as the great body crashes over.

Cato goes in like a shot as the animal, snorting, tries to roll back on its feet. The knife crosses the throat, sunlight glinting on the blade, and the blood sprays thick and high, spattering the whole bunch of them. The massive hog thrashes and shrieks against the ground. Justus breathes hard, his shirt, breeches and flesh sticky and stiff with blood. It clings to the palms of his hands, tautens, drying on the skin of his face, the hot reek of it overpowering now in the closed space. The second body settles, and the critters in the pen squeal louder than before, knowin' what's comin' for them.

Glory straightens from the hog at last, blood-smeared arms hefting his second tub. Sow's blood fills it, slopping over the brim to puddle the dirt. Takes him an' William both to git it lifted back by the storehouse wall. Steam rising from it, covering the pair of

58

them in a cloud. Some distance from them Justus stands, watching the women crowd in on the second hog. Cora the nearest, bending close to ease the knifeblade in, slicing up through the fat and flesh of the belly. Her hands, too, smoking as she reaches inside, drawing out the tangle of guts and flinging them aside.

Cora—Cato's woman.

Her long-jawed head turning, looking toward him where he stands. Cora, tall an' long-limbed, her skin smooth and ebony black. Blacker'n his, black as Chloe or Cato. Now as she turns her head he catches sight of her body, outlined through the cotton of her dress: taut, high lift of her breasts against the cloth, the nipples showing hard in the morning cold. Slim, flat belly and narrow flanks. The smooth, lean curve of her hips and thighs. Meeting his eye, she smiles—a faint, secret smile, her dark eyes half-lidded. Justus swallows, uneasy now. Aware of the harsh breathing of Cato at his shoulder. Aware too of the thickening swell of flesh at his groin that strains against the cloth of his breeches. . . .

She Cato's woman, sure 'nough. An' Sheba his. But Cora a wench to take any man's eye. Could be the strugglin' hogs, or the hot stink of spilled blood that rouse him this way. But right now, lookin' on her, he cain't help wonderin' what she like under that there dress. How her body feel to a man's hand. What she like in the crib at night. . . .

Breathes out hard, recalling Sheba. Cato's hard eyes on him as he turns away.

'Best you should quit dreamin', nigger,' the stocky black man tells him. Strokes with his free hand at the blade of the fouled knife. Eyes glinting in the smooth dark of his face. 'She for me, an' don't you forget it – not ever, you hear?'

Justus don't answer. He goes on by the man with the knife, stands ready as Mede heaves on the gate an' the next doomed hog comes flying out. Squealing like the knife already at its neck. . . .

He gets up slow, wiping the blood-stained palms of his hands on his breeches. The mornin' halfway through, an' by now most of the hogs are drained an' gutted. They save the biggest hog till last. He up there now by the gate of the pen. Slamming at the wood with his massive snout. From here Justus kin hear the clack of them tusks, an' he don't care for the sound of it a-tall.

Shoats an' sows is one thing. Full-growed boar hog, that somethin' else agin.

Behind him he hears the driver chuckle. Ugly, knowin' sound.

'Yeah,' Jacob says. Grins, his yellow eyes narrowed as he too looks to the penned hog. 'He gonna give you trouble, I reckon.'

Turns sudden, flicking out the whip in his hand so the lash snaps. Cutting at the frosted dirt.

'Let go the gate, Mede!' Jacob calls.

He sees the gate start its backward swing. Then a hairy bouldering shape surges out, like to a chargin' wall. He sees it slam Mede back with the gate as it goes by, flinging them at the rail fence beyond. Then ain't much time to see nothin', 'cause that goddamn' hog right on to him.

Springs aside as the tusked head swings, hooking for the body. Hog misses, slobber flying, spraying his shirt and breeches as it whirls half around, aimin' to come in agin. William gits in a man-sized wallop with his hickory club to the critter's head, but that jes' slows him down a little. Justus throws hisself on to the flank, hands digging for a grip in the coarse mat of hair. Hog takes off at a run, dragging him with it. Bare feet slithering in the frozen mud. Justus snarls. His face pressed to the boar's hairy back. From here he kin make out the glint of that mean little eye turned his way. Hear the clack of tusks. Away beyond him the wenches are squealin' out louder'n the hog, an' Jacob's voice bellowin' out above them. Tellin' them to hush up, or they be sorry. . . .

'Oh, God! Justus!' Sheba callin' out now, scared for him already. 'Don't let go from him, honey!'

Some chance, gal, Justus thinks.

Reaches sudden. Twining an arm under the throat of the hog. Hauling tight. Feels the jolt as the huge body tenses. Shaken half to pieces as the head flings this way an' that, spittle spattering the air. Glory comes in to help. Grabs for the head, a way too close. Point of a yellow tusk rakes him along the upper arm. Glory yelping and falling back, clutching his torn flesh as the blood spills down.

'Git to him, damn it!' Jacob yells.

Rail fence comin' up fast ahead. Hanging to the hog's back, wrestling for the head, Justus feels the breath drive from him as it crashes into the flimsy barrier. Rails splintering out as the animal slams and rebounds from the wood. Far side of him William comes in agin, his grey face savage as he lays in with the club. Him an' Glory kind of close, after all.

'Git on down, you sonofabitch!' William shouts. His breath rasping as the club comes down a second time. Three. Four. Justus counts the blows with each shuddering thrust of the hog beneath him. Last time he hears the skull-bone cave. Big hog snorts again, blood gushing sudden from the snout, making slick pools underfoot. One last shudder and it keels over, falling, Justus hanging to it as it goes.

'Oh, yeah!' That Lucy, screaming out high and shrill. 'You done it, sure 'nough!'

He gets up, flinching at the bruises on his body. Sucking the air back into his battered lungs. Down on the ground the hog lies quiet. Cato crouched by it to set the hooked knife to its throat.

'Git that goddamned tub yonder!' Jacob snarls, teeth bared like a wild dog. His shout halts William halfway towards the injured Glory, who stands clutching his gashed arm, wincing at the pain. The grey-skinned man turns to the sound, anger still in his own dark face. The look of those fierce eyes is enough. William grabs a fresh tub, heaves it over as the knife flashes and a bright jet of blood pumps from the severed throat.

'You hurt bad?' the driver asks. Met by that unforgiving stare, Glory scowls.

'Ain't nothin' but a scratch,' Glory tells him. 'Don't amount to much, I reckon....'

Jacob watches that scowling face a while. Turns, flicking the long whip out along the ground. 'Chloe, git his arm bound up,' he calls. 'Rest of you, git to it!'

His voice comes to Justus as from a distance, heard yet not heard. The big man stands, his huge frame heaving as his breath returns. In front of him the faces of the women looking his way. Relief and admiration there. Maybe somethin' else, too. Not from Sheba only. Cora lookin' at him that way, too. An' Lucy....

'That sure was somethin', Justus,' Lucy says.

Her eyes on him as she speaks, touching him like fingers on his blood-splashed flesh. Lucy ain't black like Cora or Chloe, nor yet the light yaller-brown Sheba got. Instead, she kind of reddish-coloured, like Mede. Her thick, wavy hair holds the same tawny lights. Could even be kin. Only her eyes different. Where Mede's are blue an' pale, Lucy got the same deep red-brown eyes as her skin. He stands now. Feeling their touch upon him. Saying nothing as the breath rasps in his throat, and his untamed maleness bulges under his breeches.

'You hear me, nigger!' Jacob's voice cuts through his thoughts. Brings him back to the raw cold of the morning, the stench of blood and filth all around. 'Git on there!'

He moves, heading over to join the rest. Mede stumbling back with him, bent over as he clutches the bruise at his side where the hog drove him into the fence. Justus lays hold on the gutted carcass of the shoat. Hoists it on his shoulders to make for the open storehouse door. Back in there they got the scaldin' vats an' the brine. After that, the hogs hung up inside till they needed.

Looks like they through with this year's hog-killin', anyhow.

All the same he frowns, hefting the bloody carcass on his shoulders. Unquiet time, hog-killin'. Gits a man restless an' fired up for no reason a-tall, he reckons. This time the wenches got it too. Recalling how Cora and Lucy eyed him a moment back, he licks at his lips, uneasy in the morning chill. Maybe just as well he got Sheba to keep him down. 'Cause either one of them would be hot for him iffen they git the chance. An' ain't no denyin' they comely wenches. Man could have him some fun there, sure 'nough.

Scowls, shaking the thought from his mind. Best he should forget it, like Cato says. Sheba his woman, an' that enough for him.

Leastways, that the way he figures it oughta be.

Frowning still, he takes the weight of the dead hog on his back. Stooping as he ducks inside the storehouse. Bare feet crunching in the frosted earth.

Times, he reckons it might be easier to be a hog than a man, here on Sweet River.

'THIS PLACE ain't our country,' Nestor tells him. 'Way before you born, they come over to Africa with their guns an' clubs an' all, brung us back in chains cross the big water.'

Justus squats on the earth floor, hands around his knees, wide-eyed as he listens. Dark is over the cabin, and all the candles out, but nobody thinks to ask Nestor what he's doing here at this hour. As oldest hand on Sweet River, the grey-headed slave has the run of the place, night and day alike. Now he sits hunched on the crib, his back to the wall and his thin legs dangling halfway to the ground. Justus at his feet, listening.

'How they do that, Nestor?' he asks.

'Come in boats, boy, like you never seen in your life. Big guns, too, like up on the road that time you dug the ditch.' His voice tautens, remembering. 'Once they got us in them boats we was locked down good, chained up, laid flat to the floor. Musta been hundreds of us that time, crammed tighter'n hogs in a pen. Plenty got sick once we was on the big water. Folk shittin', throwin' up every place you turn. After a while they was some dyin' or goin' crazy. An' the stink, churns me up jes' thinkin' . . . I ain't like to forget it.'

Across the darkened cabin, Glory and William glance towards him. Their faces half-laughing, half-afraid. The old man on the crib turns his head their way, touching a hand to the charm at his neck. The two brothers look away hurriedly, moving to the far wall and its empty cribs. They settle there, heads down, muttering between themselves. Nestor smiles.

'This A-frica,' Justus again, eyeing the old man uncertainly. 'What it like, Nestor?'

The hunched figure above him chuckles, one hand lifting to scratch a leathery cheek. In the darkness his eyes glint like twin shards of glass, mockingly.

'One thing sure, it ain't like Cato says,' Nestor grins wryly, shaking his salty head. 'Ain' no black folks hangin' out of no trees that I recall. No boy.' His lined face sobering. 'We got villages out there, houses. One I lived in was a sight better'n quarters here. . . . Raised us some crops, herded goats an' cattle. Come to think, ain't so different from here on Sweet River, 'ceptin' we was free.'

'That right?' Justus squints, not sure he heard straight. 'You mean, wasn't none of you slaves, Nestor?'

'Slaves? Man, we was kings! Ever'thing we growed was ours, an' we didn't have no big Massa Boss an' no driver comin' around gettin' us up come first light, neither.' His face puckers in thought, regretful. 'Had us our own gods, too. You ever hear of Legba, huh? Or Shango, maybe?'

'Shango?'

'He the god of storms, boy. He talk in lightnings an' thunders.' Nestor ducks his head, smiles knowingly. 'You figger folk gets struck by accident, huh? That Shango, he take 'em. Back home, in our village, use to kill us a goat for Shango when the rain come, keep him fed so he leaves us be. . . .'

Squatted by the old man's feet, Justus nods, frowning as he thinks it over. Somethin' in that, all right. He seen lightnin' strike a tree clean, or a man maybe. Didn't look like it wasn't meant that way. Could be more in this god talk than he figured at first.

'Spirits everyplace,' Nestor is saying, rocking himself back and forth in the crib as his voice goes on in a kind of chant. 'Get 'em in trees, in the earth, out'n the bayous—you name it. Critters too, specially snakes. Back in our country, snakes is gods too. Tell you 'bout that some time. Plenty power in a snake. He mean, like you young fellers when your sap runnin' high, know what I tell you?' He watches the young man's awkward face, laughs slyly. 'Yeah, you knows all right. You an' that Sheba, here nights. I heard you, like a coupla cats sometimes. . . .'

Justus grunts and looks down, his face grown hot. He grins, but all the same he's glad of the darkness. Across the cabin he can sense the other two and their laughter.

'Somethin' like that over here,' he says after a while. 'Like, we got us ring-shouts an' dancin', that kind o' thing. An' some of the other fellers—they reckon they go worship in a oak grove, some nights. Cato claims he seen a cock killed an' hung up one time. . . .'

'That voodoo, boy,' Nestor snorts, shaking his grey head in contempt. 'None of that don't amount to nothin'. It come from the old country, all right. Trouble is, they don' know who the real gods is no more. Back in our country, we all got names of our own for the gods, but we all knows who they is. Know who we is, too! An' we had drums. Ain't got no drums out here.' He leans forward, his glance striking sharp at the squatting man. 'You ever hear drums beat, huh boy?'

He shakes his head, not sure what Nestor is aiming at. Here on Sweet River they got stuff like bones and gourd-shakers. But drums? White folk soldiers have drums, they reckon. He can't recall seeing one on the plantation anyplace.

'Guess not,' he says, and Nestor grins.

'You hear a drum beat, you know it,' the old man tells him.

But Justus is going back in his mind to what Nestor said before. About the gods, and their names.

'Nestor, you say y' all got names for the gods back home.' His voice uncertain, faltering. He glances up to the old man as he speaks. 'That mean you ain't all the same over there?'

He sees the withered features pucker in amusement, and hangs his head.

'Boy, I had you figgered smarter'n that! Does we two look alike?' He cackles throatily, the grey head shaking.' Ain't no two of us akin here on Sweet River, let alone back there. No, boy, over the old country we got different peoples, see? My country, we was Yoruba—big nation, strong. Real big villages—Oyo, Ile-Ife, bigger'n Sweet River. Plenty spears, good in war. Worked iron real good.' He pauses, rheumy eyes half-shut in thought. 'Kin tell folk apart here, even now. Cato, I reckon he one of them Ga off the Guinea Coast. An' Mede, I figger there some Wolof blood in him someplace; he got that tall, stretched-out look Wolof have back home. Chloe now, she a Malinke, an' that kid Lucas he take from her more'n his pa. William an' Glory, I reckon they could be Ashanti, but they ain't the same. Maybe some Manding there in Glory, cain't tell for sure. . . .'

He lapses into silence, eyes closed, frowning as he thinks it over. Justus starts to smile.

'What 'bout me then, Nestor?'

'That easy, boy. You Ibo. Kin tell that jes' from lookin'.' Nestor grins, nodding, his eyes open. 'Iboland not too far off from Yoruba country. Our folk use to fight one time. . . . Ibos always was smart, wood-carvers an' suchlike. I kin see it in you too. Yeah, you a Ibo all right. Didn't know it till now, huh?'

'Reckon not,' Justus says. Then, 'An' Jacob, what 'bout him?'

'Ashanti, I reckon.' The old man scowls, irritated. 'Don' talk to me 'bout Jacob, son. He one dumb nigra, ain't got no more sense'n he was born with. Once they whupped him good, he like a white folks' dog. Now he do ever'thing they tell him, jes' like so. Huh, that Jacob!'

Justus nods, and for a time the pair of them are quiet in darkness. After so long the young man speaks again.

'Nestor, you claim your people strong. How come the white folks brung you outa there in chains?'

The old man's face takes on a bitter look. He leans, spitting on the dirt floor.

'They had help,' Nestor says. It seems to Justus, listening, that his voice trembles. 'They set one bunch of our folk against the other, sellin' guns, givin' presents, that kind of thing. We got us nigras like Jacob back there, too! Yeah, that how they done it. Me, I was drug out from my own village, an' was Yoruba men brung me to the traders. One of them was kin to my mother, come to think. . . .'

'That be some while back, I guess?' Justus puts in cautiously after a spell of quiet.

'Way back,' Nestor shakes his head sadly, thinking over time past. 'That time, white folks here been fightin' another war altogether. That Frenchman, Napoleon Bonaparte his name was . . . yeah, way back. I was comin' up for fourteen years old that time, startin' to work iron like my father done—he was blacksmith to the village. They brung me from the forge, me an' plenty others . . . mostly young folk like myself . . . an' out to them boats they had. . . .'

He sighs, letting the memory die. When he turns back to the young man, his expression is cold, somehow remote and proud.

'Ain't anyone kin be a blacksmith, back in the old country. Back there, kings work iron. They do tell Shango hisself was a blacksmith once, know that?' The mask cracks then, and he grins crookedly at the squatting figure by his feet. 'When I was growed they made me blacksmith here on Sweet River... I taught that Laban ever'thing he knowed. Kin teach you too, maybe. You got the build, an' you Ibos is smarter'n some, I reckon....'

'Sure kind of you to offer, Nestor.' Justus keeps his voice low, respectful. Chance at the blacksmith's job would be welcome, taking him from the cane and the ditches. Still he hasn't heard enough.

'That big water you tell of, Nestor. How far it go?'

'Cain't rightly tell, boy.' The old man frowns, remembering. 'Whiles, they'd have us up on deck, get us to shuffle around an' dance maybe—had fellers with whips there, like always—an' we'd get to see it then. You ain't seen nothin' like that water, chile. It go clear from sunup to sundown, not a sight of land a-tall. An' all a-heavin' an' tossin' like a wild hog under that boat. Men was throwin' up all the way across. Up there was bad 'nough, but fastened down below in the dark was worse. Plenty died off, an' times they drug 'em out to toss over the side.' He scowls, sucking his teeth. 'Bad time, that. Ain't known a worse, an' must be fifty years since. Now, I'm bout the only one alive.'

At that the young man nods, silently. No one on Sweet River up to Nestor's age, that for sure.

'Once they got us here they found us quarters, set us to work right in them canefields yonder. Split us up, too. Them that had one kinda talk—Ibo, Wolof, whatever—set off from one 'nother. No drums, no chantin' neither. After that, it white folks' talk always. You sing out in your own tongue, you take a lickin' for sure.' Nestor's face puckers to a wry, bitter smile. 'We bin here a while, they pitch in with that Africa stuff. How we always been dumb, livin' in trees an' all....' His eyes on the young man now, narrowed, glinting. 'Some of these young folks believes it all. Not me—I been there. I *seen* what it like, for true. You hear me, boy? Give us black folks a chance, an' we as smart as them.'

'You reckon?' Justus studies the man above him, none too sure.

Nestor snorts his contempt, slaps with a hand in the air as if brushing the words away.

'Boy, I know it! Heard tell of a feller once, on some island not far off from here. Some Frenchman place, I reckon. Toussaint, they call him. He run the white folks clean outa there all by himself. For a while, he even give that Frenchy Napoleon a whippin'!' He leans close, his withered features gone grim and hard, his mouth a thin straight line. 'Think about it, boy. They kin be beat, same as we kin. Right now they got lucky, is all.'

'Yeah.' Letting the word come slow. Uncertain still in his mind. Thinking about Lawrence astride the big horse, the blacksnake whip in his hand. The grey soldiers on the road. Wonders how this Toussaint would have handled them.

'You figger a man could get back to A-frica, Nestor? 'Cross that big water you tell of?'

'Dunno, boy.' For once the old man is unsure. He leans back on the cabin wall, one hand scratching in the grey bristles at his jaw. 'Times, I'd think 'bout that. More'n once I made a run. Never did make it, I guess. Now I get too old, ain't goin' nowhere. Noplace but here for this nigra, chile.'

He breaks off then, letting the hand fall. Lifts his head to look the young man in the eye.

'You now, husky young buck like yourself, that different. Just remember that downriver they's that big water. Get deep into them bayous, could be you git loose altogether.' He falls quiet, his old salty head sunk on his chest. Long hands lying still in his lap.

Down by his feet Justus frowns. Thinking. Hard work here on Sweet River. Day clean to first dark. Ditching. Cutting, Harvesting. Hauling and crushing the cane in the sugar-house. Tough, back-breaking work, going on forever. Day after day. Year after year. Until he gives out, and they bury him in that same red earth.

Then again, it's the one life he knows. . . .

'Ain't been noplace else, Nestor,' he says.

At that the old man rouses, coming bolt upright on the edge of the crib. All of a sudden his sunken eyes blaze. Looking up, Justus scents the power in him and is afraid. 'I have, boy,' Nestor says, in a low measured kind of voice that sets the young man's spine prickling. 'An' what I seen is a whole lot better'n what we got here. Was I you, I'd take out after that.' He pauses, drawing breath slow as his anger dies down. Still, the look he gives Justus makes the youngster feel small. 'You wanta live this way always, boy? Workin' yo'self dead for Lawrence an' that Jacob? Or you gonna try strike out an' live free?'

He doesn't answer, looking to the ground.

'Thinkin' 'bout that wench, ain't you? That Sheba, huh? Ain't about to leave her, that it?'

Still no answer. Across the cabin he hears Glory chuckling softly. Justus bunches a fist against the dirt floor. He looks up again to the old man, knowing his silence is answer enough.

'Up to you, boy,' Nestor tells him. He shrugs his thin shoulders, easing himself forward on the edge of the crib. 'You want her, you better stay. You run, you lose her sure. Stay, you could lose her agin, ain't no tellin'.' He grins again, humourlessly. 'One thing sure, they gonna work you while you here. Pretty soon you be played out like the rest. . . .'

'*You* lasted, Nestor,' he says. Nestor laughs.

'Ain't nobody else has.' He gets down from the crib, dusting the dirt and spiderwebs from his shirt, ready to be gone. 'No other field hand here livin' above forty year old. Jacob there, he half my age an' he old already, I reckon. . . .'

Over by the door he pauses, looking back. His eyes reach for the young man in darkness. 'Think about it, boy,' he says. ''Cause pretty soon, you gonna have to choose.'

He leaves, the door closing behind him as he vanishes into the dark outside.

OVER AT the big house, Lawrence downs another whisky.

Dark at the windows beyond him, pressing in close. Black and thick as molasses. A smothering, clammy heat that brings him out to sweating at the armpits. Moisture beads his narrow face as he drinks, scowling. Ice in the glass, its chill welcome against his lips at the rim. Lawrence swallows, the fiery liquid flooding his throat. From outside, a breeze wafts in the heavy scent of hibiscus blossoms. Further off, he hears the scraping chatter of cicadas and the distant chorus of bullfrogs out by the bayou.

'Some things here I aim to change, mighty soon,' Lawrence says.

The room is awash with yellow lamplight. He looks over to the thin, white-haired man who leans in the rocker across from him, his eyes closed. Old now, his father, and frail to the first glance. The tanned skin yellowing, pouching and lined with age. The eyes sunken, rheumy and faded. The joints of the hands are twisted, swollen atop the silver-headed cane. Painful for him now, to walk or ride. Maybe even to breathe. Still, the old man hangs grimly to the life he has left. And for as long as he can do it, he'll be master at Sweet River.

'That right, son?' Old Man Lawrence smiles, half-turning his head. The eyes are open now, narrow and shrewd. 'Just what you got in mind?'

Faced by that sly look, the young man scowls again. 'You too soft with these nigras.' Lawrence says. He swallows the whisky, setting the glass down hard on the table top. The sound of it rings sudden in the stillness. Now the young man stands looming above the frail figure in the chair, legs astride, hands clenched in front of him. 'I seen 'em too often lately, layin' the work by when it don't suit their pleasure. Every time Jacob turns his back, you got idle niggers somewhere about. An' that ole crow Nestor is usually where the trouble's at. Should of sold him downriver years back, is my opinion.'

The old man in the rocker chuckles, shaking his white head, and reaches for the half-drunk whisky in front of him.

'We had our change out of Nestor,' Old Man Lawrence tells him. 'More'n fifty years he's worked here on Sweet River. Good man, too, best blacksmith I ever seen in my life here or anyplace else. Used to hire him out one time, brought in quite a heap of dollars that way....' He smiles, nodding faintly at the distant memory. 'About this other business, seems to me there ain't no percentage in a man ruinin' his own property for the pure hell of it.

The work gets done, an' you know it. Yields are up on last year's crop, an' ain't no reason to suppose we doin' worse'n we was before. Drive the nigras, sure, I see that. But playin' 'em out in double-quick time, that ain't my line, son. Nor should be yours neither, I reckon.' He smiles again, mockingly it seems, and lifts his own glass to drink.

'Hagar!' Young Lawrence turns for the doorway, face twisted in anger. 'Fresh glasses. An' hurry it up, you hear?' He swings round again to his father, breathing hard, brushing the fresh sweat from his face as he moves. Down by his sides, his hands are clenched hard.

'I still say you're too soft,' the young man mutters. In the glare of lamplight his own dark eyes glitter like specks of glass. 'Firm hand's the one thing them dumb niggers understand. Once I'm master here, I aim to see they get it!'

'Yeah, son. You do that.' Old Man Lawrence grins crookedly, rocking himself back and forth, his eyes half-closed. All the same he watches as Hagar shuffles into the room, setting out the fresh-filled glasses on the table in front of them. Getting an old woman now, Hagar, the black skin shrivelled and puckered into deep lines around the eyes and mouth, her thick hair whitening fast on her skull. He eyes the stooped, obese shape as she turns, gathering up empty glasses on the tray to move out again.

Who'd have thought she could give him twenty years? Or that a generation back she was the hottest nigger wench in the quarters? Lawrence grins now, remembering. The smooth touch of her flesh is with him still, after thirty years and more.

'That's just fine, Hagar. You get along now, you hear?'

'Sure do 'preciate that, Mistuh Lawrence, suh.' A bent, broad-beamed black woman, hunched over as she waddles awkwardly out of the room. Lawrence grins again, shifts in his seat to where his son still faces him, glowering as he reaches the fresh glass from the table.

'That's another thing needs changin',' Young Lawrence tells him. His glance, too, follows Hagar's shuffling figure out by the door. 'That Hagar—she's way too old for the job. What we need here is a new wench to serve table. Housemaid, cook, whichever, long as she kin come when you call her. . . .'

He breaks off, aware suddenly of those sly mocking eyes upon him.

'That so?' The old man puckers his lips thoughtfully. Watching, Lawrence figures that his father can read his mind. 'Mind tellin' me who it is you got in mind, son?'

Knows damn well who I mean, the old goat, he thinks.

'Sheba,' Lawrence says. On his lips the word comes as a betrayal, and his hands clench on the glass he holds. 'She's a touch delicate for field work, I reckon. Good manners an' all. Young, too. Bring her over to the house, you'll see a difference, sure enough.'

He breaks off then, drinking hurriedly, the whisky burning his throat. Across from him the old man smiles again.

'That ain't all, is it?' says Old Man Lawrence.

'What do you mean?' His own voice is sharp, resentful. Hoarse yet from the last slug of whisky. There in the rocker the old man chuckles, shaking his head. Lawrence is having trouble meeting his eyes.

'Reckon you took a fancy to that brownskin gal,' his father says. His bleared eyes glint, remembering thirty years back, and the time he and Hagar had in the old feed barn. Then he catches the fierce expression in the face of his son, and his own look becomes sober. 'One thing, son. Don't go forgettin' she's Justus' woman right now. I got a feelin' them two are about to jump the broom, real soon.'

Lawrence stands wordless to that for a long minute, his mouth tight, breath heaving in his chest. Then he breaks out, cursing viciously, and whips forward to hurl his glass at the wall. The old man doesn't even turn as it shatters to fragments behind him.

'God damn!' Lawrence shouts, his thin face convulsed. 'Them niggers run this place, or us? The hell with Justus! I want Sheba, I take her—ain't for him to stop me....' He runs out of breath suddenly and stands, gasping, his face hot in anger.

'Hagar!' The old man calls. He turns back, peering over the silver-topped cane at the man who stands before him. Got a mean streak in him, John—no two ways about that. Worse since his mother died, but always there. The old man turns that bleak thought over in his mind, eyeing him soberly, unsmiling.

'That's right, son,' his father tells him. 'The niggers do run the place. 'Cause we sure as hell can't handle a sugar cane crop ourselves. Now you hear me, John. Them blacks is good merchandise. I don't want none of 'em spoiled or set agin us. As it is, we been lucky the army ain't called up no more of 'em for work on the roads yonder.' For a moment his faded eyes harden, glittering. 'I aim to keep 'em, son, you hear?'

Lawrence doesn't answer, glowering down at the glass shards and spilt whisky on the floor. Behind the old man, Hagar shuffles in again, looking from the mess to young Lawrence and back again. Back of the fixed, fawning mask, her deep-set eyes are hard and resentful. Hagar had thought she was through for the evening. Lawrence glares back at her, viciously, and the old housemaid turns away. Her breath comes short as she bends to gather up the mush of glass and liquor from the ground.

The old man sees it too, hears the harsh grunt of effort as she waddles out at last. His son's right. She's served her turn. Played out now. Sooner or later, Sheba will be coming over to the big house to wait on table, and do whatever else John has in mind. The white-haired man watches Hagar out through the door, his weathered face emotionless.

'That Justus, too,' Old Man Lawrence says. 'Don't forget him. He's a good husky young buck, got the makin's of a blacksmith, I reckon. We been short-handed there since Laban got himself crippled at the forge a couple of weeks back. Way I see it, we could have Nestor train the boy up a little. From the look of him he's good for ten years, I'd say.'

'Ain't got no time for neither one of them,' Lawrence spits out the words in a fury, wiping at the stain of whisky on his white shirt-front. 'Nestor nor Justus. They're both of 'em uppity niggers. They got a way of lookin' at a man that I don't care for—it ain't respectful.' He breathes out slowly, conscious of the sweat that pours off his face and soddens his shirt at the neck. The damp patches in the palms of his hands. 'They kin both use some disciplinin', I reckon.'

Old Lawrence lets go a snorting breath, and raps with his cane on the wooden floor. His dark eyes probe at the younger man like twin slivers of quartz.

'I tole you once, son, we *need* these niggers,' the old man says. 'Gonna need 'em more before we done. There ain't no other help to hand, an' our boys is farin' bad against Sherman's bluebellies yonder. We already lost Atlanta a while back, an' we ain't done yet.' He sighs, his grizzled head sinking so that his chin rests on the crossed hands above the cane. His look shifts towards the dark, uncertain land beyond the windows, his eyes suddenly brooding, wary. 'Big trouble comin', son. I kin see it. We got any sense, you gonna keep them niggers happy.'

Lawrence's thin face tautens, quivering in sudden rage. He swears again, strikes with a bunched fist down against his thigh. 'You just think what the hell you like, old man!' he shouts at the bent figure in the chair. 'Once you're gone, I'm gonna be master here—and I ain't takin' no shit from no Justus or nobody else! I want that girl, an' by God I aim to have her, you hear me?'

He turns, slamming out from the room, the door thudding shut behind him.

SWELTERING SUMMER'S noon. The canefields and bayous lying hazy, shimmering in heat. He lies between the tall rows of the canes. Flinching now and then to the lash of the sun on his back. He long since ate the food he brung along, an' now don't look like there nothin' for him to do a-tall. . . .

Looks toward Nestor, but the old man sleepin' today, hunched over in the shade of that one twisted tree atop the rise. Most of the gang laid out further on, restin' same as him. A while back he saw Glory an' William move off, but he don't know where. An' Jacob, too, he around someplace. Right now, though, place lies quiet as a grave. An' he lies with it, chewing a strip of cane straw to splinters in his mouth.

Inside, though, he ain't so quiet. Heat of the sun burns at him, fires his blood, keeps him restless, unsettled. While the bunch of them out there workin' it ain't so bad. Jacob drive 'em too hard to think long on anythin' else. But come noontime, after he rested up for a while, he gits to troublin' in the heat. Feelin' the lazy flicker of lust twitch at his groin. Thinkin' of Sheba, an' wishin' it had got round to night already, 'stead of bein' halfway through the day.

Justus grunts, irritated by his body's longings. No way he kin do nothin' 'bout *that*, he figures. Rolls over, head pillowed on his arms. Stretches out, closin' his eyes agin the sun.

Light footfall rouses him. Eyes openin' sudden, glancin' back beyond him. Cora smiles, picks her way easy through the tall ranks of cane. Her lithe, dark body rimmed in the fire of the sun.

'You lookin' at somethin', boy?' the tall black wench asks. The sly smile of her face reflected in her eyes. Met by her knowing gaze, Justus swallows and scowls, looking away.

'Reckon not,' the big man says, hoping she don't see how this heat roused him up. From where he lyin' he kin feel the bulge of his swollen manhood through his breeches.

Somewhere above him Cora laughs. Soft, mocking sound, low in her throat.

'Have it your way, honey,' she says. Goes on by him down the cane row, stalking smooth and easy as a cat after sparrows. Halfway along, she turns to look back to him where he lies. That same sly, mocking smile on her face.

'Sure you don't want to come along?' she asks.

He shakes his head, scowling, made uneasy by the light in those dark eyes. Cora grins, shrugs her ebony shoulders. She goes on down the canefield, out of sight.

Watches her until she gone. Scowls, aware of the teasing heat at his loins. That wench hot for him, he knows. Had an eye for him since hog-killin' time. Cato her man, sure, but it don't seem to bother her too much. This kinda thing go on much longer, he figures he gonna have a trouble gittin' outen her way.

Maybe he wouldn't even want to try. . . .

Snarls, angered suddenly at himself. He better off keepin' Sheba in mind. She be all the woman he like to need.

After a while the restlessness gits to him again. Justus rises up from the ground where he lies. Moves out to another path between the mass of canes. No sense goin' the same way she gone. That be askin' for trouble, sure 'nough. But right now it more'n he kin do to stay quiet where he is.

Deep in among the canes, cut off on every side from the heat of the sun, he halts. Looks about him, slow, thoughtful. Up above he kin scarce see a cloud. The whole earth shakin' in a haze of heat. Shrugs, about to go on. Then he hears the voices.

'Oh, yeah, my honey,' Glory moans.

Halts like he's struck to stone, searchin' for the sound. Cain't tell where it come from, not for sure. But it somewhere out beyond him in the thickest of the cane. On a path he cain't make out from here. Even as he looks, the noise starts up agin.

'Do that agin, William,' Glory sayin', like he gonna die any minute if William don't do what he tellin' him. 'That's right, honey . . . oh, that the sweetest, sure 'nough.'

Hears William's soft, chuckling laughter, the sharp, hurried breathing as the words die to inarticulate cries. Justus licks at his lips, uncertain. He seen the two of 'em lovemakin' before. Nights, in the quarters. But out here in daylight! He figures he didn't oughta be here listenin' a-tall. No more'n if somebody come by while he an' Sheba was gittin' to it. Same time, though, he wary of movin' less'n he disturb them. He don't want neither of 'em to think he been standin' an' lookin' on.

Turns about slow. Careful on his feet. Starts to move away as those same voices murmur in the canes beyond. He's but a few paces further along the path when comes a startled cry and sound of another, fiercer voice.

'So this what you two nigger bitches snuck off to do, huh?' Jacob says.

Sound of that fearsome voice raises the hackles on his neck. Justus freezes where he stands. Crouching low as he peers through the barred stems of sunlit cane.

'Weren't doin' no harm—' Glory begins. His voice runs out, suddenly.

'Hush yo' mouth, nigger,' Jacob tells him.

Now Justus kin see them through the canes: the twined shapes of Glory and his lover sprawled out, low to the ground. And bent

76

above them, the massive figure of the driver, the coiled blacksnake in his hand.

'God damn if this ain't somethin',' says Jacob. 'Jes' the sweetest li'l bitches, ain't you?'

Reaches down sudden, shoving William so he falls away, thudding to the ground. Jacob grins vicious as a gator. Suddenly the driver lays down the whip. Tugs at the buckle of his belt, unfastening his breeches.

'Damn if I ain't gonna join in myself,' Jacob says.

Oh Jesus, Justus thinks. Feels the bile come sudden at his throat. As if from a far distance he sees Glory pinned, helpless, as the bulk of the driver comes down on him.

'Oh, ma Lawd!' Glory howlin' out like he hurt real bad. 'Oh, Sweet Jesus, have mercy....'

Screams high as a woman. The driver grunting and bucking on him like a hog. Far side of them William don't move a-tall. The grey man covers his face. Starts to shake with sobbin'....

God damn you to hell, Jacob.

Justus turns in a hurry, loping back uphill through the tall canes. He sure as hell cain't stand to watch no more. As it is, he already feelin' kind of sick.

Once out from the field, sun is bright as ever. Summer's noon, like before. But he cain't drive what he seen from his mind. Not now. Not ever.

Justus breathes out heavy. Closes his eyes a while as the world settles about him.

Somehow, he don't reckon he gonna sleep too good tonight.

HE STANDS, his feet apart, planted in the shallow water.

Dusk coming down on the maze of bayous and creeks all around. The first stars showing through twists of thick purple cloud. Last rays of a bled sun throwing their ebbing shadow in patterns of red and black. Silver glint where the dying light strikes droplets in the water-lilies and the weed. Willows shade him as he stands there in the gathering dark, silent, fixed as stone, feeling the wash and eddy of the ripples that strike him ankle-high. Toes sunk in the mud of the bottom. Waiting, the long spear poised at the shoulder. Eyes on the faint, flickering shape in the water beneath him.

Out at the edge of vision, something moves, breaking the pattern of the trees. He doesn't turn, letting the heron pass. Tall, crested shape, stalking from sight through the grass at the water's edge. In the marsh beyond him, bullfrogs set up to croaking, the clamour of their massed voices ringing out across the flat stretch of the bayou.

Against his shoulder the shaft of the spear chafes on his sweaty skin. He grimaces, trying to ignore the hovering flies. Took him a while to finish that spear—made it from a lopped hickory bough. The wood is hard, unlike to give should he hit a snag underwater. With his hoop-iron knife lashed with twine to the pole, it makes for a handy weapon. Now he hefts it, eyeing that one point in the water where flies hover low to the surface and that large shape comes slinking upward from the depths.

He sees the dark surface pucker, telltale ripples arrowing back as the head comes up.

That same instant he strikes, leaning hard into the blow as the spear whips down through the water. He feels the weapon hit, impact jarring back along the shaft before the point ploughs on into the mud. He springs back, hoisting clear for the bank. Gaffed, the fish flies from the hoop-iron point, thudding against the soft marshy ground beyond. Scrambling ashore, he grins. Not a hope for it, now. He grabs the threshing creature by the tail, whacks it a couple of times on the willow roots close by the water. One last spasm, and the fish goes limp.

Breathes out now, leaning on the spear, holding up the fish against the last of the light. A largemouth bass, its colours already dulled, fading fast in death. Still grinning, he starts back from the water's verge to where the willows give to a natural clearing in the brush. Looks like he'll eat well tonight.

By now the fire he left has taken hold, already throwing out heat. Green boughs laid over the tinder help to hold in the flame.

Pretty soon he has the fish headless and gutted, broiling over the heated wood while he turns it with a pointed stick where it chars to the flame. He eats with his fingers, breaking morsels of flesh easily from the bone. Taste of the bass is sharp and clean against the back of his throat. He savours it, chewing slowly, licking his lips to catch tiny dribbles of water from the flesh. Behind him, dark has come down fully, blacker than velvet over the trees and the standing water. Filled at last, he sinks back against the base of a willow trunk, hands crossed on his belly, eyes half-closed.

Days in the wilderness have altered the look of him. He's leaner than he was, the ribs showing plain where his body tapers at the flanks, the belly flat and hard from long spells without food. The thick fleece of his hair shows wild and untamed, bushing out from his head to give him a fierce, lionish look. Still the power is there, in the broad, massive spread of shoulders, the deep, barrel chest and muscled limbs. If anything, he's harder, more dangerous than before.

A noise rouses him, brings him awake. For a while he listens, uncertain, taking it for thunder. A distant hollow sound, rumbling someplace far out of sight. After a time he knows what he's hearing. That noise can only come from many guns, like the ones he saw on the road a ways back, all of them firing together. Somewhere in the open, way out of this wilderness, the two white armies were fighting. Thoughtful, he frowns, listening as the echoes shiver out across the water. Then he shrugs, turning away.

That white folks' business. It don't signify nothing.

In front of him the fire has begun to burn low. He pitches a few green twigs on to keep in the flame. Took him a fair time to get it started, cutting himself a smooth stick to use for a hand drill, the way he seen Nestor make fires back on Sweet River. Next time he might do better to find himself a piece of quartz someplace. Get a spark from his belt buckle, maybe, something like that.

Firing rumbles on in the distance as he stands up, stretching, reaching for the spear beside him. He pitches the fish leavings into the bayou, where they sink almost at once. Sometime he figures he might need to store the kills. And while nights are hot right now, come the rains he's going to need a shelter of some kind. Come mornin', he could work on that.

Gunfire wavering, shaking down to its echoes in far distance. Idly he wonders how long it must be since they come back and found Burns' body. Must be a while. By now he's lost track of the days.

Not that they'd come in after him this far into the wilderness. For the moment, at least, he's safe.

Over in the far stand of trees the nightbirds call. He shivers, remembering the ghosts he dreamed of in the hollow trees, that reached for him with their boughs. Looks like he's adrift in this dead spirit country. That big water Nestor spoke of has to be a long ways off—could be he'll never get that far. He peers into the darkness, aware still of the trembling of his limbs. The wilderness is strange to him, even now. Bad as it was, Sweet River was the one home he ever had. He sloughs off the fear shaking himself like a dog. Best go see to the snares before he turns in.

He scouts the brush cautiously, alert for snakes and spiders, holding to the spear one-handed, the other resting on the butt of the revolver thrust in his belt. Ain't much use right now, that gun. Only four shells to it, and still handles kind of strange. He shrugs, pushing on beyond the willows to where the thicker brush begins.

There are half a dozen snares laid out in the thickets, in all. Bent willow saplings, set to trigger nooses made from green vine. Last time around, he struck lucky. Swamp rabbit caught there, hung up by his back leg. A blow behind the ear kills him. Getting the dead animal loose, slinging it at his shoulder, he nods, satisfied. Not a bad return, even if it took the best part of a morning fixing up the snares.

When he gets back it's so dark that all he can see in the faint sheen of starlight on the water. That is, until the fire flares up sudden and he catches sight of a standing shape beyond him at the bayou's edge: a lone deer, bending its head to drink. At the bright spurt of flame it whirls, its forked head swinging upward. For an instant he sees the fire reflected in those dark liquid eyes, glimpses a glittering spray from the hooves. A moment more, and the one sight is the white-tailed rump, weaving away to vanish in the far thickets.

He eyes the outline of shaken bushes thoughtfully. Too far off for the pistol, and with the spear he wouldn't have a hope. He goes out after game like that, he'll be needing a bow. That, too, is something to work on. Nodding at last, he turns back again to the red glare of his fire in the clearing.

It's the ghosts he fears mostly as he drifts off to sleep, hunched to shade by the willow roots with his spear across his knees. Yet when sleep comes at last it isn't of hollow trees he dreams, but of that other time. Back on Sweet River.

A DARK lowering day, sweaty and close, without a breath of wind. Threat of thunderstorms to come in the hanging cloud, pressing hard over the tips of the willow trees lining the drive of the big house yonder. Out in the canefields maybe sixty slaves bend their backs together, men and women alike, hacking and gathering the thick stems. Kids in there, too. Lucas, he sees, crouched in the shade of a lone live-oak up by the ridge, his water-bucket by him and the gourd dippers hung from the low boughs. And behind them the drivers, yelling and cursing, their long whips cracking harder than ever, hitting out now and then, when the fancy takes them. Jacob and Bob and Andy. This time of year they get driven hardest. Man have to toil like crazy to get in the cane 'fore the rains come, haul it over the sugar house to be crushed and barrelled. As he hefts the baled cane for the bed of the waggon, he turns his head, eyeing them: the black, gleaming backs, awash with sweat. Dull glint of swung steel as the cane stems fall. Row after row of hunched, toiling shapes, moving slowly forward beneath the threatening sky. He takes in the scene, quiet, glaring.

Come to think, he could take one of them cutting-knives to Jacob's neck right now.

Justus grunts, sets down the bale in the waggon bed. He turns, backhanding the sweat from his face, as his glance goes back again towards the big house. Old Man Lawrence out at Palmetto, he knows. Saw him leave a while back. Took a half-dozen slaves with him; Cato was one. Way he hears it, they gonna need more molasses barrels to take the crop they figger on gettin' in this time. Lifting again, he scowls, eyeing the outline of the big house through its willow trees. No sign of Young Lawrence neither, not yet.

Or Sheba.

At that his dark face clenches, setting the teeth hard together. Ain't seen nothin' of Sheba since she gone over to the big house to wait on table for the two white masters. Had plenty time for thinkin', though, laid alone at night in his crib by the wall, hearing the nightbirds cry and knowin' he got to stay hungry. Knowin', too, what Sheba like to be doin' over there with Young Massa Lawrence. He sucks in a breath, feeling his hands grip hard into the baled cane stalks. Like to tear a man apart, thinkin' the way he doin'.

He snarls, heaving the bale into the waggon. Perched atop the mound of cane, Glory watches him cautiously. William, too, looks back from where he holds the horses by their head-ropes.

'Somethin' troublin' you, Justus?' Glory asks.

'Not a thing!' Glaring back at them, hating even them for the moment. Coupla no-account she-men. He turns, bending for the last bale, swings it up against his shoulder.

'Have it your way, boy,' Glory says. He shrugs, catching and stacking the bale as it comes, his look almost pitying. Neither one of them can work out how come Sheba got to mean so much to him. 'Jes' don' put out yo' back, is all!'

He hears William chuckle away in front, catches Glory's smothered grin, and feels his own fists bunch in a moment. He's about to speak when the footsteps sound behind him, and the blast of the whip splits air above his head.

'Gahd dammit, nigger!' Jacob yells over the noise of the lash. 'Ain't no time fer standin' round. Git that cane haul' fer the sugar-house, an' move yo' ass, you hear me?'

Half-turning, he sees the hated figure, standing with legs astride behind the whip. His eyes meet that fierce mad-dog stare, take in the powerful set of the body, stronger and more savage than his own. Studying it all in that single glance and hating everything he sees.

The hell with you, Jacob.

He doesn't answer, climbing up to join Glory on the heaped bales in the waggon. In front of them William gets into his seat, gees up the tired horses. The waggon jolts forward, thudding into the ruts and over patches of stubbed ground.

'That better, nigger!' he hears Jacob call out after them. 'Jes' be sure you stays movin', or I gonna have the skin clean offen yo' back!'

Justus doesn't turn to look again, stays glowering with his head down, bumping and sliding as the bales shift underneath them both. William gives the horses a free rein, and the waggon swings over the last low hill, rattling down towards the sugar-house. Once out of sight, Justus hits his bunched fist into the canes, mouthing a curse as his blow splinters the outermost stalks.

'One time, I swear I gonna take a knife to that Jacob,' Justus says, hanging to the rim of the waggon to keep from being shaken off. 'Gonna gut that son like a fish!'

For a while Glory doesn't bother answering, gritting his teeth against the jolting of the waggon. Up ahead the sugar-house comes looming, a tall log-built structure same size as the quarters that house all of Lawrence's hundred slaves. Outside, other waggons are drawn up or turning back again for the fields, and other bent figures hump their bales. He sees Mede there, his long, red back standing out among the rest. Beyond, the big doors stand open. He hears the pounding of the crush-rollers, sees the bright flare of flame. The sweet stink of the boiling sugar in its vats eddies back to them, thick and almost overpowering. William grins, pulls in the horses, and the waggon jars to a halt.

'Don' take on that way, boy,' Glory says to him in his soothing, womanish voice, reaching to touch the bigger man on the shoulder. Justus shakes off the hand, snarling to bare his teeth.

'You jes' keep your hands off me, boy.'

He's first down from the waggon and ready with the first bale, when he halts in his tracks, staring. Over beyond the sugar-house there's a couple more buildings. Feed barn and stables. Outside of the barn a horse is tethered. Lawrence's horse. At sight of the animal, Justus freezes, the sugar-cane bale still on his shoulder.

From the horse his look turns, hard and narrow-eyed, toward the dark inside of the barn.

'Justus. . . .' Glory's voice reaches for him from a world away, unheeded.

He moves quickly, slamming the bale down into the ground. The packed cane bursts, loose stems spilling everyplace as the bale smashes apart. Justus kicks his way through it, careless alike of the staring blacks all around and the two back by the waggon. His face is twisted into a mask of murderous rage, his great fists clenched. Bare feet smacking against the earth, he makes for the nearby barn.

'Justus!' Glory's voice rises behind him, desperately. 'Justus! Where in the hell you goin'?'

The shout goes under, drowned by the thunderous din of the rollers in the sugar-house, washed away in a tidal wave of noise that echoes the roar of the blood in his ears. Already he is past the throbbing doorway of the sugar-house itself, past the leaning hipshot horse and approaching that other door, giving on to darkness. Gripping the wood of the lintel-post, he eases into the barn.

That same moment he sees them.

Over beyond a ruck of hay bales, close up by the wall where the shadow hides them. Sheba bent over with her hands to the wall. Her dress pulled up on her back, her smooth buttocks gleaming. Lawrence with his hands on her narrow flank, his breeches half-way down, thrusting furiously into her from behind. Head back, eyes shut, already close to coming. From outside nothing of this would be seen, still less heard against the battering of the rollers in the sugar-house beyond. Here, though, he catches their voices. The strange yet familiar animal sounds. She beneath him, shuddering, groaning: Yassuh, Massa, you give it to me now. Harder, harder. Ah, that *so* good . . . And he: you bitch—you bitch—you bitch! Talking through his clenched teeth, tight, close to strangling the sound. Even as Justus looks on, Lawrence cries out in a harsh, hoarse voice and gasps, falling against her as he spends himself inside. Sheba moaning and smiling as she takes his weight, her eyes half-closed, her smooth body shaking. For a while they stay that way, the two shapes locked together, white into black.

Seems like Justus can't move at all, standing there and staring like someone hit him with a sledge between the eyes. The rage boiling up in him hotter than the sugar in those steaming vats, throbbing back of his eyes, bringing the smell of blood to his nostrils, threatening to burst his head apart. Yet some other unseen thing, holding him. Making him watch as it happens in front of him.

Lawrence moves then, sliding away and out of her, his manhood limp. And with that move the last thread breaks that holds Justus back from him.

He starts forward, in across the strewn hay, seeing their shocked faces turn at his approach, the anger and the fear. His own face merciless, terrible in rage. Something in him, now, like to the power he seen in Nestor: a force, filling him, telling him for sure that he can take Lawrence and any other man on earth.

'What you doin' here, nigger?' Lawrence, wrestling still with his breeches, his thin face uncertain. Afraid behind the hatred.

First time he's seen that, and it makes him feel good. He says nothing. Smiling. Coming on with his big hands clenched. Behind Lawrence he hears Sheba scream softly, the sound choking in her throat.

'You git out, nigger, you hear?' Lawrence's voice quivers, the fear showing plain. From the belt of his pants his hand darts suddenly to the whip he has lain down on a nearby bale of hay. Speaking as the hand moves. 'Gonna tell you but one time. . . .'

Ain't gonna tell me nothin', he thinks.

For a big man, Justus is fast. Lawrence has grasped the thick handle, but he's still bringing the blacksnake up for a cut as Justus gets to him. His fist takes Lawrence hard in the mouth. He feels it strike, feels the satisfying jolt that travels all the way back along his arm to the shoulder. Lawrence stumbles backward, legs tangled in his half-dropped breeches, and thuds over to the ground. Justus snarls and goes in after him, hacking with his fists for the body and head. Beyond him Sheba screams again, cowering back against the wall.

Lawrence has lost the whip in falling. Now he rolls, flinging up

85

one arm to protect his mauled face. Justus comes down astride him, fists clubbing at the body beneath. Too far gone in anger to aim for the groin or the covered face, he slams one murderous blow in for the ribs, and hears Lawrence squeal like a stuck hog as it thuds home. His fist hammers the protecting arm aside, hands reaching to lock at that thin neck. Life pulses against his grip and he squeezes, throttling in a frenzy of rage. Red mist before his eyes. Sweat and a struggle for breath under his hands. Lawrence bucks and thrashes, his eyes bugging. Arms flailing helplessly for that huge shape that straddles him. His blows hit Justus and rebound, unheeded as the spatter of rain on a log roof. The big man snarls, his grip growing tighter, fighting to crush that flesh he holds. . . .

'Git him loose! For Chrissakes, git him outa there!'

The sudden shout cuts through the noise about him, half-heard against his own snarling cries. Next minute a heavy looping blow thumps at the side of his head, and arms are coming at him from all sides, hauling him up off the body. Justus grunts, struggling like a madman in the clutch of many hands, still gripping Lawrence's neck. Someone has grabbed up the fallen whip, dealing him a whack across the head with the thick stock. Now the same man cracks him hard over the fingers and he lets go his hold, yelping at the sudden pain. The mass of black, sweating bodies cling to him, pinning his arms, hauling his backward, away from where Lawrence staggers shakily to his feet, choking for breath by the far wall. Sheba still cringes there, screaming, her dress up around her waist. For a while he goes on struggling, straining against an arm that locks around his neck from behind. Then the rage goes out of him and he sags, his breath coming harsh and fast, glaring about him. Glory and William are among those holding him, gripping like grim death. Not for Lawrence's sake, he knows. For his. What he's done is already more than enough.

He looks for the man with the whip. Finds him. Nestor meets his eye, the long blacksnake laid back at his shoulder. The old man's face is bare of all expression, his grey-filmed eyes giving nothing away. Justus sighs, his head sinking. Nothing else he could have done, short of getting all of them killed.

The sound of his laboured breathing seems to fill the barn,

echoing harshly in the new-fallen quiet. Beyond them, in the sugar-house, the rollers keep up their endless pounding. From Nestor his glance travels to the pair by the wall. By now they're decent. Sheba has pulled down her dress and Lawrence is through buttoning up his pants.

Lawrence turns towards the man they have held between them, one hand massaging his raw throat where the marks of the fingers still show red against the flesh. His face is marked, too, the torn lip still dribbling blood. He coughs, spits loose a broken tooth. His eyes are on Justus now, narrow and murderous with hatred. For the first time Justus knows a twinge of fear.

'You gonna be sorry for this, you nigra bastard,' Lawrence says. He takes his stand in front of the held man, lashes his open hand across Justus' face. A backhanded blow hits from the other side. The heavy ring furrows his cheek and Justus feels the sluggish trickle of blood. He makes no sound, meeting those vicious eyes with a hate-filled look of his own. Lawrence steps back, his thin face twisting. For a moment his clenched hands tremble at his sides. 'Jacob!' The voice rises to a womanish scream. 'Jacob! Git in here, an' fast!'

He turns, gesturing to the nearest of the slaves as other figures start to pour in at the entrance of the barn. Jacob is among them, whip in hand, his massive shape bulking above the rest. At sight of him Lawrence's face creases in a thin, unpleasant smile.

'Git a rope over that beam,' Lawrence calls out as they drag Justus across the barn towards him. 'An' tie his wrists good at the loose end. I need him strung up for what I got in mind!'

Now he struggles no longer, aware of a sick empty feeling at the pit of his belly. The rope is brought, one of the slaves whose face he cannot see in the gloom lashing it tightly about his wrists. The other end is slung over the main beam of the barn. At a word from Lawrence, a bunch of them begin to haul on it. Justus grunts, the pull taking his arms way above his head as both feet leave the ground. He hangs there, breathing hard, his wrists taking the body's suspended weight. Around him the other slaves give back, silently. Those at the far end of the rope make it fast to a heavy block on the ground.

'Ain't gonna touch you no more, you black buck nigra trash,' Lawrence tells him. He stands in front of the dangling man, smiling viciously up into that pain-racked face, rubbing one hand against the other. 'Your kind ain't fit for a white man to dirty his hands on. Still, you gonna be sorry. What you got to say now huh?'

Justus doesn't answer, glaring back into those narrowed eyes. Over Lawrence's shoulder, at the edge of the other onlookers, he can make out the figure of Sheba, her fearful, tear-stained face turned towards him. Justus snarls, his lip curling, and heaves helpless in his bonds. Lousy black bitch—couldn't wait to git her dress pulled up. Maybe he ought to have killed her too. . . .

Lawrence sees only the bitter look levelled at him, and his temper runs out. Abruptly he leans forward, spitting up for the face. Justus feels the spittle strike, mingling with the blood as it runs down his cheek. Rage fills him suddenly and he pushes again at his bonds, flinching as pain flares in the bound wrists above his head. He clenches his teeth, fighting back a cry, and Lawrence smiles once more.

'Have it your way, nigger,' Lawrence says. 'You gonna sing out loud enough 'fore we're through.' He looks to the hulking figure of the driver, waiting back of the bound man, his long whip lifted. 'Y'all ready there, Jacob?'

'Yassuh, Mistah Lawrence.' Jacob chuckles, eager to earn his corn. 'I whip him good, boss, you bet yo' life. . . .'

Lawrence nods, reaching to take his own whip from the hand of Nestor. Then he sees the look in the old man's eyes, and frowns.

'Somethin' botherin' you, old man?' Lawrence asks. His tone cuts keen as a blade. He doesn't care for Nestor overmuch.

At the sound of his voice the old man shrugs, bending his grizzled head so as not to look his master in the eye. 'Ain't no business of mine, boss,' Nestor says in the whining lapdog voice that only white men get to hear. 'Jes' come to mind as how yore pappy don' know 'bout this. He come back, could be he not care to see his nigger spoiled while the crop bein' cut.' He glances up carefully, smiling. 'That all I got in mind, Mistah Lawrence.'

For a minute Lawrence holds off from speaking, one hand on the handle of the whip as it is offered to him. Then the thin face tautens, darkening in rage, and he snatches the blacksnake from Nestor's hand.

'Is that right?' Lawrence's eyes are slitted, hard and keen as shards of splintered rock. 'You listen to me, Nestor, and listen good. My pa ain't gonna be here too much longer. An' when he goes, ain't gonna be no one around here for me to answer to. I'm your master here on Sweet River, an' if you niggers ain't learned it yet, you better catch on fast. You hear me, old man?'

'Yassuh, boss. Sure do hear you good.' Nestor cowers, ducking his head and backing away.

Hung as he is, feeling the rope bite painfully into his wrists, Justus finds time to wonder at how the old man manages to carry off the deception. For the moment, it's enough. Lawrence's mouth curls in a sneer. He nods, satisfied.

'Just so you know it,' Lawrence says. He turns again to the man who dangles helpless from the beam, his toes scrabbling air in a vain attempt to reach the ground. 'Now we're gonna put us a few knots into this black bastard's hide.' He grins, nodding across to the driver beyond. 'Lay it on him good, Jacob!'

And Jacob lays it on.

He hears the hiss of the whip through the air, but he still isn't ready for it when it lands. It hits with a blasting sound, slamming across his back, the lash biting deep in his flesh as it pulls away. His whole body shakes to the blow, the breath driven out of him in a great gasping sound. His face contorts as he fights to hold down the pain. . . .

No time. The second cut comes in, raking him clean across the back. Feels like the lash goes all the way down to the bone. This time his head throws back, teeth grating together. Somewhere beneath him Lawrence laughs softly.

'That's it, nigra. You get a good taste of that blacksnake, you hear?'

Sucking in breath, his chest heaving. Fighting through a thickening haze of pain to find Nestor's face across the barn. He catches a glimpse of the old bent man before the whip snakes in again. Seems like the eyes are trying to tell him something, but he can't tell what. Hang in, boy, maybe. Somethin' like that. The long whip hits again, Jacob grunting with the effort, and his eyes and mouth alike go wide to the searing lash as it takes the skin from his back. Nothin' Nestor can do for him now. This is one whuppin' he have to take himself.

Another lashing stroke. Another. By now he can't tell how many. He lost count soon after ten, agony wrenching all other thought from his mind. The blacksnake cuts raw flesh now, blood spattering as it lands. He feels it run thick and sluggish down the line of his back, soaking into the cloth of his breeches. Seems like he can't stand this no longer, pain flowering sharp and bright as white-hot metal behind the eyes. In his wrists feeling is gone altogether, the bonds so taut that the blood is cut off from his hands.

Under him somewhere in darkness the others, murmuring. Glory's voice among them.

'Oh, ma Lawd!'

'Jes' lookit that boy's back!'

'Cain't stand to see it, Caleb, I tellin' you.'

'Cut him clean to ribbons—Oh, Gahd!'

'Hush it up, you niggers!' Lawrence's voice coming harsh above the rest.

So far, he knows, Nestor hasn't spoken a word.

His back now a flaring mass of pain, throbbing searing through him to the brain. And the whip keeps right on coming, Jacob making hoarse panting noises behind him. The same kind of noises Lawrence made when he lay on Sheba in the dark. Thinking of that, he makes to set his teeth tight again.

Lawrence snarls from beneath him. 'Come on, you dumb bastard! Sing out! Keep it comin' Jacob, you hear me?'

A vicious curling stroke, ploughing deep in the raw flesh. Justus throws back his head and yells, a harsh, bellowing, animal sound. Again. The shout throttles higher this time, almost a scream of agony. Below him he hears the other slaves groaning, as if feeling the lash themselves. And through a falling veil of darkness, the mean victorious voice of Lawrence.

'Let him down!' Then, as the rope goes slithering loose, 'Hurry it up with that salt bucket!'

He's moaning still as he comes down, hands catching him, lowering his torn body to the ground. Facedown. Stray hay stalks jab in the cuts, and he cries out again. He lies, his bloody face close to the dirt floor of the barn, unable to move. Can't even think for the terrible pain. Someone cutting his hands free, kneeling above him. When the bonds are loosed he roars out at the agony of the returning blood that the rope had cut off. Over beyond him, footsteps coming back. A sudden halt. Lawrence there, standing above him. Back of him the other slaves, waiting.

'Take a good look,' he hears Lawrence tell them.' 'This gonna be a lesson for you all.'

Then the change in the voice. The sudden barked command.

'Get to him, an' salt that nigger good!'

Someone upends the bucket on his back. The pain blinds him, shooting like fire along the fibres of every nerve. Justus screams like a woman, heaving and thrashing against the ground. They're kneeling over him now, rubbing the salt into the raw, bloody gashes carved out by the whip, holding him down as he bucks and shrieks at the unbearable agony he's suffering. After an age, it's done. The screaming stops. Justus whimpers, sobbing like a child with his face to the ground. Tears running unchecked, salty in the cut on his cheek, puddling in the dirt by his head. His raw back heaves, the shoulders trembling.

'Gonna bear them marks till you die, nigger,' Lawrence says softly from above him. The white man is sated now. He has what he wanted. Justus and Sheba both. He chuckles, low in his throat, turning away. 'Be 'long time 'fore you cross me agin, I reckon.'

Justus doesn't answer, whimpering still with his face to the ground. Around him it's growing dark. The pain is getting worse, it seems. Vaguely he senses their retreating footsteps as they leave. Those other hands that reach to lift him from the ground.

Then the pain seizes him hard, and the world goes black about him.

When he comes awake he's back in the quarters, slumped in his crib by the wall. Nestor has laid him facedown on the makeshift bed, and now he's laying something on to his flesh that burns him like fire. He lets out one gasp, holding to the sides of the crib.

'You stay quiet, you hear,' Nestor tells him. 'This gonna hurt, I reckon.'

He shakes his head, his eyes filling with tears again. He can't speak for the pain. All the same he calls out high and loud when the hot, stinking mass comes down on to him.

'Ain't nothin' but a herb poultice, boy,' the old man says. He smooths the dressing, binding it up around the body with torn strips of cloth. 'Help draw the flesh a little, keep out the bugs an' dirt. Salt in them cuts should do the rest.' He halts a moment, sucking in his breath, lets it out again in a thoughtful sigh. 'He right, that Lawrence. You carry them scars on you till you daid. That Jacob sure whipped the hell outen yo' back. . . .'

Justus says nothing, biting down on the pain. One side of the crib, his great fist clenches. Nestor sees the move and shakes his grey head, smiling ruefully.

'You lucky you ain' git yo'self kilt, chile,' the old man tells him. 'Lay a hand to a white man, an' you sure askin' for a rope about yo'neck.' He steps back, his task completed, looking down on the prone figure of the youngster. 'Guess you learned somethin' from it, anyhows. . . .'

At that the big man rears up, striking at the wood of the crib.

'Gonna kill him an' Jacob both!' Justus grits through his teeth. His face twists as pain sears in his back and the mouth comes open in a gasp of pain.

Nestor sighs, shaking his head, reaches to lay one gnarled hand on the thick curled fleece beneath him.

'You oughta thank him, boy.' Nestor's rheumed gaze holds level, serious and unsmiling. 'He shown you the way it is, you an' Sheba both. . . .' He catches the murderous gleam in the younger man's eyes, meets it unflinching until Justus looks away. 'Up until he have Jacob lay that whip to you, I figger you been livin' someplace else.'

His back, it seems, is no longer part of him. A mass of roaring flame, scorching into his flesh. Justus groans, sinking down on to the crib, hiding his wet face in the cornshuck mattress beneath him.

'Talk sense, huh?' Nestor says. he stands close, stroking the curly head of his friend, his dark glance gentling. 'You ain't gonna do nothin' to Jacob, nor Lawrence neither. Ain' gonna be good for nothin' a-tall for nigh on a week, I reckon. An' once you up, best grease yo'self good 'fore you put on a shirt, you hear?'

He moves back from the bed, one hand scratching his own salty hair, and squats down in the corner where the shade falls coolest. Justus turns his head, questioning, his hot eyes on a level with those of the crouching man.

'Tole you once, boy,' Nestor is saying. ''Bout that wench, an' all. Now it plain. You done lost her, an' you took a fist to Young Massa Lawrence. One thing sure now, he gonna be out to git you, an' sooner or later he gonna nail you clean.' He pauses, his eyes narrowed and glinting, fixed on the man in the crib. 'You mind what I tole you, boy, 'bout runnin' or stayin' here on Sweet River?'

Justus doesn't speak. His head nods once, grimly.

'Choice is yours, chile.'

'I made it,' Justus tells him. At the hard level sound of his voice the old man's face draws into sober lines.

'Uhuh,' Nestor grunts, pushing up slowly from the wall to stand at last. 'That good 'nough, I reckon. Jes' make sure you think it through, is all.'

'I done all the thinkin' I'm like to do,' Justus says.

Over by the door the old man halts, looking back. His dark, slitted gaze scans the prone body draped across the crib. Nothing in those eyes to betray the thoughts behind them. 'I was you, I'd catch up on some sleep now,' Nestor tells him. 'Pretty soon, you gonna need all the strength you kin find.'

Justus lies back hearing the door swing shut. For a while his eyes glare at the log wall across from him as if willing a way through to the open fields beyond. Already the pain is dulling, losing its razor edge as weariness takes over. Slowly the head sinks down.

He sleeps, sprawling over the crib, for a while forgetting the gashes in his flesh. And those other deeper wounds inside.

OUT BEYOND the doorway of his shelter, the rain comes down in a solid sheet.

He sits crosslegged back of the overhang, where water sluices and spatters on the sodden ground, watching the downpour as it strikes. A wall of rain hits the live-oak woods, tall trunks whipped by the wind. Blurred, uncertain outlines in a sea of grey, whose hissing drowns out all other sound. Water spilling in freshets downslope, carrying twigs and stems and half-sunk pebbles along with it, in among the live-oak roots that give to the bayous below. He hears it drum on the roof of his shelter, droplets spitting down here and there through the odd small chink. Overhead, the split gourds he's hung around the outer wall are swinging, filling to overflow on to the soaked earth. By his feet Burns' upended hat spills water over the brim. Ain't gonna be short of a drink this time.

Frowning, he turns from a world awash with rain, hefting the arrow on his open palms. It's the last of a round dozen he's made these past few days, fashioning them with his knife from chopped palmetto stems, slit near the base to take a fletching of egret and heron feathers. This one, he figures, is a mite handier than the rest. For a point it has a shaped piece of flint he came by the day before last, almost stumbling upon it among the woodland roots. Notched and tied fast, it promises to be his best arrow yet. The others have points from splintered bones, or just the palmetto wood itself, honed to an edge. Eyeing it, he nods at last, satisfied. Reaches behind him into the gloom where his other arrows lie, wrapped with the pistol and the unstrung bow and the spearshaft in a parcel of rabbit and muskrat skins. As he lays it beside them, his hand rests a moment on the bow, almost tenderly. Made him a fair weapon there. Wasn't too hard to find the bow wood. Cut himself a supple branch from a hickory overlooking a swamp further into the trees yonder, and whittled it to a shape. The bowstring was a whole lot tougher. None of the animals he took in his snares were big enough—sinews wouldn't stretch far enough

94

for somethin' this size. He ended up using his knife to fray strands from his belt, binding them in with a coarse, tough grass he's found growing on the slopes. Tried it out a couple times, and it seems to handle good. Yet to test it on anything the size of that deer he saw.

He moves, lowering the skin cover back across the weapon, keeping it from the wet. Frowning in thought. No doubt of it, he needed a bow. Couldn't hope to live forever on muskrat and rabbit and fish; even they ain't so dumb as they look. Had to keep shifting his snares every once in a while, if he hope to catch anything at all.

Up above his head the long meat strips hang, shivering on their grass ropes when rain hammers the roof. Swamp rabbit, mostly. Had the stuff smoked in this place while the weather held good. Ought to keep for a while. Took him a day and more to set up the shelter, using a frame of willow saplings lashed crossways into a kind of dome, tying them with ropes of grass and vine. The outer layer he covered with moss and leaves and turves of grass, with a stretched skin here and there for added protection. Seems like it works for the moment.

All the same, he's glad he got to make the bow. Gives him the chance to move around. With the hut and the snares, he was beginning to feel tied down.

Looks out into the drumming rainfall, his face set into sombre lines. Watching the water rebound in a fine spray from the mud. Beyond him, a grey curtain shuts off the world, even the trees lost to sight now.

Not a soul to be found out here. Only the wild critters. And the ghosts. This here wilderness is full of spirits. Drowned folks, rotted away someplace in these bayous. Lynched niggers haunting the trees they was hanged from. Spirits everyplace, Nestor tell him that time. All around him, with the night-birds, the snakes and all. He hears a bull gator, barking out someplace in the lower bayou, and shudders. Touches a hand to the rabbit foot strung at his neck. Figured it might serve him as a charm, keep off the worst of the ghosts. Somehow it don't seem to have the same power that Nestor's had; he still gets scared come nightfall. Times, he wakes crying out, thinking they come for him.

95

By now he pines for company. Missing the comradeship back on Sweet River. He thinks of them sadly. Mede and Cato, Glory and William. Nestor most of all. Sheba. Even now, he still thinks of Sheba. Something good he had once. Now he got nothin' a-tall.

He leans, scratching a sudden itch in his scarred back, sweating in the humid heat. This lonesomeness gettin' to him. Like to eat a man away, rememberin' how it was.

Musta been crazy, makin' a run. Where he think he gonna git, anyhow?

He waits until the worst of the empty feeling passes. After a while the hardness returns. A grim determination in his look as both hands clench to fists on his thighs.

Ain't done yet. He wait out these rains, an' make a move. Come the time, he try again for the big water.

He eases back inside the shelter, lays himself down on the piled skins. Sleeps.

Outside the rain sheets down without end on the bayou country.

AFTER THE whipping, he's a while getting back to the fields again. Still, he makes good use of the time they give him.

Nestor right enough. First couple of days he don't feel good for nothing. Sicker than a kitten, an' no more strength in him than a wet hen. Whiles, he throws up the food they give him. Rest of the time, just lies and suffers, sleeping when the pain allows. And once the worst time is over and the poultice and bandages come off, he finds the old man was right again: his back is a mass of knotted scars, crossing one over the other where the whip came down. Crusted and bloody from the salt, they fade in time to a dirty white, dead marks cut into the living flesh. Once up, he stays quiet, wary of betraying himself. Letting the hatred stay hidden, unspoken, festering viciously within him.

He don't go back to the fields straight off. Over at the forge they still short-handed. Laban's hand took a turn for the worse and he ain't up to workin' his old blacksmith job. For a while he works there under Nestor's eye, the old man showing him the simplest ways of heating and working the metal. He don't learn too much, but enough. Fixes up a few busted tools, shoes a coupla horses. With Nestor to show him, he gets by.

It's while he's working at the forge he comes on that stove-in molasses barrel back of the sugar-house. Splintered planks, mostly, but what catches his eye is the hoop-iron binding, busted with the barrel to a ragged edge. Nobody about to watch him that time, and a good wrench takes it loose. Long enough for a knife, he reckons. He stows it in his breeches, takes it with him to the smithy. There, while Nestor looks on, his withered old face expressionless, Justus sets a file to the jagged hunk of metal, honing it to a point and sharpening it along both its sides.

'Got a use fer that, I reckon,' Nestor says.

The big man nods, not answering.

'Gonna need a handle of some kind on it, boy,' the old man tells him. 'Less'n you wants yo' hand cut up bad.' He reaches down into the plank box where he keeps his own handyman's materials. 'Got some twine here iffen you want it, serve for a haft, I guess.'

'Thanks, Nestor.' He grins, taking the offered bundle, binding it hurriedly about the thick end of the metal. The old man nods. He doesn't smile.

'Now git it stowed, an' fast,' Nestor says. 'You an' me got work to do.'

A few days more and his time at the smithy is up. Lawrence don't trust him too much in the old man's company. He wants Justus back in the field, under Jacob's eagle eye. When the time comes, Justus says nothing, setting back to the canefields with the rest as Laban takes over once more at the forge.

Come nightfall, he's found new ways to pass the time.

The knife he has hidden in the cornshucks of his crib, where neither Lawrence nor the drivers would think of looking. At nightfall when they're shut in, he slips the honed blade from the mattress, edging over to the far wall beyond his bed. There in the deepest of the shadow, he works at loosening one of the logs in the wall. He picked it out a while back: a thick, rough-hewn piece set halfway up from the ground, well into the shade. He don't have to work on it too hard. Chinks in the wall aren't caulked up much, and the damp and the insects have got to it, part of the timber rotting from the outside inward. It gives way easy under the slow, relentless sawing of the blade. Pretty soon he can push it back and forth much as he pleases. Wouldn't take but a minute to kick loose, come the time. Justus grins. He sets his blade for the log above it, the iron rasping on the outer skin of the wood.

Glory and William are both there in the cabin with him, squatted on the ground, the blanket laid out ready under them both. They smile, touching each other gently in the way lovers have. They only look to Justus once in a while. From where he crouches, working by the wall, he hears their low-voiced chuckling speech.

'What you figger he doin', Glory, huh?'

'Cain't tell, honey.' Glory's voice catches in a laugh, struggling. 'Don' pay to ask. He a mean man, William, you heah?'

'Sure whale into Young Massa, but good.' William grins at the memory. 'Like to bust him apart. Catch him with he breeches down, too. . . .'

'Y'all see that thing of his? Some whang, huh? An' they reckon us niggers is big. . . .'

'Set him loose in the pasture, figger we could raise us a stud farm,' Glory says.

He hears their choking laughter but works on, unsmiling. Even now, the welts in his back are enough to remind him it wasn't no joke. Under the pressure of the blade the second log starts to give, rocking loose. Now Justus smiles, setting it back into the slot he's made. Reaches for the log beneath the first.

Startin' to git someplace, I reckon.

When the work is finished, he scoops the wood shavings and punk into a hole in the dirt floor. Fixes the logs so the sawn edges don't show too plain. Turning slowly, he leans to thrust the blade back in among the cornshucks, out of sight. When at last he gets to his feet again, his look goes across the cabin to where Glory and William now lie under the blanket, their arms about each other. For a time he glares at their dark heads, silently.

'You two seen nothin', you hear?' he says at last.

'Don' trouble, honey.' Glory's voice betrays the sly smile at his lips. 'Ain' payin' you no mind.'

He stands a while at that, thinking it over. Presently, he too smiles. 'Yeah,' Justus says. 'I figger I kin trust you, at that.'

He eases back across the crib, settling, his hands laid flat over his belly. For a while he lies that way, looking up to the darkened roof over his head. Across from him he hears whispers and murmurings, and soft rolling movements. Across his belly the big hands lock tighter.

Long time since Sheba come here. Since the whipping, none of the other women in the quarters will risk spending time with him, a trouble-maker that he is, and with the return of his strength, his male need is beginning to trouble him again.

Justus shuts his eyes, willing the thought of Sheba's urgent flesh from his mind. The image he has before him now is of those loosened logs, and beyond them the woods and creeks and bayous that lead away from Sweet River into the wilderness.

Come the time, that the way he goin' to go.

NIGHT. HOT and smothering, darker than molasses. It lies heavy on him, as he twists and turns his aching bones in the bed. Alone. Unable to sleep. Weather like this, a man should have someone by him. Take his mind from the heat and the sleeplessness.

Frogs croaking in chorus somewhere beyond the willows, and from the trees a lone owl calls. Gator barks again from the bayou, and Old Lawrence curses, rolling over in his sodden sheets. Seems like the whole night filled with noise enough to keep a man awake. And the gnawing bite of rheumatism in his bones don't help none. That, and the thought of a lithe young wench in the sheets alongside him.

Never used to bother him, the nights. Soon as the sun went down he was over at the quarters with a hot wench—nothin' like it. Still ain't, even now, though he don't get to manage it much. Mostly now it's Beth who pleasures him, evenings when Hagar ain't around. An' often as not he cain't git it up too well. Lately, his craving has been for that young pussy of hers. Seems like he kin taste it at his lips this minute. And that remembered taste sets him to rolling and turning again.

Beyond the thin wall that divides his room from theirs, he hears those others: his son and his new wench, Sheba—one that use to be Justus' woman, 'fore John took the whip to him. Low murmur of their voices. Slow whisper of turning bodies in the bed. Old Lawrence groans softly under his breath. Shifting position yet again. They ain't no help to him neither. Not right now.

He don't care a-tall for the way things are goin' on Sweet River nowadays. John got this mean streak to him, an' it sure like to cause trouble in future. He already got Justus all fired up at him takin' his woman from him, an' then havin' Jacob whip him 'fore all the hands. Not that he had no choice there. Nigger lays a hand to his master, punishment got to come there an' then, so they all know who's boss. No, that ain't it. But if John had gone about his lovin' a little more cautious-like, the way he used to when he was young, wouldn't have been no need for all that trouble. Justus is a good nigger, and they git the work from him. He turns mean on them, that's work lost, an' money too—an' all on account of one man's pleasure. . . .

Troubles him more than a little, these days. Place is slippin' from his hands an' into John's. Had to come some time, but the way John has of runnin' things, Sweet River could be played out inside the next few years. With the war and all, and the way things goin' for our boys, there just ain't no tellin'. . . .

Not so long back, he'd have stood up agin the boy. Faced him down, like he done before. Not now, though. He a way too old for that. Best to stay clear, let John git on with matters any way he pleases. However dumb it might look to him.

Turns again, breathing hard as he brushes the thick sweat from his face.

Could jes' wish he had him a hot wench with him tonight, like John got in the next room.

Far side of the wall, in the room beyond, Lawrence eases over sidelong in the sticky sheets, smiling in darkness as he reaches an arm across the girl beside him.

100

'You awake, Sheba?' he asks.

Grins wider as the wench nods, sliding her lithe moist body up beside him. Lets his own hands move around to cup the smooth globes of her breasts.

'Kind of different, huh? Up here at the big house?' Stroking slow as he talks. The nipples coming up hard against him. Smiles again, guiding her smaller hands down to where his manhood rears from its bush of hair. 'Quite a change from the quarters, I'll bet. How you likin' it, Sheba?'

'It jes' fine here, Massa Lawrence,' Sheba says.

Her practised touch rouses him, moving feather-light on his swollen stem, riding him until his upright flesh strains and pulsates against the smooth mound of her belly. Lawrence moans softly, clenching his teeth as his eyes close tight on the spasm of pleasure.

'Yeah,' Sheba tells him, as his hand slithers down to touch between her thighs. 'It jes' fine up here. . . .'

Slides over him easy as he rolls on his back. Hoisting herself on his standing root. Straddling, lets him enter her slowly, inch by inch. Beneath her Lawrence gasps and grunts, biting his teeth together. Already close to his time. Poised above him, the brown-skin wench grins sly. Starts to move herself back and forth on to him.

Under the bucking force of their combined thrusting the bed sings out, jolting as the springs twang and whine. A fresh sheath of sweat covers them both, spraying from them as they lunge and heave hurriedly to climax. Harsh sound of their breathing echoing in the darkened room. . . .

Up against the wall, Old Lawrence twists and turns, plucking at the sheet. Sighs a little, eyes half-shut, dreaming of Beth and the times he had with her a while back. Far side he hears Sheba as she screams out shrill in climax, and the harsher, heavier groaning of his son. Crash of their joined bodies in the bed slams at his senses, threatening to shake the world apart. Old Lawrence drags the sweaty sheet over his head, trying to shut out the noise of their breathing and moaning as the pair of them settle at last. He don't make it. Under the sheet, the same noises go on, reaching him in spite of it all.

Ain't right, the old man thinks. Feels the growth of a dark

thought in the back of his mind, like a cloud hung over him. It ain't right. She like to his half-sister. Man shouldn't go layin' with his own flesh an' blood. It ain't healthy. . . .

A sin, too. Ain't that what the Bible said?

Sure, John don't know the pair of them got the same father. But it's a fact, all the same. And *he* knows it. Old Man Lawrence cain't git away from that. 'Cause he done sired the both of them.

Wouldn't be so bad, maybe, but sound of their lovin' back there is gittin' him all hot an' fired up. More'n he oughta be. Whiles, he lets Beth's image slip from his mind and sees *her* there instead: Sheba, standing up there naked before him. That sweet yaller-brown body of hers catchin' the light. Holdin' up her pussy for him as he ducks his head forward between her thighs. . . .

Rouses from the image wild-eyed, sweat standing out on him. He shakes his head. He got no business thinkin' that way. My God, she his own child!

All the same, cain't git that picture of her from his mind. Lies, staring up at the dark roof above as the murmuring voices fade at last. Still seeing her there. Waiting for him. Smiling. . . .

Groans, flinging-back the sheet. Stays still a while, the raw breath rasping in his throat.

He ain't about to git no sleep tonight.

ONE MORNING at first light, the horn blowin' to call them out. And when he gits to the door of the shack he shares with Glory and William, they out there waitin' for him.

'Come on out boy,' Jacob tells him. He grins, the teeth bared in his broad, splayed face. 'Massa Lawrence got somethin' special in mind for you.'

Both the other drivers standin' back of him. They grinning too. The whips laid back easy to their shoulders. Justus studies them warily, one by one. Bob the oldest, he guesses. Hair salty white, an' he's running' to fat, with a greased look to his mahogany flesh and a gut that hangs over his belt. The eyes still shrewd, though,

102

sunk in the pits of flesh. Far side of him Andy stands quiet, stroking the butt of his whip. Thin, dark, leathery man. Hard to tell how old or young he is. One thing sure. He kin make that blacksnake sing.

And there between them the massive wide-shouldered bulk of Jacob. Big and powerful as Justus hisself. More so, maybe. Right now, he don't aim to find out. Jacob alone would be enough for him, he reckons. Agin three drivers, he got no chance a-tall.

'What you mean?' He asks. At once the smile fades, the yellow eyes narrowing.

'Ain't for you to ask,' Jacob says. He gestures with the coiled whip in his hand. 'Now move it. We don't aim to be kept hangin' around.'

Back of him Glory and William stand framed in the doorway, looking uncertainly toward him. Meeting their eyes, he shrugs. Nothin' they kin do, nor him either.

'I'm comin', Jacob,' he says.

Steps out ahead. Jacob leading as the other two follow close behind. Wonderin', as he walks penned between them, what in hell they gonna do with him.

Path they take leads away from the quarters and the canefields both and snakes on into shade of a bunch of live-oak trees. There in a clearing a hut stands, new-built from log and clapboard. Light glinting faintly on the shingles of the roof. At sight of it the group of them halt, Jacob turning to him, smiling agin.

'This where you gonna be stayin' for a while, boy,' the driver tells him. He taps the whip-stock lightly on the big man's shoulder. 'Best git on an' look it over, huh?'

Touch of that plaited hide on his shoulder recalls the other time, and Justus stiffens in a moment, the hair standing up at the nape of his neck. Biting back the snarl that threatens to come to his lips. Seems like he kin still feel that lash rip into his back every time he sees Jacob there in front of him. That memory, and what Nestor tole him, 'bout his mama and the way she died. Remembering, his great fists bunch again. Catching the move, Jacob steps back easy, slipping the blacksnake out to slap against the ground.

'Don't you try nothin' foolish, nigger,' the driver tells him. 'Stay quiet, you feel a whole lot better, I reckon.'

He don't say a word to that. Instead he goes along with the three of them as they steer him to the hut. Ducking the low sill of the door, he steps inside.

Kind of dark inside there. No candles he kin see. Room enough for one, but not much more. Crib by the wall, an' a pail left longside it.

'Left that for you to piss in, looks like,' Jacob says. Grins, raising a hand to his mouth. He and the two drivers stay back by the door, lowering their whips. By now they got the job all but done.

'Ain't gonna be locked in,' Jacob tells him. 'But don't try nothin'. One or other of us be around, day or night. You hear?'

'I hear you,' Justus says.

Stands back as the door closes, leaving him in darkness.

He don't come out from there all that day.

Towards evening Cora comes to the hut and he lets her in. She got food with her, an' lays it down. Leaves without a word. No call for him to talk with her, neither. Andy out there in the doorway behind her, the whip hung loose and ready in his hand. When they're gone he eats up. Food like he ain't never had before in his life. Steak an' eggs. Molasses. Fresh milk. They sure as hell feedin' him up, he thinks. But what they got in mind for him?

Stays. Taking this new kinda life as it comes. Eatin' the food they bring him. Usin' the pail every once in a while. Sleepin'. Thinkin'. Still he cain't figure it out.

Three days later he's still there.

Before too long he gits to hungerin' for a woman agin. Specially at nights.

FOURTH NIGHT he's there—or maybe the fifth, he cain't rightly tell—comes sound of a scratching at the door of the hut.

He rouses awake to the sound, lifting from his bed of corn-shucks, his body a deeper wedge of darkness in the walled gloom. Eyes wide. Nostrils flared. Every pore of his flesh alert as he halts there, listening again. And again, the same scratching answers him.

'Sheba?' Sound of his voice comes hoarse, thickening with need. From the time he been put in here, he ain't seen a woman. Lack of it has begun to trouble him some, these nights.

'Sheba, that you?'

No answer. Silence a moment, then comes that scratching again. The way she did before when she come to him in the quarters. Justus crouches halfway to his feet, dark eyes fixed on that unopened door. His broad heavy-jawed features still puzzled, uncertain.

Cain't be her. Not Sheba. She up at the big house—with *him*!

Feeling the hatred flare in him a moment at the memory of how it was, the big man sighs. Last of his anger ebbing as he looks again to the door. Not Sheba, huh? Who else it gonna be?

'You out there, Sheba honey?' He licks at his lips. The hot, swelling need already starting to fire his blood, pulsing hard at the root of his groin. Maybe it's true, maybe it ain't. He sure as hell wants it to be. 'Come on, gal! Ain't you gonna answer me?'

No answer, like before. Quiet. Then the scratching starts up again.

Bites on his lip at that, the sweat breaking out on his brow, sheathing the skin. Outside in the night a gator barks someplace, and the frogs sound away in the bayou. Justus gets to his feet slow, heading for the door.

Has to be Sheba, he thinks. Ain't none of the others would know....

Scratching stops as he lifts the bar. The door easing open a crack against the dark. Shows him the lone figure, standing there, holding a lit candle in her hand.

Ain't Sheba, after all. This one a way too tall for her, and darker-toned. Gleam of the black, smooth skin and upturned eyes send back a reflected shimmer in the light of the moon. Coal-black, this one. Slender an long-limbed. His look touches on her now. Rests at last on the hands that hold the candle, with their long, tapering fingers.

'Let me by,' Cora tells him. She smiles slow and lazy, her lean

105

face lit by candle-flame. 'Got somethin' for you, big boy . . . somethin' you ain't had for a while. . . .'

Slips by him as he stands there. Edges into the unlit room to set down the candle on the sill. From the door he watches her, frowning and unsure, knowin' this ain't what he wanted.

Knowin' too, that maybe part of him does want it all the same.

'What in hell you doin' here?' he asks.

Cora smiles again, turning toward him. Long hands to her neck as she works on the fastenings of her dress.

'Shut the door, Justus,' Cora says.

Hand to the door, he stands, makes as if he's about to speak. Cora's smile goes kind of sly. She stretches, pulling the dress up over her head, lets it fall crumpling to the floor.

'Ah, Lawd. . . .' Seeing, he swallows. His look crosses the lean smiling face with its black frizz of hair. Slides downward to touch the sheen of the taut breasts, the flat belly and softly swelling mound with its triangle of fur. That place draws his eye, up between her long, slim legs. Cora sees it, and smiles. One thin-fingered hand falls to cover it from him.

He closes the door. Sets back the bar in its place.

'Ain't answered me yet,' Justus says. He aims to make it come out sounding rough, but the thickness in his throat don't let him. Moving back towards the rumpled pallet, he feels the need surge up inside, the manhood hardening to throb against the cloth of his breeches. Knowing she sees it, too, and cain't be fooled. 'What you come here, for, Cora? Thought you was Cato's woman before. . . .'

Cora meets his gaze steadily, her dark eyes asking him other questions. The hand stays quiet between her legs. 'You troubled over Cato?' her voice purrs softly. One with the secret smile. 'Scared of him, maybe?'

'He don't worry me none.' Justus' voice is harsh. Hands sweating as he lays them flat to his thighs. She sure one hell of a wench, and it been a long time. . . . 'Jes' thought you was his gal, is all.'

The long-limbed woman shakes her curled head, her eyes half-lidding as she smiles. 'You know why I'm here,' Cora tells him. 'An' Cato ain't no part of it.' The sly look reaches out for him again, mocking. 'What wrong with you tonight, honey? Ain't you got no sap fer a little pleasurin', huh?'

Keeping that sly gaze on him, she starts to rub the furred patch with the palm of her hand. Gently.

Heat of his pulsing maleness strains at the cloth, the sweat breaking out afresh at his palms. Justus swallows hard in his throat, fighting to meet the stare of those knowing eyes.

'This ain't the way it should be,' he tells her at last. 'Sheba my woman, you know it. An' you comin' here, it ain't right. . . .'

'Sheba ain't your woman no more,' Cora's soft voice strikes at him harder than a blade. 'Massa took her long since, up to the big house. She for him, now.' Smiles, licking with a wet tongue-tip around the inside of her lips. 'Reckon you know that, too.'

For an instant his great hands bunch into fists, clenching. Justus snarls, choking back the fury that threatens from deep within, hearing his teeth grate together as he checks the words. Ain't no one he'd have took that from. No one but for this dark, long-legged wench who stands to face him in candle-light. Sight of her rousing his blood, spite of himself.

And even from her, it hard to bear.

'You a mean bitch, Cora, you know that?' Hate mingles with desire, choking his speech. He spitting the words from him like so much venom, as if to void the thought of Sheba and Lawrence, and how it got to be. The way he caught them in the sugar-house, locked and thrusting, sweating as they came. Or maybe lying close up in his bed there, smooth and sticky from loving, laughing at him too, maybe. At the thought of it he snarls again, shaking his massive head. Breath heaving from the huge muscled chest. After a while the fury passes. The big hands unclench. On Cora, though, his dark-eyed look stays hard as diamonds.

'Best you should git from here, gal,' Justus tells her. 'I aim to have me some rest. You hear me good?'

Turns from her, laying himself down again on the rumpled pallet, moist already from his sweat and from dreams of Sheba. Flat to the ground, he lies there, glaring at her as she leans by the clapboard wall of the shack, her sly gaze still upon him.

Ain't no way, though, he kin hide the swollen bulge at his groin,

107

the glistening at his upper lip, or the deeper dark that threatens, back of his eyes. Cora sees, like always.

'Don't aim to give me none of that, huh?' Cora asks, eyes touching on his loins as she speaks. At the imagined touch he flinches, the need like a clenched fist at the middle of his body, drawing him taut together.

'Reckon not.' Sight of her dazzles him, choking the words. Her slim, lithe shape outlined above him, a gleaming, polished black. Tight, lifted sheen of her breasts. Slow, satin curve of hip and belly and thigh. And below and between, the soft, glistening mound itself.

'Git from here, wench,' Justus says, grinding the words out tight-lipped, teeth clenched. 'You ain't gonna git nothin' from me.'

Above him Cora laughs, a low chuckling sound in the semi-darkness. The long-limbed wench moves from the wall, sinks catlike to her knees, her smooth thighs spreading wide to catch the light of the candle-flame. Hand to the place, she eyes him, smiles again. 'That right?' she says. Then, looks down slow to where her hand and its long fingers rest. Same hooded glance coming up again to meet him.

'Reckon I'll have to do the job myself,' she says.

Fighting the terrible surge of desire, Justus watches. Sees those long, dark fingers stroke downward in the bush of hair, reaching the moist core, the woman of her. Cora murmurs softly, deep in her throat. Fingers easing back the flesh of the outer lips to touch at the swelling bud within. Justus, with a choked wordless sound, reaches for the candle stub. Her other hand drops gentle on his muscled wrist. Puts it by.

'Leave it be, honey,' she tells him. The smile curves her lips. Eyes slitted, nearly closed, she fondles the smooth bud of flesh beneath her hand. 'That way you ain't gonna miss nothin'. You hear?'

Strokes again for that slippery bud. Tremors at the touch, head thrown back. 'Yeah, that better,' Cora says.

Outside, his eye to the crack in the hut wall, Lawrence holds down a shiver of breath. Already he's beginning to sweat in the

108

humid night—and not from just the heat. Was his idea to send Cora in to him this time. His orders, too, to make sure the candle stayed lit. With what he got in mind, he don't aim to miss nothing either.

He got plans for Justus, sure enough. And it gonna do him more good than that black sonofabitch could ever know.

Watching as that long-backed body moans and thrusts, urgent against her fondling hand, the plantation owner grins. Licks at his lips. Ain't no way that one gonna hold out against her. No way. Come to think, he's getting kind of hard himself.

Lets his own hand slither down the wooden wall for the bulge in his pants. Stroking it gently over the place. Feeling his heat through the taut-drawn cloth.

Flat on the cornshuck bed, Justus feels the sweat gather cold on his upper lip. Licks at the salty taste. Across from him, Cora leans way back, heaving herself upward against the fingers of her hand, eyes closed, smiling now as she moans and shudders for breath.

'Yeah, honey. . . .' The words coming from her in a strangled gasp. The dark head shakes as a fresh spasm goes through her. 'Ain't gonna be long, big boy. . . .'

Looking on, he sees the sudden sheen of moisture that slicks her moving fingers and falls to mingle with the gleam of sweat on her thighs. Cora's eyes open wide, seeming to roll back in her head as the long tremors shake her body all its length. Her mouth opening to yell out loud as her fingers churn in a frenzy. The bush of hair awash with the onset of her coming. . . .

'Oh, yeah! . . . Sweet Jesus Lawd! . . . Oh, yeah. . . .' Her voice giving out a succession of harsh, inarticulate cries as her body heaves and shudders, like it about to shake itself apart. Abruptly Cora slumps, going limp as her dark head sags forward on her breast. For a moment she stays that way. Eyes closed, as the breath comes from her, harsh and echoing in the enclosed space.

From where he lies he feels his own breathing quicken. Sudden hammer of heartbeats on his ribs. He stays still, watching as her eyes open, slow and easy. Sated, looking toward him, lazy as a cat. The woman smiles.

'That please you, boy?' she asks.

Makes to speak, and again the words don't come. Feels like his throat blocked by swallowin'. Like all of him drawn down tight and hard to the root of him, hot and swollen huge in his breeches, like it about to bush him wide open. Justus swallows. Wipes a moment at the sheath of sweat on his face.

'Come here to me, gal,' Justus says.

Seeing the charged look of his eyes, she chuckles, a soft furred sound. Cora eases on back, thighs wide as her wet hand holds the lips open, showing her innermost flesh gleaming sleek and pale in the candle flame. With her free hand she beckons him, those long fingers curling to invite him closer.

'No,' Cora says. The sly cat-smile at her lips. 'You come here to me.'

Reaches for him as he gets up on his knees. Leans to meet her. Justus draws a long shuddering breath as his palms light on her smooth bare shoulders, the sweet touch of woman-flesh finding him like a taste through his own calloused skin, all the more welcome after his days and nights alone. Same time her own hand moves. Slips to caress the uncontrollable bulge at his groin. Threat of his pent-up need beneath her palm is all but unbearable. Justus closes his eyes, groans softly.

'Gonna have to do somethin' 'bout that,' Cora murmurs, her own voice sharpening a little now in anticipation. Deftly her hand works at the buckle of his belt, laying him bare. Justus shivers as she slides the breeches down over his thighs, her smooth palms soft as touching shadows along his flanks. She makes a kind of low purring sound, deep in her throat, shifts his hands to cup her breasts. He fondles the taut flesh, stroking the nipples until they turn hard against him, watching as her eyes slowly close. Cora lifts the hand away from her wet secret place and lays it to his lips. Rank, musky scent of her filling his head until he drunk with the smell of her. Same instant her other hand goes low beneath him, reaching down to the root of his manhood, sliding easily upward along the taut, pulsing rod of flesh.

'Easy, gal.' He all but whimpers at the touch. She sendin' him clear outen his haid.

'Anythin' you say,' Cora tells him.

110

Lifts herself forward so the hot, moist core of her is poised over his upright stem, then eases down, arms at his neck now as his urgent flesh goes into her inch by slow inch, sliding easy, her own inner warmth closing about him.

Touch of the pleasure drives him wild. Justus bellows like a maddened beast, lifts clear from the ground as her long thighs lock on him at the waist. Kicking from the breeches, he stands, pushing her hard to the wall of the hut and thrusting furiously inside her, Cora grunting softly with the force of each rhythmic lunge that slams her against the clapboard wood.

'Oh yeah, honey,' Cora moans, feeling already the slow spiral of her own pleasure build again. 'That a way better. . . .'

Bites on his lip as he plunges in her. Long nails clawing, raking furrows in the flesh of his back. Justus tastes the salty tang of blood in his mouth, feels her own hot mouth close over his, her tongue probing, exploring inside. Lower down, his pleasure surges swiftly to its peak. Ain't gonna be long now, he knows.

Locked on him, her smooth heels climbing the scars of his back, Cora squeals out sudden. Fierce shrill sound, almost like she hurt bad. Same time lets down her hand to fondle at him as he thrusts, taking him with her over the edge. Justus snarls, shaking his head as the sweat flies from him. Yells aloud. He drowns in the scalding joy, the blazing flight of his pleasure, as he spurts and pours himself into her, filling her with his jissom, the last jetting spasm draining him, leaving him spent.

Cora hangs to him, moaning still in the aftermath of her own coming, the two of them sliding down slowly and, lying at last on the bare dirt floor, bodies bound tight together with the sweat and sap of their loving.

'Sure was somethin',' Cora says at last.

She leans over, raising herself on her elbows above him, cradling his head in those long-fingered hands, stroking through the thick, bushy mane of hair. Justus lies quiet. For one thing, he's a way longer gettin' back his breath. Then, too, he's rememberin' things. Like, when his time come a moment back, he didn't see Cora there a-tall. Was Sheba in his mind. . . .

Still, when his eyes open to see that thin, coal-black face above him, he ain't any too worried. Whichever way you look at it, was good for him too.

'Best you should rest awhile now, I reckon,' the tall woman tells him. Smiles again softly, half-sated and half-aroused. 'Git up yo' strength agin. . . .'

'How 'bout you?' He wants to know. Reading the question in his face, Cora laughs.

'Us gals always quicker'n you men,' Cora says. 'Pretty soon we ready to start over. Ain't Sheba never tole you that?'

This time mention of her name no longer brings rage. Right now, he way too tired. All the same he smiles a little as she eases over toward him, sliding up against his body. Cora shifts herself a shade higher, cups a sleek breast in her hand and brings it to his mouth. Justus takes it, feathering the nipple with his tongue, drawing the hard, shivering tip of her into his mouth. Tasting, he hears her moan, feels her smooth thighs clamp on his own outflung leg. Slithery, moist touch of her inner flesh smooth against him as she moves now and then, starting to rouse herself, her free hand falling to lie a moment on his own slack flesh.

'Yeah,' Justus tells her. Looking upward, he too smiles. 'See what you mean, gal. . . .'

Cora doesn't answer, but brings the breast to his mouth again. As he feeds on her she takes his own hand and draws it upward to the moist place between her thighs.

Warm musk of her woman-scent reaches him again, strong in his nostrils, as his fingers find her, her inner wetness closing on him. She tightens and relaxes, moving against him, then after a while rolls from him, lying on her back. Lifting on his elbow beside her as he works, fingers awash with her moisture, watching the changing expressions of her upturned face. All at once Cora shudders. Heaves with her body to meet him as the movement quickens, the pleasure gaining speed as she climbs again to her climax.

'Oh, ma Lawd. . . .' Cora moans out the words, head falling back as she seizes on his hand, working him hard against her in a frantic haste. Her other hand closes on his manhood as it begins once more to rise. At the touch he trembles, feeling his need grow afresh. Right now, though, he figures it ain't the time. 'Cause she already there.

Stroking, he feels the final shudder of orgasm as it takes her, shaking her like a fish on a hook. She screams out high and loud, locking on his hand as she comes at last. Justus feels the slippery pulse of her wet flesh at his palm in the instant before she moans and goes loose, falling back. For a while her breathing is the one sound in the stillness.

Outside, Lawrence sucks in his breath sharply, the sweat running into his eyes, his shirt and pants clinging to him in the close heat of the night. Watching their locked bodies as they rear and plunge, he works in frantic haste with the fastenings of his breeches and eases the stiff, throbbing member out into his hand.

God damn! Ain't seen nothin' like this, not in all his life. The buck and that nigra wench gettin' him so fired up, he knows he ain't gonna be able to wait no longer.

Should have brung Sheba down here maybe. Smiles at the thought, his dark mean eyes narrowed for the moment. Could have been kind of interesting, havin' her watch them with him, 'fore he did the same to her. Come to think, he might just do that anyhow, once he gits back. . . .

Throb of the urgent flesh against his palm dissuades him, taking his mind from Sheba for a while. Eyes fixed to that candle-lit crack in the wall, Lawrence starts to pump and jerk, hand clutched to his pulsing root as it thickens and swells, hoping somewhere far back in his mind that they don't git to hear his breathin' from where they laid down. . . .'

Inside, Cora's deep eyes open, looking to the upreared figure of the man beside her. The tall wench grins softly, lets her glance shift to where her own hand lies with its fingers curled at his roused manhood. She touches him lazily and the dark column rears up against her hand, stiffening, seemingly huge in candle-light. Cora runs her tongue around the inner side of her mouth and smiles again, knowing.

'Your turn, I reckon,' Cora says.

She rolls up on to her bare knees suddenly, her hand feathering beneath him, and bends to take him into her mouth. Flick of her tongue tracing wet circles over the swollen head, then that moist welcome warmth takes him in. Long fingers still stroking at him, upward along the shaft, Justus draws a shuddering breath. Swallows, looking down as the dark head goes to work. All feeling in him drawn to those sweet sensations that start to shiver through him at the root.

'Cora, honey. . . .' Words giving out sudden, the breath leaving him. The pleasure surging, rushing swifter and swifter towards fulfilment. He grits his teeth, sweat gathering on him, fighting to hold off, to prolong the incredible sweetness of her mouth on his flesh. For a while it works, but only for a while. Cora looks up at him slyly, flicks with her expert tongue at the underseam. Laying an unsteady hand on her curled hair, Justus lets go his breath, lets the pleasure take him soaring high as a hawk. Cries out as he comes again, gushing hot and thick into the warm, wet cavern of her mouth. She swallowing his jissom, holding him in her lips as he throbs and goes limp. Sinking down as strength ebbs to the afterwash of loving. Both of them lying there, twined in each others' arms, sweat-sheathed, sticky with sap of their mingled ecstasy.

'Yeah.' Justus breathes the word. Right now, seems like it the only thing he kin find to say a-tall. What they just done said a whole lot more.

Glancing up into his raptured face, agleam in the candle-flame, Cora nods. Reaches to touch him with a slender, dark-fingered hand. 'Sure was,' Cora says. Grins soft, hugging him to her. 'An' the night ain't over yet. . . .'

Outside Lawrence hauling at his rampant flesh in a frenzy of lust, eyes shut, teeth clenched. Hungry already to come, like they just did. Again the while feeling the hate build in him, knowing this the way it was with him an' Sheba, an' how far short he is of this goddamned nigra buck. Knowing too that however he gits off this time, ain't nothin' to what the pair of them got in there right now. . . .

Hate powering, blocking him. Fighting with that other driving need that cries at his root. Lawrence curses under his breath, struggles to throw the images from his mind until only Sheba is left—a vision of her waiting for him, up there at the big house, flung out on his bed with her thighs spread out wide, an' that sweet, furry little pussy of hers laid open for him, wet-lipped and ready. . . .

Feeling of rising pleasure comes back and he smiles, his hand working urgently, eager for that final plunge over the edge of his climax. . . .

In the dying flicker of the candle-light, Cora stirs again, sliding her sinuous body free of the big man who holds her. Rears up over him as he too smiles, lazy and contented, reaching up for the touch of her taunt, lifted breasts. For a while she waits, letting him fondle there, her eyes lidding to the pleasure of his fingers at her flesh. Cora shakes her head at last. Catches at his hand to put it by.

'How 'bout you should do somethin' for me, big boy?' Cora says.

Raises over him, lifting one leg so that she straddles his face. Lowers herself down, hands clutching at his mane of hair. Cora feels the first lapping touch at her inner flesh, opens to him, murmuring as his tongue goes into her, rousing her. His whole mouth on her now, licking and sucking at the swelling bud of flesh. Cora moans. Starts to move her long thighs against his face as the rhythm quickens, her hands leaving his hair, flailing as she bucks and heaves across him. The dark wench lets one hand slip down between her spread thighs, touching herself as his lips and tongue work from beneath, her other hand reaching backward to cup his fallen manhood. Fingers stroking and teasing until, glorious beyond belief, he begins to rise again. Feeling him swell up against her hand, the woman smiles in triumph. Head flung back, eyes shut as her own moment approaches yet again.

Beneath her, drunk with her musky woman-scent, Justus tastes as she cries out and goes slack, moving on him. Juice of her coming like warm syrup down either side of his face. A heartbeat later, and his own teeth clench on a tide of fresh, unexpected pleasure. . . .

This crazy, he thinks in the moment before he comes his third time, spilling thick into her hand. But it sure as hell happenin'. . . .

Outside, Lawrence watches for a splinter of a second. Then the dark wave takes him and he too comes. Spurting sudden to spatter on the wall of the hut. Stands as the last sensations ebb from him, eyeing the slimed mess on the wood. Feeling the first flickers of self-disgust. Loathing at the slack emptiness of his sated flesh. . . .

Snarls like a whipped dog, turning back to fasten up his breeches. He seen all he needs. This idea he got for Justus gonna work, all right. An' when it does, he figures he'll be the one to enjoy it, sure enough.

He starts back from the hut in the gathering dark. Heedless now of the murmurings inside. Sooner he git from here, the better.

Maybe Sheba kin do somethin' like it for him, later tonight.

LIGHT FROM the window wakes him, high overhead.

He lies a while without moving, sprawled across the crib. Been a busy night, he guesses, an' Cora near 'nough wore him out. Stretches lazy, savouring the bruises: the marks of her teeth on him, the long, raking claw-scars on his back. Smiles easy, sated. Remembering.

Off by the quarters the cowhorn sounds, callin' them out for the canefields agin. He don't heed it. Lying, listening to the birdsong of early mornin'. Not for him, he reckons. Whatever they got in mind for him, ain't the canefields. That for sure.

The troubling thought returns then, nagging like to a thorn someplace, at the back of his mind. Justus scowls. Swings his legs off the bed, gets up.

His breeches are still on the floor where he left them, kicked off a few hours before. Seeing them there he grins, but only for a moment. That other thought with him now, an' he reckons he gonna need an answer to it soon. Frowning again, he hauls the breeches on, buckles the belt at his waist, stretches to his full height, yawning as he crosses the room. Sure been some kind of a night.

Far side the room's the water-bucket they left him. Souses his hands and face in the tepid, muddy-coloured water, shaking himself dry. Somethin' goin' on back of all this—has to be. But right now he don't know what it is. Least he kin do is enjoy hisself.

He's already turned, headed back for the rumpled crib, when the voice halts him.

'You 'wake there, boy?'

Comin' from beyond the high window, out of sight. At sound of it he grins all the same, crossing the narrow room.

116

'Nestor.' His voice gone up a notch and his face lights. Kneels on the crib, hands to the clapboard wall. 'Nestor, that you? What you doin' here?'

Far side the wall he hears that throaty chuckle like before.

'Jes' seein' how you makin' out, boy.' Nestor says. 'It's all. How you doin'?'

'Well, now. . . .' Hesitates a while. Not too sure what he oughta be sayin'. How much does the old man know? All of it, like enough. 'They been feedin' me good—stuff I ain't so much as caught a scent of 'fore now. Steak an' eggs an' all. . . .'

'That right?' He catches the glint of amusement in the other's voice. 'So they treatin' you good, huh?'

'Reckon they are,' Justus tells him.

Outside comes a momentary pause. When Nestor talks agin, his voice got a wry sound. 'Yeah,' the old man says. 'They sure as hell treatin' you good, Justus.'

Inside, leaned to the wall on the crib, he frowns, thoughtful. Nestor knows it, sure 'nough.

'You wanta know how come?' the old man asks him.

Breath comes from him in a long, heavy sigh. Justus nods slowly. Like Nestor kin see him through the wall.

'Sure would 'preciate that, Nestor,' Justus says.

Another silence. Shorter than before. Only this time when Nestor answers him, ain't no humour in his voice a-tall.

'It's this way, boy,' the old man says. 'Cain't be sure what they got in mind, but I got a suspicion. An' I reckon I ain't mistook. Lawrence had you put out here, an' he ain't no friend of yours or mine, right?'

'That right 'nough.'

'So it got to be somethin' that good for Lawrence, right?'

'Guess so.' Frowns deeper on that, shaking his head. Out beyond the window comes that dry chuckle again.

'Got you thinkin' there, boy,' Nestor says. At once, though, he's serious again. 'No. Way I see it, Lawrence got you in mind to breed his wenches. Any wenches—you take my meanin'?'

For some while after that he don't say a word, struck like to dumb at what he heard. Then all he kin feel is the hate an' anger

117

firin' up inside him. So hot, he cain't hardly breathe a-tall.

'Sonofabitch!' Grits it out through tight-clenched teeth. His huge fists bunched so tight the knuckles showin' clear through the skin. Seems like he cain't find nothin' else to say, the hate so strong inside.

'Sure is,' Nestor agrees. 'Right now, though, that don't count much either way, I reckon. That be why he feedin' you up good . . . an' that why he sendin' in the wenches to you nights. Way I see it, it got to be, boy. . . . Cora last night, huh?'

Justus catches the sly hint in the voice and frowns once more. That Lawrence playin' him for a sucker, sure 'nough. 'Yeah, that right, Nestor.' Anger plain in his voice. 'Was Cora come here.'

'Uhuh.' Nestor's voice gentles at that. 'That Cato's woman, mind. An' he a mean son hisself. Once you git back in the quarters, you watch out for Cato. You hear me?'

'I hear you,' Justus says.

'Listen to me good, boy,' Nestor tells him. 'Lawrence, he got you figgered to be his breedin' man, I reckon. Like to a stud hoss, or a bull maybe. Right now, that how it gotta be. Ain't no way you gonna git loose from doin' what he got in mind for you to do. . . .'

'So what you tellin' me?' the big man asks, bitterness in his voice.

Outside, beyond the wall, he hears the old man sigh like he tired of life.

'Hear me, chile,' Nestor says. 'Ain't nothin' wrong with what you an' Cora done, no more'n what you done with Sheba before. What a man do with a wench, ain't for nobody else to judge, I reckon. Same with this breedin' business he set up for. I heard he been takin' bets from some of them other planters round about, how you kin serve their wenches too. Reckon he aims to make quite a heap of dollars from it.'

'God damn, Nestor!' His shout rings in the trapped space, fury building in him like it about to explode. 'Ain't *no* man gonna do that to me! I ain't no hoss, nor no bull neither!'

'Sure you ain't.' The other voice touches on him, soothing. 'I knows it. Lawrence, though, he gonna have you do that thing. You be sure of that.'

'Gonna have to kill me first!' Justus yells.

'Quiet down, boy,' Nestor tells him. 'An' don't talk that way. Give Lawrence a chance like that, he might like that, he might jes' take it.'

Hearing the rebuke in that voice, he nods. The breath shuddering from him.

'Yeah, you right,' Justus says at last.

'Sure I'm right.' The old man sounds impatient. 'Now, stay listenin', 'cause this should count for somethin', I reckon. Whatever happen to you, boy, jes' stay free inside yo' haid, you hear me? Lawrence kin do anythin' he like with you, same as he kin with every other nigger in this place. Kin work you day clean to first dark. Kin whip the skin from yo' back. An' he kin set you to breed the wenches he wants, iffen you care to or not. One thing he cain't do, not less'n you let him, an' that's make a nigger of you inside your own haid. He ain't never done that to me, 'cause I don't aim to let him. Don't you let him do that, you hear me?'

'I won't,' he says.

At sound of his taut-strung voice, the old man chuckles softly. 'No, boy. Reckon you won't, neither,' Nestor says. 'Now you jes' remember. What he git you an' them wenches to do, it ain't you an' it ain't them oughta feel bad over it. 'Cause ain't nothin' wrong in it, yo' side. Anybody in the wrong of it, it that sonofabitch Lawrence. 'Cause he set you to it, an' all the meanness in him 'fore any of this started off. You listenin', Justus?'

'You bet,' the big man tells him.

'Good 'nough,' Nestor says. 'So make sure you stay free inside your haid, like I tole you. That what count, boy, more'n anythin'.' While you free there, ain't nothin' he kin do to touch you. 'Cause you free yet, an' no way he kin win. You reckon you kin do that?'

'I reckon.' Knelt at the crib, he smiles slowly. 'Thanks, Nestor.'

'Jes' tellin' you the way it is, chile,' the old man tells him. 'I figger I kin count on you to do what I tole you. You too smart to do nothin' else.'

'How 'bout if he should send up another wench?' Justus wants to know.

Out beyond the wall, he heard the old man laugh.

'That what we all here for, boy,' Nestor says. 'Ain't nothin' wrong with that. Tho't I tole you that more'n once already.'

Justus is still grinning at that when he hears the other voice outside.

'Hey, old man!' That Andy, shoutin' sudden from close to the hut on Nestor's side. 'What you think you doin' here? Git from here an' fast, you heah me talkin'?'

In the silence that follows, Justus catches his breath.

'You talkin' to me, Andy?' he hears Nestor ask.

'You heard me, I reckon,' Andy says. He's slow to answer, an' when he does it comes sullen, like he knows he beat already. Hearing him, Justus starts to smilin' again.

'Well now,' Nestor's own voice is level. assured. It holds, too, the hint of a threat. 'I know you, Andy. Knowed you from a chile. An' you ain't got near enough meanness in yo' whole body to go talkin' to ole Nestor that way. You oughta know better'n that, I reckon.'

'You tryin' to threaten me, ole man?' Andy's voice struggles, tryin' to sound tough, but it don't work. He don't scare Nestor none, an' by now he knows it.

'What you think?' the old man asks.

This time the driver don't answer him a-tall.

'That a way better, Andy,' Nestor says at last. 'Sometime you oughta go ask Jacob how he talks to ole Nestor. Jacob a way tougher'n you is, boy. More mean piss in that nigger'n you gonna find in a hundred years, I reckon. An' I ain't never had no talk like that from him. 'Cause he know this ain't jes' a ole man he talkin' to. Iffen you want to sleep easy, boy, you better know it too.'

'Okay, so I know it.' Andy sounds sulky, like he been whipped good. 'Jes' leave me, be, ole man. I jes' doin' like they tell me. . . .'

'Sure you is.' Nestor sounds like he's holdin' back from laughin' out loud. 'No offence, boy. I was goin' from here anyhow. . . .'

Inside at the wall of the hut, Justus hears the shifting sound as the old man eases away from the wood. Next minute, that same voice floats up to him.

'So stay free, chile,' Nestor says.

He moves from the wall. His steps and those of the driver fading together.

Once they're gone Justus stays there, leaned at the wall, the smile still to his face. Yeah, he thinks. Nestor right, sure 'nough. He ain't nobody's nigger, 'cause he free in his own haid. An' it shows plain. Any other nigger on this here plantation, Andy'd strip his back clean for less'n what he took jes' then from-a bent old man. There somethin' to this stayin' free, sure is. . . .

That the way it gonna have to be with him.

He gets down from the crib, grinning as he stretches upward to the sunlight.

Come nightfall, the scratchin' at his door agin. Justus goes to lift the bar like before. Outside, sees Lucy standin' there. Like Cora, she holdin' a lit candle in her hand. Light of it fallin' on the reddish colour of her hair an' upturned eyes. Seeing him stood there in the open doorway, she smiles.

'You gonna let me in, Justus?' Lucy asks.

Justus stands there a while, lookin' on her. Lucy ain't so tall as Cora. More like to Sheba's build, he guesses. Slim and medium high, her head up to a level with his chest. Recallin' Sheba an' how it was, he sighs. Times, he wishes it didn't have to be this way.

But only for a moment. Lucy quite a looker. That reddish colour she got go with her high-boned face. An' look of them red-brown eyes decides him. What we all here for, Nestor said. . . .

He steps back, leaving the door wide open to her.

'You better come in, Lucy,' Justus says.

Watches as she goes on by him, smilin' up to him from half-covered eyes. She been waitin' a while for this, he reckons—way back to hog killin' time, maybe. Shrugs on the thought, turns, following her inside. All the better, he figures. Be a sight harder if she couldn't stand the sight of him.

She's set down the candle in the moment he drops the bar. Turns toward him in that wavering light, the smile sunning her face. Eyeing her carefully, he too smiles.

'What with the candle?' Justus asks. Already sight of her lithe, firm-fleshed body turns his insides to water and sets the hot pulse beating at his groin. 'You reckon you gonna miss somethin', maybe?'

'I don't aim to miss nothin', Justus,' Lucy tells him.

Pulls the cotton dress over her head in a single swift move. Under it she naked as a jaybird. Same red-brown colour to her all the way down to her toes. 'Cept for where the hair turns darker rusty red at the place between her thighs. She got fuller breasts than Cora, he notices. An' her belly kind of rounder, not so flat. But she got a good slim-hipped shape to her, an' from here it enough to set his mouth to waterin'. Once he had one wench come to him, seems like he cain't git enough.

'Jes' hold on, gal,' he tells her. 'I'm comin' right over.'

Reaches to her as he crosses the room, taking that slender body into his arms. He feels the shiver that runs the length of her as his own great hands touch on her naked flesh. Lucy murmurs against his massive chest, closing her eyes. At once he lifts her, bearing her for the crib by the wall.

'Don't you worry none, honey,' Justus tells her as she looks up into his face. 'It gonna be all right.

'Who tole you I was worried?' Lucy asks.

Her own hands eager on him as he lays her down. Touching and finding her wet and ready for him, Justus breathes hard, feeling his manhood surge up stiff and hard. Lucy peels off his pants in a hurry, letting them drop to the ground. Lying back on the crib, she takes hold on the upright rod of flesh. Cups it in her two hands. Fondling as he fondles. The two of them close already to time.

'Come on in, honey,' Lucy says.

Lifts herself to him, her thighs spread wide as she guides him into her. Legs closing to grip his waist as his throbbing organ sinks its length. Justus gasps. Stands with spread hands balanced on the wood of the crib, Lucy hanging to him as he thrusts fiercely in the heat and moisture of her innermost flesh, force of his rutting slamming the frail crib into the wall. Beneath him she moans out, reaching to lay his hands at her breasts, her own hands clawing at him in frenzy as their joined bodies heave and plunge rapidly towards climax. Justus sees the candle-light shimmer on the reddish waves of her hair as Lucy's head thrashes on the bed, eyes closed tight as she gasps and moans.

'Oh yeah, honey . . . oh, Justus . . . oh, that sure is good, Justus, honey. . . .'

122

Feels the fierce wave as it starts to rise, towering up to cut him off from all other feeling. Justus sweats and groans in turn, driving hisself into her like he ain't never gonna stop. Senses that sweet, thick pleasure as it rushes and builds, too furious now to hold. Lucy shrieks out under him, clasping hard about his waist as she shudders and comes, her scented juices trickling into the hair of his crotch. Same instant Justus hollers harsh as a mountain cat and bucks into her as that high wave takes him, shooting himself into the warmth of her in a gushing, draining spasm of ecstasy. . . .

Sinks to his knees by the crib as Lucy slackens, her legs sliding from him. For a while the two of them stay that way, sound of their shuddery breathing the one thing to be heard. After a few minutes feels her light touch on his hair. Looks up to see her smiling face above him.

'Best I ever had, Justus,' the red-headed slave wench says. At the light in those eyes Justus grins, the slow sated feeling warming him to the bones.

'Got us all night, honey,' he says.

Eases forward. Brings his mouth to the wet, musky sweetness between her thighs. Feels her fall back above him. Breathing out softly as his tongue goes into her.

Up by the crack in the wall of the candlelit room, Lawrence watches them again.

'GOT ME an idea, 'bout that nigger Justus,' Lawrence says.

He gets up from his cane-bottom chair and steps out along the porch a ways, halting at last by the wood pillar at the far end. Leans there a moment, studying. Out beyond the clapboard shade the canefields swelter in the murderous heat. Mid-afternoon, the sun high in a sky the colour of brass. A hazy heat above the willow trees, overset by dark insect clouds. Further off, the live-oaks by the water all but blurred from sight. Reek of blossom and bayou scum mingled with the scent of earth. And in among the canes, the black, toiling shapes of men and women, cutting and carrying,

123

heading back and forth by the looming sugar-house, whose dull rumbling noise pounds on without end.

Up by the doorway, perched in his rocker in the shade, Old Man Lawrence twists his head, looking to the man against the pillar. Somethin' in John's mind here, he knows. Always gits restless when he figured out some new trick or other. An' Justus.... Frowns on that a while, his pouched faced sagging into the familiar folds of age. Ain't no love between John and that buck, not since Sheba an' the whuppin' he give him. Could be this son of his got something real unpleasant to tell him.

'So tell me.' He lets himself sink back in the chair, his white head settling again, eyes closed, the thin, parched lips quirking in somethin' like to a smile. 'How's he been makin' out, since you done took the skin offen his back?'

'Was Jacob did that, on my word. Wouldn't soil my hands.' Lawrence all but spits out the words. Abruptly he turns from the pillar, stalking back along the porch. The first spasm of annoyance past, his lean features return to their former cruel humour. A vicious glint to his dark, narrowed eyes.

'Last I heard, he was helpin' Laban at the forge,' Old Lawrence murmurs. Eyes still shuttered against the sun, he starts to rockin' gently back and forth, one hand easing down for the half-empty glass of lemonade by his feet. Lately his rheumatics been playin' him up some. He ain't been out by the quarters to see what's goin' on. 'You had anythin' special lined up for him since then, John?'

At that the younger man smiles colder. That same mean glint to his eyes.

'Yeah,' Lawrence tells his father. 'You could say that....'

He moves back easily, flopping down in the chair. Reaching for the chilled glass at its foot.

'Laban's back at the forge now,' Lawrence says. He sips at the cool liquid, his lean face sobering as he drinks. 'Justus now, I had him brung from the quarters. Set him up all by hisself in this hut. I had built special for the job. Fed him up some—steak an' eggs, molasses, fresh milk. Then few nights back, I sent Cora in to him....'

He pauses, smiling faintly as he savours the aftertaste of his

124

drink. Savouring too the alarm and disbelief in the old man's face as his father heaves upright against the arms of the rocker. Staring at him like he cain't believe what he hears.

'Do I hear you right, John?' Old Man Lawrence's voice comes hoarse, breathless, his wizened features still stunned. Too shaken yet to be angry at what he's told. 'Cora—why, she's Cato's woman, ain't she? That gonna be trouble, for sure. An' steak an' eggs? What in hell you doin', son? Carry on that way, he'll be eatin' up here at table with us. . . .'

'Hear me out, old man,' Lawrence tells him.

The curt, brutal sound of his voice in the hot afternoon hits the other like a blow. Old Man Lawrence puckers his face and looks down, sinking back into the chair. Seems like he a way too old for this kind of argument. Specially when the sun is high.

'I was around when Cora went to him,' Lawrence says. He smiles now, the gleam of bared teeth keen and vicious as an unsheathed blade. 'I saw it all, old man. Everythin' them two niggers did. Let me tell you somethin', pa. That was the hottest damn thing I ever seen. You ain't seen nothin' like it yourself, I reckon.'

The old man sighs a moment, his eyes half-closed. The words of his son bring back memories of Beth in the house at nightfall: her lifted skirt and spread thighs. Soft, musky warmth of her, wet against his face. Old Man Lawrence shudders, aware for the first time of the clothes that cling to him in the sweaty heat. He downs the last of his drink, thankful of the cool taste that quenches fire inside. Wishing already for the night.

'Could be I wouldn't be too surprised, son.' His own eyes slitted, hard and shrewd, as his lined face crumples into a knowing smile. 'I been down them quarters in my time. Reckon I know the way it is. They got nothin' else much to use for pleasure anyhow.' Chuckles, shaking his white head in sunlight. 'Tell truth, John, there ain't no better pleasure on this earth, far as I know. If there is, I ain't heard it yet. . . .'

Across from him in the other chair the younger man frowns momentarily, irritated at the interruption. Trust the old fellow to go on about how it was.

'Next night, I sent him Lucy in,' Lawrence says. 'Ain't nobody laid claim to her yet.' He too shakes his lean, dark head, starting to smile again. 'Shoulda seen the way that black buck handled her, too. Like he ain't never had a woman for six months. You better believe me, pa. After what she got there, she like to turn up her nose at anybody else.'

Slumped in the rocker, sweating hard, Old Lawrence looks up to him, suspicion in every furrowed line of his face.

'Just what's in all this for you, son?' the oldster asks. 'Thought you didn't have no time for Justus. Matter of fact, I coulda sworn one time you hated that buck like poison.'

'You got it, old man!' Lawrence's smile is gone. He bites the words back through his clenched teeth. For a moment, facing the stare of those black, narrowed eyes, the old man feels a chill touch of terror, aware suddenly of the younger man's hatred. And his own helplessness.

'Sure as hell ain't his pleasure I got in mind, pa,' Lawrence says at last. He eases the drink to his lips, the dregs of liquid sliding slowly down his throat. When he comes to set it down the thin smile cuts his face again. 'No, what I'm thinkin' of is a whole lot better than that. I'm talkin' 'bout money, old man. Hundreds of dollars. Thousands, even. I reckon even you gonna have to like the sound of that.'

'Ain't sure I read your meanin', John.' The old man's voice is shaky for once, his look wary as he gazes on the darker, taller figure of his son. 'How come we gonna be makin' money from him?'

He sees the look on his son's face, then, and at once he's even more troubled than before. 'You tellin' me we gonna put him to stud? Like to a hoss or somethin'?' Now he frowns in earnest, the yellowing skin gone taut at the corners of his eyes. 'That's somethin' we ain't never done here on Sweet River, John. Cain't say as I care for the sound of it, neither. . . .'

'Happens anyhow, down by the quarters.' The younger man still smiles. His stare, though, holds cold and hard on the man across from him.' Sure—most of 'em git to jump the broom in time. But way I see it there ain't no difference. Man gits to serve the wench, either way.'

'Yeah, but usin' a man like some kinda stallion—wearin' him out to no purpose. . . .' The white head shakes. Uneasy. 'That ain't the same, John. An' it don't take no 'count of his feelin's. Could ruin us a good nigger that way. . . . I don't see no percentage in that, John. Noway.'

'Will you hush up an' listen, old man?' Lawrence's voice suddenly bites, impatient again, his black, pitiless stare boring into the slumped figure in the rocker. He leans forward in his seat, hands gripping tight on the arm-rests. 'This here is money I'm talkin' on. Justus is but one nigger, right? Even should he be wore out, you got plenty more. Besides.' His grin turns cruel and knowing. 'I seen that buck perform. He gonna take some killin', believe me. There's money in this, pa, an' you know it. After what I done with him already, I reckon Lucy an' Cora be carryin' for him in a while. His sap's good, you bet. That's dollars in the pocket for sure, come the time.'

'Sure, but nothin' like the money you talkin' 'bout,' Old Lawrence begins. That fierce, black gaze cuts him short in a moment.

'You're right.' Lawrence hasn't lost his smile. 'I got somethin' a whole lot bigger'n *that* in mind. A while back, I met up with Billy Devereaux in Palmetto. You know him—'

'Feller from Blackwater? Sure,' the old man mutters. Sullen. His head sunk on his chest.

'That's him.' Lawrence nods, the keen smile slicing his face. 'He got a couple of wenches ripe for servin', he tells me. Ready to pay hundred dollars each for the buck to do the job. From what I hear, there's one or two more interested. Lacourbe for one, and Harcourt from over at Jericho. When I saw Devereaux, I gave out word for a meetin' here. Tole 'em to bring their wenches along.'

'When?' The old man's voice is a hollow croak.

'Three weeks from now.' Lawrence nods easily, assured. 'Thursday. Up by the old feed barn. Devereaux, he already laid a bet my man cain't serve three wenches in a night. If the others come in, could be more'n a thousand dollars ridin' on the one meetin'.'

'You didn't tell me nothin' 'bout this, son.' Seems like Old Man

Lawrence cain't find nothin' more to say. Across from him his son hears defeat in the tone of his voice, and smiles sharper than before.

'Guess not.' Settles back easy in the chair, his thin shoulders set to the wicker and cane, head back as the hatbrim tilts over his eyes. 'Don't signify now, pa. You a gentleman, always was. You know once a man lays a bet, ain't no goin' back. Ain't that what you always tole me?'

'God damn. . .' Old Lawrence breathes the words, sinks, hunching lower in the mahogany seat. Right now he figures he ain't felt so drained an' empty in all his life. Shoulda known somethin' like this would happen sooner or later. All the same, wishes he didn't have to be around to see it.

'What you aim to do with him, before the meetin'?' he asks at last.

Leaned back in the chair across from him, young Lawrence chuckles softly.

'Nothin' special,' the dark, lean-faced man tells him. 'He kin go back to the quarters agin for the next coupla weeks, I guess. Come a week fore the contest, I'll have him set back in the hut. Feed him up like before, keep him starved of wenches this time. When they bring him to them nigger bitches in the barn, he's gonna be hotter'n a stallion. . . .' Laughs again, meanness in the dark glint of his eyes. 'Sure gonna see somethin' *that* night, I reckon!'

Slumped in his chair, the old man don't answer. All at once he feels so bone-weary he could sleep for a hundred years.

'Could sure use a whiskey,' Lawrence mutters. He sits up sudden, pushing back the hat from his face. 'Sheba!'

Watches her as she appears in the doorway, stepping out on the porch, lithe and slim and silent as a cat on her bare brown feet. Seeing that look, Sheba smiles, her dark, gentle eyes cast down to the boarded floor.

'Somethin' I kin do for you, Massa Lawrence suh?'

Sure is, the dark man thinks. But he don't say it. Instead he leans to pick up his glass from the floor, handing it to her. The lean-lipped grin cuts his face and his eyes touch on her body like the stroke of a hand.

'Go find me a glass of whiskey, honey,' Lawrence says, his dark glance tracing her body outlined under the calico dress. 'Ain't no hurry. I ain't goin' nowhere today.'

'Sure thing, Massa Lawrence.' Sheba takes the glass. Their hands touch and she too smiles. Lawrence watches her go, slipping smooth as a shadow back inside the house.

Got me your woman anyhow, Justus, he thinks.

And pretty soon you gonna have to do just like I tell you.

Settles back into his seat. Stretches a while, lazy and content in the afternoon heat. Looks like things gonna be goin' his way from now on.

Beyond him the canefields simmer in the fearsome heat as the black figures go back and forth, and the beat of the sugar-house rollers pounds ceaselessly on.

AFTER THAT time Lucy come to him, he left to hisself for nigh on a couple of weeks.

They feed him up, like always. Lucy or Cora bring it over most times, but every time they got a driver longside them so they ain't no chance of doin' nothin' else. Best they kin do is give him a smile as they lay the platter down or take it up agin. Come mornin', one of them empties his slop-pail. Sets fresh water for him to wash. That apart, he don't have sight of a livin' soul.

Left to hisself, time gits to weigh heavy on his hands. Whiles, he'll pace the board floor up and down like he aims to wear it through, chafin' some at bein' penned in this place. Other times, jes' lies on his crib. Drowses. Dreams, maybe, of Sheba mostly, an' what he had once. The other wenches they sent in to him— Cora, Lucy—they both fine, but they jes' ain't the same. Him an' Sheba was lookin' for somethin' more. They was hopin' sometime to go jump the broom. Now, he don't have that no more.

That bastard Lawrence done took it from him.

Memory bringin' back the worst of the anger. Times, he gits up

129

to beat on the wall with his fists. Ain't no use. Shakes it some, but the wall don't care. An' mostly he ends up with his knuckles bruised an' the hate simmering on under the skin.

The days in this place have changed his looks. With the good food they given him buildin' up his body, his black skin gleams smooth now, like it been oiled, the muscles showin' sleek mounds in the flesh of his arms and breast. Huge as he is, he got a handsomer look. But for the callouses on his palms you wouldn't know him for a field hand.

That, an' the knotted marks of the whip-scars in his back.

Yeah. Recallin' that time, he feels the hate seethe inside him. Ain't nothin' ever gonna wipe out the marks that sonofabitch left on him. Only blood.

Lawrence's blood.

Sinks again on the groaning crib, breathing out hard, feeling the sweat cool on him from the force of the rage within. No way he kin git to Lawrence, nor Jacob neither. One chance is to run. An' right now, that lookin' like no chance a-tall.

Whiles, Nestor comes by. Talks to him through the window set high into the wall. Same talk as always: stay free, don't let 'em git to you. He heard it all. Taken it in long since, Jes' don't know iffen he kin keep to it, is all.

Nights alone, the lack of a woman grows to a torment, goading the flesh. Times, he lies awake, struggling to sleep, fighting the urgent need of his upright maleness. Throb of the stiffened flesh swelling so taut it pains him sometimes. The images his mind calls up made the more hard to bear. That, and the thought that he's a pawn in Lawrence's hands. Movin' when the Massa says so. Goin' hungry when he don't. . . .

He could solve it, he guesses. He found ways before. But right now, cain't bring hisself to do that. Not makin' love with his hand—not after what he known. Ain't no way he gonna spite Lawrence. One way or another, that sonofabitch gonna have him do jes' what he wants. An' if he don't, they's allus Jacob an' the whip. . . .

'Course, he knows what they got in mind, ever since they sent in Cora and Lucy to him. That, an' what Nestor tole him. Sooner or later, he knows, they gonna come for him.

All the same, when the time comes he ain't ready.

Crash of the heavy whip-stock on the door brings him awake. Justus groans, rousing from the crib, hearing sound of the voice beyond.

'Come on out, nigger!' Jacob calls, mockery in his tone. 'Massa waitin' on you, boy.'

Draws breath at that, the cold thought striking home. It come at last. Justus shrugs his massive shoulders. No way of gittin' out from it, not now. Naked in darkness, he reaches to haul on his breeches, buckles his belt as he gains the door. Already the sweaty heat of the night grabs him by the throat.

Outside, that same heat presses down upon him. Thunder rumblin' in the low-hung clouds. There the three of them wait for him, jes' like before: Jacob straddle-legged at the centre, Bob and Andy out to either side, the bunch of them holding to their coiled whips. Seeing those grinning faces, the big man scowls, hating them.

'Come on, now.' Jacob's yellow eyes got a mean glint of humour. He pops the whip as the first blast of thunder rackets in the distance. 'Hurry it up, there. Ain't you hot for them wenches, big boy?'

'Don't know why he troubled to put his britches on.' Lean-faced Andy chuckles from far side of him, stroking the leathern thongs of the whip. 'They gonna have 'em offen him soon 'nough. . . .'

Grits his teeth, hearing the bunch of them break into laughter. Right now, he'd give one hell of a lot for the chance of gittin' his hands to their necks.

Jacob sees the look, and his smile fades. The huge driver puts a calloused hand to the other's shoulder. Shoving him forward so that for a moment Justus struggles to keep his balance.

'No call for you to keep us hangin' round,' Jacob tells him. 'move yo' ass, nigger!'

Starts forward at the word, hearing his teeth grate hard together as he moves. The drivers close in about him, shepherding him away from the quarters an' heading for the old feed barn and its outbuildings back of the sugar-house. From above comes a sizzling explosion of blue-white light that blinds the world for the fraction

131

of a second. After it, the deafening blast of thunder. Jacob glances up to the sound, his splayed face puckered in a scowl.

'Storm gonna break any time,' the driver says. Then, in a sharper tone, 'git on there, you sonofabitch,' half–raising the whip.

The big man meets that yellow stare, his own hate showing plain in the eyes, his face a fierce mask. Jacob won't use the whip this time, he knows, but threat of the blow is enough to make him bristle up with rage. Moving ahead as the first rain spatters down in flat, heavy drops, he feels his insides churn, full to bursting with that explosive mix of hate, fury and animal need.

Overhead comes another blue-white blast, forking seemingly into the ground by their feet. Racket of thunder following fast, all but bursting the eardrums. Around him the drivers quicken to a run, feet slapping as a sheeting downpour turns the earth to mud. He follows, loping to where the dark, low outline of the barn rears through a drumming curtain of rain.

Weight of the downpour strikes on him like a blow, water stinging as it sprays back off his body, steaming where it hits the ground. Justus slams through it, head down, blinded, sheathed from head to foot in moisture that smokes upward from his shoulders and his hair, sweating still in the close, humid heat. Either side of him the other two drivers slither and curse in the clinging mud, hurrying for the open door of the barn. Jacob panting like a hound as he pads along close at his back.

Up front he glimpses the barn through the rain, the doors flung back, ablaze in torchlight. From inside, a baying chorus of voices. Blurred by the hammering fall of rain, it comes to him like the sound of a pack of hunting beasts. Justus licks at his lips, feeling the hairs prickle up along the back of his neck.

'They comin'!' one voice calls high above the rest, like to a hunts-man whooping on the hounds to a kill. 'Here they comin', fellers!'

'Bring that buck nigger sonofabitch in here!' somebody else shouts.

Thrust up toward the open doors, he snarls—low, vicious sound in the back of his throat. White bastards, all of them. Then comes the thud of Jacob's whip-stock in the small of his back. Justus sucks in his breath, the snarl dying.

132

'Don' play dog with me, boy,' Jacob mutters. 'I whup dogs, you heah?'

He don't answer, letting them push him forward into the blaze of light.

Torches light the barn, trussed into brackets of pine along the walls. Out front they made a bed of straw. That be for what they got in mind, he knows. Justus studies it but a moment, his hard-eyed glance moving on for the group of white men who lounge on the hay bales and the wicker chairs far side of the bed of straw: red-faced, sweating men in shirtsleeves and pants, some still wearing their wide-brimmed hats even beneath the roof of the barn. Justus catches sight of Lawrence leaned back in a chair, swigging from a half-empty whiskey jug. Far side of him the old man hunches, his pouched face weary and resigned. Other faces, glimpsed for an instant: a big florid-featured man in a white store suit, straw hat topping his head. Mean blue eyes like to a pig's, sunk deep in the flesh, and a tight mouth half-hidden in rolls of fat. Dark, swarthy little feller, black-eyed and moustached, waving his ringed hands as he reaches for the jug from Lawrence. Same moment all their eyes fix on him and Justus looks down. Knowin' if he look them once in the eye, he a daid man.

'This the nigger, huh?' It's the fat, ruddy-faced one who asks. Got kind of a high voice to him, like he ain't hardly a man a-tall. Steaming in the sudden enclosed space, hearing the rain pound on the roof overhead, Justus stays looking at the floor.

'Sure 'nough a fine-lookin' critter, ain't he?'

'Not so sure of what he is like under the breeches,' says the smaller, darker man, sly humour in his voice. At once the bunch of them break into laughter. He hears it. Head down in a reek of whiskey fumes and choking cigar-smoke. Nails biting into the palms of his hands. Hating them.

'You gonna git your turn, Lacourbe,' Lawrence says. Chuckles, already drunk, slumping back in the chair. His eyes, though, hold a wicked glint. 'Any more of you gents still reckon he cain't do the job?'

'Not even him,' another voice says. 'Not for three wenches in a night. Put me down for a hundred, Lawrence!'

'You already got my money agin it,' the dark-faced Lacourbe tells him.

'Good enough.' Lawrence grins his lean-lipped grin, dark eyes glittering. Turns to the heavy-set florid-faced man across from him. 'How 'bout you, Devereaux?'

'Was me made the wager, remember?' Devereaux says, his high voice mean and petulant against the thrash of the rain.

Old Man Lawrence looks up slow from under his hooded eyelids.

'That nigger gonna catch his death,' the white-haired oldster says. His speech is soft, almost a whisper. All the same it cuts through the other sounds. 'Best have him rubbed down, John, or he ain't gonna manage nothin' tonight. . . .'

'Reckon you're right, old man.' Lawrence scowls, the thin smile fading. He sets upright in the seat, looking to the drivers, who stand quiet, soaked bodies steaming in the warmth of the barn. 'Jacob, git that nigger rubbed down, you hear me?'

Shade of a fleeting anger crosses those savage features. Only for an instant. 'Suh.' Jacob keeps his eyes down. Glances around him for somethin' to use.

'Kin have my shirt, boy!' one of the watching men calls out. Cackles as he mouths the words, all but spilling drunkenly from the hay bale where he perches. Other hands reach to haul the shirt over his head, the bunch of them laughing now like kids let loose. 'Take it, nigger!' the half-stripped man calls out. Lolls off the hay bale, the others catching him as he falls. For a while he lies there, laughing still as he gasps for breath.

'Yassuh.' Jacob takes the rumpled shirt. Starts to wiping the rain and sweat from the other man's body. Justus stands quiet, feeling the touch of those hated hands upon him. Feeling too the rage as it surges up afresh inside him. Slither of the stained shirt moves over his upper body, soaking up the worst of the wet. Abruptly Jacob steps back. Lets fall the sodden garment to the ground.

'That'll do, Jacob,' Lawrence says. He lays back in the chair, reaching inside his coat for a long-shafted cigar. Eyes on the driver, he lights up, real slow and lazy. 'Now git from here. This white folks' business.'

'Yassuh, Massa Lawrence.' Jacob bows his grizzled head.

134

Turns, signalling to the men behind him. The three of them move out from the barn and back into the hammering veil of rain.

'Let's see him stripped, Lawrence!' It's Devereaux who calls out. Listening, Justus reads an eagerness in his voice that ain't healthy. From the corner of his eye he catches sight of that red, sweating face. The tight mouth open now, moist where the inner part of the lips curls back from the teeth. Swallows, feeling disgust rise in him together with the rage.

The rest, though, take up the shout. Seated in his wicker chair, back of a curling stream of cigar-smoke, Lawrence nods his head.

'Haul them britches, nigger,' Lawrence says.

He complies. Breeches slide from him to the floor. Straightens, hands down by his sides. Touch of heat and air on his unclad flesh rouse up that other hunger. Justus draws breath unsteadily, feeling the thick erect stem of his manhood rise, pulsing as it stands out from his body.

Stays motionless. Hearing the shrill noise of their whoops and hollers as they too see what is to be seen.

'God damn, some whang!'

'Kinda well hung nigger, ain't he, boys?'

'More like to a stud hoss, I reckon!'

Hears their mocking voices as if from a distance, hazed in the smoke and the whiskey fumes. He got to git through it anyhow, he knows. All the same, when fat Devereaux rolls to his feet and starts toward him, the big man feels his body tense, his skin prickling suddenly.

'Reckon I'll take me a closer look,' the red-faced planter says, and leans forward, his plump hands reaching for the tall figure in front of him.

Justus stands, feeling his teeth grit of themselves as the seaty palms knead the muscles of his arm, slide over his chest and back, lingering a while on the knotted scars. Devereaux nods, his mean little mouth wet and loose now as his touch goes lower. Fingers probe at the flat belly of the slave. Rest for a moment on the stiff, upright member. . . .

Justus sucks in his breath. His dark face murderous. Some day, he'll git to this bastard too.

'That's enough, there!' Lawrence calls out sharply. From where he sits his black-eyed stare cuts at the red-faced man in front of him. 'He ain't for sale, Devereaux. Nor for nothin' else, neither!'

The words bring a fresh outbrust of laughter from the seated men. Hit by their mocking glances, Devereaux's face goes a deeper red. The fat man straightens, wipes his sweaty hands on a flowered handkerchief, his features sullen as he turns to move away.

'Looks like you marked him good,' Devereaux mutters. 'Wouldn't be no good to sell anyhow.'

'That ain't why I'm keepin' him,' Lawrence tells the fat man. Grins around the cigar that smoulders at his lips. 'He ain't marked where it counts, I don't reckon.'

Pauses, his look turning to the huge black man who stands before him, fighting still to hold down the hate and fury inside him. Justus endures the look of those eyes. His own stare fixed on the ground.

'This here Mister Devereaux,' Lawrence tells him. 'Come all the way up from Blackwater to see you perform, nigger. Mister Lacourbe, too, from Willow Bend, and Mister Stoneham from Magnolia. There's a whole number of white gentlemen waitin' on you, boy. Lot of money, too, you hear?'

'Suh, Massa Lawrence.' The words taste like scum on his tongue. All the same, he gits them out. Lawrence nods, snake-eyed, back of the lit cigar.

'Best make it good, nigger. That right?'

'Sure will, Massa Lawrence,' he says.

'Time to bring in the wenches,' somebody shouts from beyond him. At once the baying clamour sets up again. Justus stands. Letting it wash over him like slop from a bucket, trying to disregard the throbbing heat at his loins. All the time burning each hated face into his memory.

God damn you to hell. All of you.

'Okay,' Lawrence's voice cuts over the rest. 'Send 'em up here, now, if you want 'em served.'

Signals to the white overseer who stands behind them, the coiled whip in his hand. The man grins, turning from him. Out back of the barn where the shadows are deepest, other shapes move forward into the light. Four of them, walking in line, hands down by their sides.

All of them women.

Torchlight striking on them as they gain the open space by the bed of straw. Falls soft and smooth over their unclothed, gleaming flesh. Justus looks them over, one by one, feeling his hot groin tighten almost to a pain. Feeling too their own eyes upon him.

Close up, he sees they ain't none of 'em the same, no more'n the wenches here on Sweet River. Nearest to him is kind of small, an' blacker even than Cora. Glister to her smooth ebony skin like to polished wood. Narrow-waisted an' full-hipped, the breasts taut and high. Like a boy almost, the short hair curled and tight to her head. One beyond her tall an' willow-stem slender, her skin pale almost to a tawny gold, the dark hair thick and waved, down to her waist. Eyes a deep brown, sad, quiet-looking. Catches his eye and looks down, one hand covering the soft growth of hair below her belly mound. Third one a brownskin gal, plain and homely lookin', but built heavy an' strong. Good breeder, is how they be thinkin'. Last one more to yellow-brown, the hair straight and Indian black with a bluish sheen by torchlight. Sharp cat eyes she got, greenish coloured. Slant to them like an Indian's, or one of them China folks he heard Nestor talk of one time. . . .

Black wench looks to him. Grin of her bared teeth white and wide in the dark of her face. Darker gleam of eyes on him, appraising, hungry. Watching, he sees the faint tremor that shakes her belly and breasts. Feels again the pang of unsated need. This one as hot for it as he is, he kin tell. . . .

'Yeah.' Lawrence's voice cuts through the momentary dream, harsh and loveless as the stroke of blacksnake whip. 'You look 'em over good, boy. They all waitin' for one thing from you, an' I reckon you kin give it to them. Ain't that right?'

'Yassuh, Massa Lawrence.' Eyeing the black wench as he speaks, the breath starting to come harder at his chest, like a rope drawn tight about him. Ain't had him a woman in one hell of a while. . . .

Back of his mind, some other voice talkin' to him, warnin' him.

He got four wenches here. Hot as he is, how in hell he gonna have enough for that many? He ain't gonna make this, it a way too hard. . . .

Pushes the thought from his mind a while, studying the sleek black body of the first wench. She smiling back at him, hands to her sides. Dark, smooth slit of her pussy showin' plain through the wispy hair. Seeing, he swallows, eyes shut to the unbearable pulsing of his manhood.

'She's Georgie,' Lawrence tells him. 'She belongs to Mister Devereaux here. Zenobia, now—' he indicates the quiet, sad-eyed girl with the tawny skin—'She's an octoroon, you hear? Property of Mister Stoneham. Other two are Mister Lacourbe's—this here's Paulette, other's called Eunice.'

Hears without listening, his gaze fixed on the first of the wenches. Right now, full as he is of hate, it don't count for nothin': the voices, the mean, laughing faces of the whites who drink and puff smoke and mock at him, they ain't none of 'em there. They watchin', is all. What gonna happen here, it for him and for them wenches who stand lookin' to him. Waitin'.

Ain't no wrong in it, Nestor said. Folk like Lawrence who put us to it, they wrong. Jes' stay free inside your head, like always.

Draws breath, Catching the dark, vicious glance of Lawrence from the chair beyond. The lean-faced planter bares his teeth, spitting out the remnant of his cigar. Crooks a hand on the whiskey jug as it comes round again.

'So git to it, nigger!' Lawrence says.

The others startin' up to whoopin' and yellin' as he speaks. Faces mean an' slobbery as mad dogs about him. One, the half-stripped feller who was drunk a while back, lolls over to the ground, hunches on all fours to puke up what he taken.

Black Georgie lookin' to him. The wide grin splitting her face.

'Let's go, honey,' the black wench tells him.

He don't answer. Goes to her blind, clasping her to him like he about to bust her apart. Georgie's mouth fastens on his greedily, her wet tongue probing. Seems like she been without for long enough herself. Sets her teeth in the lobe of his ear as he cups her breasts. Reaches an arm about her to lift her from the ground.

Georgie arches her back as her feet leave the floor, twines her legs at his waist as he holds her poised above him. Fingers on her hand fasten gently on his straining maleness, guiding him into her as she opens. Already wet for him.

Justus groans. The rush of pleasure so fierce he cain't hardly control it a-tall. He sinks to the ground, she still hung to him. Rears on his palms above her, thrusting powerfully into that sweet gulfing moistness, the woman of her. Georgie screaming out as she claws at his heaving shoulders. Legs gripped on him as her heels climb on his sweating back.

Clamour of voices all around, and mocking laughter; stink of spew mingled with the smell of his sweat, the whiskey and cigars—he don't heed it no more. He far from here. Him and Georgie locked one into the other as the twin climax nears for them both.

Beneath him, Georgie's dark, upturned face convulses, the eyes closing, lips drawn back from her teeth as she heaves up to meet him. The cry breaking from her, long and drawn out. Her body shaking under him, out of control. Justus feels the long shudder run the length of his back as the pleasure hits, taking him over the peak. Hollers out, driving deep as he shoots himself into her. Force of the spasms ebbing slow as the jissom drains from him. . . .

'That wench served, sure enough,' someone says.

He feels the weight of the stillness that follows. His struggling breath the only sound as he lies prone. His sweating face in the straw. Georgie gone from him someplace. Right now he cain't tell where. Stays there, wisps of wet straw clinging to him as he waits for his strength to return. Above him the murmur of voices sets up again.

'Wager still stands,' Lawrence is saying. 'Hundred a time if he gits through three of them wenches. An' twenty-five for each sucker they carryin' for him nine months hence. Up to four, it gonna have to be another fifty a head. What you say?'

'Count me in,' Lacourbe still isn't convinced. 'He done a good job there, sure, but three—no way. He's tired out already. An' four? Has to be crazy, Lawrence.'

'How 'bout you, Stoneham? Devereaux?'

'Ain't backin' out, an' you know it.' The high voice of Devereaux is still sulky. 'Man makes a wager, least he kin do is stick by it, I reckon.'

'Goes for me too,' Stoneham says.

The drunken man don't say nothin'. Just sets to groanin' a little where he lies.

'Okay, nigger!' Lawrence's voice rings out hard and clean. 'Git on up. You still got one man's job in front of you, an' I don't aim to lose on it.'

Justus rolls over. Sits up, breathing hard. How long he lain here he cain't tell, but it have to be a while. Torches look to be burnin' lower than they was before. As he moves, catches sight of the three standing wenches who wait for him. At once the heat of his groin stirs afresh, the stalk of his manhood thickening again as it swells and rears up from its bush of hair.

Someone pushes Zenobia toward him as he gains his feet. Meeting the wench's look, he reads fear in the sad brown of her eyes. She scared half outta her mind. Chances are she ain't never had a man on her before, and in front of this bunch. . . . Feels the pulse of his anger return, hard in the pit of his belly. Wasn't so bad for Georgie, maybe, but this gal scared bad. An' she bein' made to act like a hot mare or somethin' for these white sons of bitches who actin' worse than animals themselves. Bites on his lip, letting the anger fade. He got to git through tonight, an' hate won't help too much. . . .

'Don' heed 'em, gal,' Justus says. Reaches gentle for her hand, drawing her to him. 'Jes' look to me, you hear?'

Tears well in Zenobia's eyes. Wordless, the tall gold-skinned woman nods, unresisting as he takes hold of her and lays her down gentle on the bed of straw.

Lies by her, one arm about her as he strokes his free hand over the full curve of her breasts. After a while the nipple tautens up beneath his touch, and the stiffness goes from her body. Zenobia starts to breathin' sharper, quicker than before. Justus leans over to take the erect nipple in his mouth. Holding her to him as his hand slides down easy for the moist warmth of her unclothed loins. He feels her hand move to stay him and lets his own halt a while. Draws on the nipple, fluttering it with his tongue. Zenobia moans out soft, her hand slipping aside. Lifts up to let his fingers find her,

140

moving inside. Justus fondles the bud of flesh within, stroking until his fingers are full wet. Zenobia moans again, starts to move against his hand. Her own hand shifting to rest on the tall column of his root. Justus catches his breath, his blood firing up again. Moves over on his side against her, taking his mouth from her breast, still touching her clitoris as she reaches to guide him in.

Thrusts hard as he enters, feeling the momentary resistance. Like he thought, it the first time for her. Hears her sharp cry of pain as she clasps and clings. Then he through, an' it don't matter no more. Goes deep in the tight warmth of her, driving strong and steady. Hearing those other voices set up agin beyond.

'Oh, yeah! Lookit that buck nigger go!'

'Gonna make two of 'em, anyhow!'

'Could use a piece of that myself, I reckon!'

Man on the floor is pukin' agin, but he don't heed. His hand in her long hair as she moves to time her thrusts with his, the pleasure building sweet and slow as her bud goes slippery wet and her head throws back. She calling on him. Gripping hard. Close now to her time. Justus heaves, arches against her, his frenzy growing. Feels like the top of his haid about to blow off at any moment. Hears her shrill cries and in the instant he comes, gushing fierce, pouring his seed into her. She gone wet and loose against him as the wave goes over her in turn.

Thuds over in the straw, as other hands reach to haul her from him. Zenobia calling out to him as they drag her away. Another time he'd feel anger, but right now he a way too tired, he figures. Instead, he sprawls there, gasping, sucking back his breath, as a blast of thunder rattles the barn roof and the thick sweat cools on his skin.

'How 'bout that?' says Lawrence. 'She be carryin' for him, sure, 'fore the next year's out.'

'We ain't done yet,' Devereaux reminds him. Sullen sound of his words got a different cast to it now, like he startin' to git worried. 'He got another to go.'

'But one more,' Lawrence says.

'He ain't gonna do it.' Lacourbe's voice. Not so sure, though, as before.

Harsh rasp of his breath seems to fill the barn, echoing in the new-fallen quiet. He still lyin' there with his eyes halfway closed when they shove Paulette forward, the brownskin wench falling on her knees beside him. At the sound Justus glances up, unsure. From above him, Paulette smiles back. She been here before.

Lies still, unable to move seemingly, as she reaches to cup his slack flesh in the palm of her hand.

'Ain't gonna make it,' Lacourbe says again.

Paulette bends over him, takes his half-grown penis into her mouth. Kneels, lapping him with lips and tongue as her hand slides up along the shaft.

Yields to it, eyes shut, relaxed, as his flesh slowly grows hard to her urgings. When his staff throbs and butts huge against the roof of her mouth, she draws away. Moves to straddle over him, his manhood going into her slow as she settles on him.

'Git to it, nigger!' somebody yells out.

Don't answer. Lying. Feeling the ache and the pent-up need grow in him as Paulette arches and thrusts on him from above, her heavy breasts falling against his hands. Justus fondles them as the movement quickens. Touches between her thighs, feels the knob of flesh slithering at his fingers, stroking there until she cries out and tremors, her sweat falling like dew on his face and chest. When she gasps and goes loose he rolls over. Turning her on to her back. Rears to plunge into her as his time nears yet again. Paulette still shivers in her final throes as he yells out, jerking as the come spurts from him. Force of it rolling him aside at last, like a spent husk. For a while, seems like the thunder is inside his head.

'God damn!' It's Stoneham's voice. 'That sure as hell some nigger you got there, Lawrence!'

'Time to collect, I reckon.' Lawrence is jubilant. 'Makes four— five hundred in all, an' another hundred on the suckers. Six hundred. You gents prepared to go any higher?'

'Well now. . .' Devereaux is none too sure, scowls as he hands over the money, his mean-lipped mouth drawn tight. 'Okay, I'll go along. Four's *got* to be too many.'

'Yeah, you right,' Lacourbe says. 'You kinda hard to put him to it, I reckon.'

'Count me in,' Stoneham says, and other voices murmur agreement.

Only Old Man Lawrence says nothing. Sits there quiet and old in the wicker chair. Right now he looks kind of sick.

Lawrence grins, thin-lipped in triumph, and stows the thick wad of dollar bills inside his coat.

'Thanks for the contributions, gents. No offence, but I'm sure glad I brung the pistol along.'

Slaps a palm on the gun-butt that thrusts from his belt, still grinning. After a while his look goes back to Justus, who still lies inert and sweating on the straw. 'Give him a while, an' he'll go to it,' he says.

Flat against the ground, Justus hears him. Feels the surge of hate return so fierce that for a while he reckons he gonna bust apart from holdin' it inside him. Snarls a moment, his great fists clenching. God damn you, Lawrence, he thinks. I ain't no bull, nor no stallion neither. Chance ever come to me, you gonna be sorry for sure....

Same time that he feels the anger, feels his own man's strength come floodin' back, like he got back his breath somehow with Paulette, an' now he kin go on all night. Looks down to his thick, heavy maleness. Sure enough it hardenin', startin' agin to rise. So Lawrence wants a stud bull, huh? That what he goin' to git.

The big man gets up from the straw, grinning plain now as he gains his feet, and the huge manhood stands out from him for the bunch of them to see.

'Jee–sus!' Stoneham says. 'I reckon he gonna do that job after all.'

Rest of them struck to silence as he stands there, looking to the one who is left. The wench with the black Indian hair and the green slanted eyes. Eunice grins back at him, eager to begin. Crouches on all fours to offer her haunches to him. Justus kneels behind her. Lays both great hands to her smooth flanks, entering.

He gonna make it, sure enough.

'Nother fifty dollars apiece, I reckon,' Lawrence grins like a gator, lighting up another cigar. 'Brings us to four hundred clear. That's one thousand dollars I took tonight, gentlemen. Easiest money I ever made!'

Stoneham says nothing, staring wide-eyed to the bed of straw, where Eunice shrills in climax, Justus groaning as he falls across her. The two of them slump to the ground. He been around, but he ain't never seen nothin' like this before.

'Last time I bet agin you, Lawrence,' Devereaux says. Puckers to spit in the straw as he forks out another fifty from his billfold. 'That nigger ain't human, you hear?'

'Never said he was.' Lawrence keeps his grin, pocketing the money. 'Tell you somethin', though. That buck gonna sire a good child on that wench of yourn. You'll be glad you brung her over, come the time.'

'Like hell I will,' Devereaux says. Then, 'Pass that goddamn jug!'

Lawrence laughs again. Turns to the slumped white-headed man across from him. 'Looks like we done it, pa,' the dark man says. 'How's that for easy money?'

The old man looks up as he speaks. For a moment the stare of those black eyes turns Lawrence uneasy.

'Git him out of here, son,' Old Man Lawrence says. 'He done what you asked, an' more, I reckon.'

'Ain't gonna be no use after this,' Lacourbe ventures. Like Stoneham, to the huge black figure on the bed of straw. Catching the look on his face, Lawrence's grin returns.

'Coupla days rest, he'll be fine,' the lean-faced planter says. 'After that, he kin go back in the quarters for a while. When I need him agin, I'll take him. *Jacob!*'

His shout brings the drivers running. Framed in the doorway as the rain crashes down behind them, the three men look to the prone shape on the ground, the expression of their faces half wonder, half disbelief.

'Git him outa here, Jacob,' Lawrence says. Leans back, drawing on the cigar he holds. 'Take him back to the hut, and fast.'

'Sure thing, Massa Lawrence.' Jacob ducks his head and he and Andy get a hold on Justus at the armpits, dragging him to his feet, hauling him out through the door while the white planters cheer and whoop, Bob following after with the coiled blacksnake whips.

Outside, thunder booms over the bayous, momentary flares of

lightning touching the canefields and live-oaks to a white sizzle of flame. Jacob and the drivers hurry him through the mud and the deep rainwater pools, feet splashing to the ankles as the fall of rain slams on them like a repeated blow. Caught in their hold, Justus sags limp. By now, he's plumb out of strength.

'Sure as hell been busy tonight, ain't you, boy?' Jacob mutters.

Says nothing. Letting them drag him on by the quarters to the lone hut among the trees, feeling the slow venom of hatred seep its way back into him until it fills him utterly, claiming him.

One day he gonna tear out Jacob's tripes. An' that goes for Lawrence too.

Flung into the hut, he lies unstirring on the floor. Stink of wet earth and bayou scum sweeter to his nostrils than the spew and whiskey of a few moments back. Stays there, hearing the rumble of thunder shift away at last, the downpour slackening to a steady spattering fall. . . . Now it's over, little of the pleasure remains. Only the hate he got for them. The knowin' what they made him do. An' how he done like they tole him.

They made a stud bull of him, sure 'nough. But for Zenobia, maybe, was no more in it than in two critters couplin', an' that bunch of bastards lookin' on while they done it. But Zenobia? What they gonna do with her now? Like enough, she be birthin' him some chile like the rest. To grow up jes' the same, brung up like an animal on some plantation. Doin' like he tole to do. . . .

If she don't die in the birthin'. It been known.

Rears up sudden, striking at the wood of the wall. Hate in him scorching like flame.

God damn! He have to get from here!

FIRST NIGHT back in the quarters. He lies sprawled on his crib by the wall, feel of the hidden hoop-iron digging into him through the cornshucks of his bedding. Touch of it remindin' him what he gonna have to do 'fore long. Scowls on that, his eyes shut against the hot sticky night that slicks him in an outer skin of sweat. Too hot for him to sleep yet a while, he reckons. Kind of hard gittin' used to bein' back here, in a way. Not that he ain't glad to be back. Wenches is one thing. What Lawrence been settin' him to just lately, he gonna need to rest up 'fore he kin think of makin' a break for it anyhow. . . .

Recalling Lawrence, he snarls. Thick, vicious sound in the depths of his throat. His teeth shut tight. Even now cain't drive them faces from his mind. Them white bastards there in the feed barn, smokin' an' drinkin', laughin', layin' their wagers, lookin' him an' the wenches over all the while, like at some stud bull servin' a heifer. God damn them to hell! Regrettin' now he didn't have nothin' like the hoop-iron ready to hand when they brung him out, that time. Coulda been worthwhile gettin' killed, he figures, jes' to try the blade out on Lawrence's gut. . . .

Sighs, letting the vain thought pass. Waste of hate, is all.

At the snarling sound the two twined figures in the blanket pause, looking over to him.

'You okay, Justus?' Glory asks. Smile at the dark man's lips as he speaks. By now they all of them know what he been put to in the old feed barn that night.

'I reckon,' Justus says. Half-turns on the groaning crib, his eyes opening a slit. Sight of that smiling face don't improve his temper none. 'Be a whole lot better iffen some folks didn't grin at me like they doin' right now.'

Back of Glory, shrouded in the blanket, grey-skinned William laughs softly. Reaches his arms about the neck of his partner. 'Come on back here, Glory. Don' you mind him right now, you hear?'

'Jes' a minute, honey.' Glory still sounds amused, his dark eyes on the big scowling man by the wall. 'Don' know what got into you, feller. Man gits to serve the number of wenches you done, figure he oughta be jes' a little thankful. Ain't that right?'

'Leave me be, Glory.' The snarl is back in Justus' voice. He heaves up slow on his hands, balanced with his huge back to the wall, like he about to jump out cross the room any time. 'Ain't in no mood for foolin' round, you hear?'

Seems like Glory don't hear a-tall. He stay right like he is, that

146

same grin to his face as always. William still fightin' to haul him back down under the blanket.

'Guess it ain't none of my business,' Glory says at last, amusement still in his voice. 'Wenches ain't my style anyhow, Justus. You know that. . . .' Grins again, holding back the laughter. 'All the same, boy, ain't many of us niggers git your kinda chance. Least you kin do is be glad you got it. Every wench on Sweet River like to be after you now, hollerin' for you to haul the drawers offen her ass. . . .'

'God damn you, Glory!' Justus shouts.

He's down from the crib and halfway across the room, his great fists clenched to clubs of bone, ready in a moment to strike out, to crush and maim. Glory and William spring up out of the blanket as he moves, the pair of them cowering up by the far wall as his great shadow falls across them both.

'Jes' funnin', Justus,' Glory says. His dark eyes, though, are wary. 'Didn't mean nothin'!'

'Oughta bust yo' mouth,' the big man mutters.

Looks like he's about to say some more, but he don't git no further. 'Cause they all turn their heads for another sound. Like somebody scratchin' on the door.

'Jee-sus!' William says, his grey face disbelieving. 'You got 'em comin' heah already?'

Another time Justus might have twisted his neck for that, but right now he lookin' to that door like the rest. And his broad dark face is unsure.

'Who in the hell kin that be?' the big man says.

Heads for the door all the same, hefting up the bar. Nowadays Jacob an' the other drivers ain't too particular who comes an' goes at night. They all got their own wenches, an' long as nobody tries to make a break, ain't no harm done. Wooden shaft eases clear and he lays it by, opening the door on to the night.

Stands a while like before, starin'.

Met by the puzzled look, the woman smiles.

'What the trouble, boy?' Cora asks. 'Way I recall, you was glad enough to see me last time I come over. . . .'

Seeing him move to pin back the door, she shakes her head.

147

'Not in there, honey,' she tells him. 'Way I hear it, you ain't alone.'

He grins at that, sensing Glory and William behind him in the doorway, their faces like his was a moment back, wary and uncertain.

'Don' care to have these two lookin' on, huh?' Justus asks. Facing him, the tall coal-black woman shakes her head, holding to her smile.

'They ain't my kind, I reckon,' Cora says.

Turns as she speaks. Moonlight pale on her long, slender limbs as she steps away from the darkened hut. Over her shoulder Cora looks backward, her dark, sly glance reaching for him.

'You comin', boy?'

Met by that probing look, he stands, unsure still.

'Out here, Cora? You crazy or somethin'?'

'Hot 'nough night, ain't it?' Her narrow-eyed gaze mocks him. She stalks on by the corner of the hut, half-hidden in a spreading pool of shadow. 'Anyhow, I know a place. You comin', Justus, ain't you?'

Slides on into the shadow, vanishing. That last glimpse of her sleek limbs decides him. Justus draws a breath. Heads out from the door.

Halfway out, the voice of Glory halts him.

'Don't go after her, Justus. . . .' Glory's voice comes kind of shrill. Framed in the dark wedge of the doorway, his upturned face catches the light. Whites of his eyes showing wide and scared. 'It don't smell right, you hear?'

For a minute he wonders if the other nigger gone outen his haid. Then Justus sees William push into view back of his friend, and the look if his face is serious enough. Ain't no joke, he figures. Not to them, anyhow. Still, the big man smiles.

'Come on now, Glory,' Justus says. Wonderin' same time, back of his mind. 'Why she do that to me? You jes' cain't stand women, is all. . . .'

'It some kinda trap, sure 'nough,' William says.

He pauses at that. Face screwed up as he looks from one to the other, studying. Far side of him the figure of Cora halts in the

148

shadow, looking slowly back to him. 'Hey, Justus!' That same low, catlike sound, reaching for him. 'You gonna come with me, or you gonna stand all night chewin' the fat with them two? You want a man to pleasure you, all you gotta do is tell me, an' I be goin' right away. . . .'

'You hush yo' mouth, you hear me?' Justus tells her.

By now, though, he quit wonderin' in his mind. The big man grins at the two in the doorway, shaking his head.

'Don' you trouble over me, Glory,' Justus says, his glance shifting to Cora in the far dark as he speaks. 'Reckon I'm gonna be doin' a way better'n you, tonight.' Turns, following that lithe, long-legged shape into the night.

'Jes' you watch out there, boy!' Glory calls out behind him, sound of his voice already faint, dying away as he leaves the shadow of the hut.

Following Cora where she leads. Sweating already in the thick, humid night. Cora slips out ahead, swift and soundless as a ghost, halting every so often to glance back and find him, makin' sure he stays right behind. Sometimes the sight of her standin' there gits him back to wonderin' agin 'bout how much Glory knows 'bout all this. He don't think on it too long, however. Sheen of moonlight on that tall wench under the trees got his blood fired up hotter'n before. Following her in among the live-oak trees, he starts again to smile. . . .

She goin' back to the hut, Justus thinks. Recallin' how it was, he grins wider. Could be he gonna have a good night of it this time, anyhow.

He's into the trees now, dark, upright trunks shadowing him on either side. Sweat slicks him as he moves in the sultry heat, gleaming where light of the moon breaks in at the crowns of the live-oaks above his head. Justus' breath comes sharper, his step quickening, his bare feet sinking in the soft earth under the trees. Up ahead Cora halts a moment before the closed door of the hut, and moves to ease it back.

Justus grins again, starting to hurry after her, balancing hisself with the flat of a palm when the tree roots trip him. He gains the hut as she vanishes inside, ducks his maned head to push through to the darkness beyond. . . .

The blow takes him high up on the forehead, impact of it gashing the flesh. Justus grunts with the force, falling sidelong to hit the wall as pain knifes through his skull. Hits the board floor, shaking his head savagely. Aware already of the thick flow of blood into his eyes.

Cato rears up in the dark above him, a heavy-bladed cane knife in his hand. Short and squat as he is, from here he looks like he big an' wide enough to fill the hut. Sight of his dark, vicious face close in the unlit gloom. Justus gits up to his haunches, fighting the pain, and the sudden lurch of sickness in his gut.

'That jes' a li'l somethin' to start with,' Cato says. He bares his teeth like to a mad dog, his eyes glaring wild, closes in again with the thick knife lifted. 'Now, I reckon you best git to sayin' your prayers. . . .'

'No!' Cora's scream rings out shrill, back of them both where she cowers by the far wall, one hand to her mouth. 'Don' kill him, Cato honey! Let him be!'

'You button up yo' mouth, bitch!' Cato's voice is venomous. Cora goes quiet, shrinking back by the wall.

He gonna have to figure this out for hisself, Justus thinks. The big man brushes the sticky flow of blood from his eyes, smearing the back of his hand as he crouches, watching the squat, powerful figure of Cato start in again with the knife poised. Pain jabbing hard in the back of his skull, he tries to gauge his distance from the shorter man in the dark, enclosed room.

'I got no quarrel with you, Cato,' Justus says.

'The hell you ain't!' Harsh sound of the other's voice hits back at him like a blow. Cato's black face contorted to a snarling mask as the knife lifts up again. 'Done bedded my woman, you black sonofabitch! Ain't no way you gonna git from here alive!'

'So what you aim to do?' he asks.

All the while his eyes rake the dark room, searching. For anything—a way out, some kinda weapon. Ain't nothin' there to find. Only Cora, huddled over in the corner yonder, comin' out with a weepin' noise, her hands to her face.

Above him, that other shape gathers itself behind the glittering blade.

'Gonna take you all to pieces, lover man. . . .' Cato grits out the words, leaning close above Justus, who crouches, penned by the wall, the blood dripping slow from his face to form darker stains on the boards beneath. The squat nigger grins, thinner than the edge of the knife he holds. 'Bit by bit, you hear me? An' hold on to yo' pecker, 'cause that gonna be last, I reckon. . . .'

Thick, broad-set body starts to raise up as he speaks, all that pent-up hate inside him, building ready to explode. From where he crouches, the bigger man sucks in his breath, feeling his own gut tighten. Two ways for him to go: if he hit in close, that knife gonna beat him. Have to git from it. Either way, it gonna be close enough.

Makes his move in the moment that squat body tenses, whipping up and back. Justus flings over backward for the wall, wide shoulders hitting the solid wood as pain rings again in the hollow of his skull. Same instant the knife carves a white slice in the darkness, hissing to cleave air where his head was a moment back. Justus hears the tip of the blade snarl splintering into wood above his head. His feet slam up for the groin as Cato lunges. With the thud of impact, the shorter man howls, lifted halfway off the ground, crashes into the wall, the thick blade clattering from his hand. Justus squirms out from under. Ploughs back on to Cato as he scrambles on all fours, groping for the glint of steel. Weight of the bigger man drives Cato back into the wall, the breath whooshing from him as he strikes the wood a second time. Justus kicks out to send the knife slithering out of reach. He gets a hold on the other man's hair, forces the snarling face downward from sight.

From below him a hand slashes backward, raking with spread-fingers for his crotch. Justus clenches on a yelp of pain as nails dig through his breeches to strip skin from his inner thigh. Grabs the arm with his free hand, hauling it hard up Cato's back. Under him the shorter man sings out high as a wench, his body buckling forward against the wall. Straddling above him, Justus pushes his face into the dusty boards.

'Lie quiet, Cato,' Justus says. 'Or by God, I'm gonna tear yo' arm off clean. . . .'

Beneath him the other man shudders and goes limp, his breath

151

muffled, whimpering against the ground. Justus crouches over him a while, the breath heaving fierce and raw in his throat and chest. Gets up slow, lifting the fallen knife. A few last drops of blood fall as he moves, spattering the dark form of Cato under him. Seems like the cut already crustin' over, kind of sticky an' itchy on the gashed skin of his brow. 'That be enough, I reckon,' Justus says.

He stands, the knife held out in front of him, its blade level on Cato's waist as the squat man rises in turn, gritting his teeth as he flexes the twisted muscles of his arm. Across the room his dark narrowed eyes reach toward Justus, glinting keen and merciless as the knife itself.

'Like to bust my arm, you bastard!' Cato says.

'You try me agin, I do that,' the taller man tells him.

Meets those eyes as he speaks, reading the hate at their depths. One heap of poison in Cato, Justus thinks. He recalls the hog-killing time. The look on the short man's face as he slit the critters' throats. Swallows on a foul taste. He won this time, but Cato ain't through with what he started. An' they both of them know it.

'Gonna take this here knife out with me, Cato,' Justus says. It still kind of hard for him to talk, what with him bein' out of breath an' all, but he gits through. His own eyes fierce on the squat, unarmed man across from him. 'You come followin', an' maybe I take it to you. You hear me good?'

'Sure I hear you,' Cato spits in defiance. 'Ain't allus gonna go yo' way, neither. Was my wench you had, back there. . . .'

For a minute his look goes to Cora, who stands in the doorway, her dark, fearful eyes on them both.

'Didn't go lookin' for her,' Justus says at last. 'She come to me. An' tell you somethin' else. You beat up on Cora, I sure as hell come back for you agin.'

Heads past them for the door, through with talkin'. Cora reaches to stay him as he passes. This time, her eyes plead with him.

'Was Cato forced me to it, Justus,' Cora says. She licks at her lips, slim fingers touching on the flesh of his arm. 'Should you need me, honey, I come back with you.'

He spares her but one look. Long and hard. Sighs in weariness.

'Not this time, Cora,' Justus says.

Steps into the warm night. Walking back slow through the live-oaks to the quarters. Pain dulling now inside his head, blood itching as it dries. Halfway to the hut he stops. Pitches the cane-knife with all his strength into the bushes beyond. Scowls as he hears it fall.

Nestor right, like always. There too much hate here on Sweet River. Lawrence the worst, sure, but he ain't the only one. There Jacob too—what he seen in the canefield, an' the way he heard tell his mama died. An' now Cato, wantin' him daid. No doubt of it, he cain't stay here. He got to win free. An' it have to be soon.

The huge black man shrugs at last, shakes his bloody head. He starts back to the hut where Glory and William still stand waiting, his massive figure catching the white-fingered light of the moon.

THE NIGHT he chooses at last, he tells no one. Waits till long past midnight, then slips from the creaking crib and to the floor, going quick and silent as a snake for that shadowed space by the wall. The honed knife in the belt of his breeches ready and edged for use. Glory and William away in the dark beyond him, sleeping heavy under the blanket. He reckons he hears one of them stir, turning over slow, as he levers the uppermost log. His own glance darts back, finds nothing. Justus grins, easing the wood clear of the gap. Glory and William ain't so bad at that. Might even come to miss them in time.

The logs themselves are good and loose. The rotted one comes away clean without a sound. Only the last, the one beneath, gives out a faint splintering that jars huge in the still night. Justus waits out the echoes, sweating. No answering sound. He shoves the sawn logs aside, going flat on to his belly. Slowly, carefully, he slides out through the gap in the wall.

Once up on his feet he don't stay to look, running hard as he can for the nigger graveyard back of the quarters. There among the grave markers and live-oak trees he leans, panting for breath, aware already of the sweat turning cool on his skin in the moist night air. About him, the graveyard seems to stretch on forever. Uneven sprawl of mounds and memorials to those slaves who never got to see beyond Sweet River. Some of the graves are unmarked altogether. Most have been set up with crosses made from lashed sticks. A few, older than the rest, are carved into strange shapes—bird beaks and spreading bull horns. Somehow, they seem out of place in this strip of Louisiana earth. From what Nestor told him, he senses that these are markers for the Africans, the ones who made it alive across the big water, only to perish in this strange country far from home. For a moment he stands, thinking about that, hearing the noise of his own breathing in the stillness.

'Don' move from there, nigger,' the voice says behind him.

He swings round at the call, crouched, one hand dipping for the haft of the knife. In the darkness his eyes show wide, terrified. For a while he figgers he got a ghost in this place with him. Then he sees them, standing motionless in the massive live-oak shade, and breathes again.

'Think you git loose 'thout us knowin', huh?' Nestor eases forward, cat-footing it from the shadow of the tree. His weathered features break into a wry smile, the stumps of his teeth showing as he grins. 'Justus, you dumber'n you look, you hear?'

He shakes his head, still not fully understanding. Behind Nestor, his eyes make out the taller, slim shape of Mede, carrying something in a cloth that hangs down from his hand.

'How come y'all heard 'bout this?' he asks. 'Didn't say nothin'....'

'Ain't one of us didn't know, boy.' Nestor wags his salt-grey head, still grinning. 'You been edgier'n a hot wench, ever since sunup. Had to be tonight, we all knows it. Only Jacob, he ain't guessed it, an' he don't know nothin' a-tall.'

Beside him, Mede steps forward. For an instant he looks Justus in the eye. Plenty to read in that look of Mede's. Admiration is there, and envy maybe, And more than a little sadness.

'Gonna be hungered, where you haided,' Mede says. He thrusts the covered bundle into the big man's hand, looking away. 'Got you some eats from the other hands — they's sowbelly, coupla hunks cornbread. Y'all take it, y'hear....'

154

He takes it, speechless. All at once it's kind of hard for him to say a thing. When he looks to Nestor his eyes are filled up.

'Glory an' William, too?'

'Them too,' the old man says.

'Tell them thanks, huh?' Justus says. 'You too, Mede.'

'You our kind, Justus.' Mede sounds kind of choked himself, looking out across the graveyard. 'Wasn't nothin' else we coulda done. . . .'

He moves away, edging back into the live-oak shadow. Nestor fronts the big man now, his old, faded eyes scanning the face before him. The thin hands lift, resting a moment on the huge shoulders of the younger man.

'Gonna wish you luck, boy,' Nestor tells him. ''Cause you sho' as hell gonna need it. Jes' remember, this the easiest part. The stayin' loose, that a way harder'n gittin' out. . . .'

A night-owl calls in one of the live-oaks beyond them, and the young man shivers.

Nestor looks him hard in the eye. Nods at last, satisfied.

'Now run like hell, nigger,' the old man says, 'Iffen you wanta stay free.'

He steps back, lowering his hands, looking on as Justus turns and starts away downhill through the sprawl of graves. Halfway down the slope, the big man halts, looking back.

'Don' be dumb, chile.' Nestor smiles, blinking his tears away as he speaks. 'I ain't no age to come runnin' with you no more. Git goin', you hear?'

Justus swings back around, brushing with one hand at his face. He makes downhill at a run, the cloth bundle jolting against him with every step. The image of the frail, salt-haired old man, standing silent in the mass of graves, goes with him in his mind. The last sight he has of Sweet River.

Close to an hour later the hounds are on his track, and the hunt begins that takes him into the wilderness.

THAT MORNING he gets up early, before daybreak.

Light still grey and uncertain as he pushes out from the shelter, the bow slung at his back. Last stars faint and cold in the dimming darkness overhead. Down on the lower slopes, the woods are screened in a heavy mist. He stands, breathing the cool, moist air, nostrils wide to the scents about him. Pretty soon, he knows, it gonna be hot enough.

He takes the long-barrelled pistol with him, thrusting it in his belt with the hoop-iron knife, the arrows tied in a bundle by a braid of grass that he holds in his right hand, hanging back across the shoulder. The hickory spearshaft he leaves behind. Need both hands for the bow, he reckons. Spear along too, that goin' to clutter him.

Going downhill through the trees, light-footed, the dew stinging his bare soles. Tall, lithe shape, flitting in and out by the live-oaks and the cottonwoods, black of his body gleaming smooth among the standing trees. Up above his head the birds are already singing. Sounds like a dove in the nearest of the branches, its call answered from further up the slope behind him. Halfway down he halts, pulling the bow over his head and into the grip of his left hand. Goes on in silence, ducking the lower boughs with their grey trailing streamers of Spanish moss. In front the live-oaks give way to more scattered clumps of cypress and palmetto, and the line of the Atchafalaya shows through the gaps in the trees. The snaking stretch of water runs outward from sight, shining in the early morning halflight and still, steaming as the mist comes up off the bayous.

Down there he sees the drinking hole he had in mind, sheltered space where tall cypresses surround a quiet inlet. The deer are drinking, heads bent to the water. Through a splay of palmetto stems, he sees the sheen of their red-brown coats, the telltale white flicker of rumps as they shift uneasily, one of them darting up its head to sniff the air, alert to danger. He nods, frowning. Weaves away sidelong to work upwind of them through the thick underbrush, fitting the first arrow to string as he goes, the bundle rope gripped in his teeth. Watching where he puts his feet in the shadows, wary still of dozing snakes.

Takes him a while, and more than once the deer glance up from drinking. But they're still by the hole when he comes in close to find his place, back of a nearby thicket that gives on to the waterside. Slowly he brings the notched arrow back against the string. He's found himself a target: half-growed buck, nearest to him, its head sunk for a moment to the water. Leaves him all of the flank to aim for, come the time.

Down by the hole comes the churring scrape of grasshoppers in the underbrush, and in the trees the chorus of birds grows stronger. Over beyond him, at the far side of the river, he makes out a massive shaggy outline that bends to scoop with a paw in the water, and sucks in his breath. That a bear of some kind, he reckons. Sure don't aim to tangle with nothin' that big. All the while thrusting on the bow, the braided rope coming back past his chest.

A spider runs over his planted foot, its furred legs tickling him as it moves. He lets it on by, swallowing as the feeling passes. It want to bite him, it sure as hell would have done.

Across from him the grouped deer shiver, sensing trouble. The buck standing closest flings up his head, dark eyes darting as his muzzle spatters water. Uhuh. The feathered palmetto stem is up by his ear as he lets fly, the string hissing heavy against his cheek.

His best. The one with the flint head.

The deer leaps, stricken, stumbling with his forefeet in the water, the arrow shaking, sunk half its length in the creature's flank. Frantic, he reaches for a second as the buck lurches up from the hole. White rumps bob away into the thickets as it staggers, hooves slipping in the mud of the back. Sweating now, he notches the second palmetto, draws the string back. Got to take him down this time, for sure. With the threshing sound of the shot the deer snorts, going down on its knees. This time he aimed lower, front of the hind leg, and the force of the arrow took it clean down to the feathers. For a long instant the buck sways, as if unsure whether or not to fall. Then it leans, crashing over on its side, one flank shuddering as the life ebbs out of it. Up in the treetops the birds break loose, wheeling and clamouring.

Steps out from the brush, dragging the bow back over his head. Ain't gonna need it no more, that for sure. The other deer are long gone, the drinking hole empty but for the circling birds. Silent, he walks by the upturned head, its eyes dark and accusing. Blood running from the mouth and nostrils, puddling in the soft ground by the head. Crouching down by the exposed flank, he pulls his knife, digging for his arrows. For the flint-headed shaft, sent cleanly between the ribs, his luck holds good. He digs it out whole, cutting it away from the flesh. The other is sunk too deep, and when he lays hold it wiggles like it busted. He shrugs, letting it go. A bone-headed one. He kin make another. Lucky the deer fell away from him and didn't roll on both the arrows.

Squatting on his heels, he's aware of the thickening sweat that streaks his face and body, coating the palms of his hands. Good thing he didn't pick him a critter too heavy to drag home, he thinks. And at that, ain't gonna be no easy job.

Day coming up over the bayou country. Sun falls hot as syrup through the boughs of the cypress trees, burning in his lap. Feels his groin stir at the unexpected warmth, and scowls. Ain't got no time fer that kinda fool stuff, not now. He lays a hold on the deer's head, pulling it back to show the white of the throat, and with his knife makes the long cut down the belly. He works fast, gutting and flaying the carcass where it lies. Blood sticky and warm on his hands as he moves, spatting at times on his breeches and the black gleaming flesh. About him the birds hover closer, and he yells, thrashing his arms to drive them off. When he's through he flings the guts into the water, wraps the bloody hide around him. The deer carcass he takes up on to his shoulders, heedless of the weight and the running blood. Starts back through the thickets, going uphill the way he come.

Pushing up that slope under the heavy burden on his shoulders, shaking his head at the gathering flies, he senses a sudden move in the thicket out on his left. Halts a moment, unsure, breathing hard under the load he's toting. Same instant the sudden squall of birds in the far trees tells him he ain't wrong. Heavy snorting noise and the thicket shakes, bursting open. Dark, low barrel-shape breaking out like a bullet, coming at him head-on.

Wild hog!

One raking look sees all: the heavy-snouted head sunk low, mouth open to bare the long yellow tusks. Mean little eyes aglint in the flesh, scenting his blood. Behind the head the dark boulderlike body looks a mile wide. Shoulders up, bristles standing stiff along the razor back. Snorting hard as it comes, its cleft hooves churning up clods of earth. Knows he ain't got time to turn aside.

Swinging round as it hurtles for him, knowing he a ways too late to get his bow loose. Shoulda brung the spear along after all. Mind skittering back to the other hogs he's seen, panicking. He knowed a hog take a man's leg clean off with them tusks once, back on Sweet River. And that warn't even wild. Too late now—the beast is nearly on him.

He pulls the gun, aiming hurriedly on the space beyond the sunk head. Thumbing the hammer. Hands awash with sweat, fighting the shakes, he presses the trigger.

The blast of the gun is deafening in the enclosed space. He reels back, echoes racketing off the trees around as the butt hammers his palm, all but blinded by the sweat in his eyes. In front of him the hog shudders all along its body, jolting to a halt as the shot smashes it back on its haunches. It snorts, the sound huge as the echoes die, then smashes down with one shoulder brushing the ground, the nethermost of its tusks slicing earth like a blade. He aims again, gripping the gun in both hands as the massive head swings for him, the glitter of those mean eyes terrifying at close quarters, the thick snout spattering blood. A second ear-busting boom as the hammer falls, rocking him on his heels. Through a thickening haze of smoke he sees the force of the slug slam the hog over against the ground. For a moment the tusked head threshes at the earth, scattering clumps of turf beyond him. Then abruptly the body stretches out and is still.

Around him the quiet is almost unbearable—as loud in its way as the din of the shots a moment before. He stands, coughing in the smoke, the stink of cordite foul in his nostrils. For a minute he feels like he's gonna throw up. The smell of blood lies on him, all

159

along his shoulders where the deer carcass slid on to the ground. His legs suddenly give out on him, and he sags on his haunches against the nearest cottonwood bole. Seems like he can't stop himself from shaking, the pistol spilling out of his hands.

He sits a while, helpless, eyeing the dead hog and the fearsome blood-welling holes in the carcass, torn by the heavy slugs. First one smashing the chest and the near shoulder, ripping out some-place low in the back. The second blasting through the ribs and out the far side. Puddles of blood lie spreading on the ground. Faced by the sight of the terrible wounds, he shivers. Good thing that white-trash patroller Burns didn't get to use the gun on him.

In time the earth settles, and his stomach with it. He leans to pick up the long pistol and stow it in his belt as the last of the smoke clears about him. Overhead the sun comes blistering through the trees, the birds setting up their song. Down by the waterside fresh shapes are gathering, herons and egrets, stalking fish in the quiet pools. He sees their pale outlines distantly, moving in and out between the boles of the trees. Justus grunts, getting up. He prods the hog's corpse over with a thrust of the foot. Kneels to slit the softer skin at the neck. The flies already busy round him as the knife shears into the flesh.

Takes him most of the day to get both kills butchered and carry them, piece by piece, uphill to his sod-roofed shelter. Most of the cuts he hangs up, unwilling as yet to gorge himself on the meat. Afterwards he's fouled over with blood, has to go back and wash himself clean again at the water's edge. Smell of sweat is one thing, but the sweeter stink of blood on his body gits to turn him sick.

Coming back up the slope, he halts for a moment by the fly-blown corpse of the hog. Black clusters of them busy at the wounds, settling to hide those staring eyes. He looks on for so long, his face twisting in distaste. Ain't nothin' pretty 'bout the way you end up here, that for sure. Turning, he trudges upwards to his camp. Soon, he knows, there will be little enough of the hog left behind. Critters got a way of cleanin' up out here in the wilderness. Bear, or wolf. Cougar even. Or smaller yet—birds and ants maybe. One way or another, that hog soon gonna be gone.

With nightfall comes the ache of loneliness. Dark falling on a world gone quiet as the graveyard that hid him when he first got loose. He sits, the deerhide round him to ward off the sudden chill in the air, watching the green wood as it spits and crackles to the flame. It's getting to him, this being alone. With each day it gets harder to bear. Times, he feels like screaming out loud against the hush that falls over the wilderness at this hour. He's the one man alive for miles around. He scowls, fitting the hoop-iron back on the spearshaft, fingers biting into the wood until his flesh cries out in pain, teeth clenching on his lower lip.

Pretty soon, he reckons, he gonna be goin' outa his haid.

Dreaming, he sees Sheba come to him again, smiling as she lays her naked body by him, their joined flesh throbbing as they touch and fondle and kiss together. Drowning in memories of other times, he groans and writhes on his bed of skins, his need tormenting him, demanding release. In his hand the rigid thrust of his member, its pulse thunderous against the flesh. . . .

He wakes suddenly, moaning as the jissom spurts from him. Lies trembling at last, his thighs awash with his own hot, sticky seed. After a while the feeling passes and disgust and emptiness take over. For a while the sense of loss is numbing, hard to bear.

She ain't here, Justus, nor ever will be. You ain' never gonna see the wench no more! He gets up before dawn breaks, stooping out through the entrance of the shelter. Going down to wash at the waterside before the first light.

'LAFAYETTE HERALD', MAY 27th 1865
AN END TO HOSTILITIES
Generals Agree To Terms

TERMS OF SURRENDER WERE AGREED YESTERDAY FOR ALL CONFEDERATE UNITS STILL IN ARMS WEST OF THE MISSISSIPPI RIVER. THE TREATY WAS SECURED BY THE SIGNATURE OF GENERAL KIRBY-SMITH, COMMANDER-IN-CHIEF OF THE TRANS-MISSISSIPPI FORCES OF THE CONFEDERACY, WHOSE MEN LAID DOWN THEIR ARMS THE SAME DAY. THE SURRENDER WAS ACCEPTED BY GENERAL JAMES H. WILSON, COMMANDER OF THE UNION FORCES IN THE REGION.

LOOKS LIKE IT'S OVER AT LAST, THIS WAR THAT HAS COST THE SOUTH SO DEAR IN THE LIVES OF HER SONS. OUR BOYS HAVE FOUGHT LONG AND HARD FOR THOSE NOTIONS WE ALL OF US HOLD SACRED, EVEN NOW. THE RIGHT OF A MAN TO MAKE HIS OWN DECISIONS, FREE FROM INTERFERENCE FROM A DISTANT CAPITAL. HIS RIGHT TO DISPOSE OF HIS OWN PROPERTY AS HE THINKS FIT. SOVEREIGN INDEPENDENCE OF EACH STATE OF THE UNION. AND THE PURITY OF SOUTHERN WOMANHOOD.

THEY FOUGHT WELL FOR US, AND RIGHT NOW IT LOOKS LIKE THEY LOST. BUT THE MESSAGE OF THIS PAPER TO ALL OUR READERS IS NOT TO GIVE WAY TO DESPAIR.

ONE THING IS SURE, FOLKS. THE SOUTH WILL RISE AGAIN.

BODY FOUND

SEARCH PARTIES IN THE WILDERNESS SOUTH-WEST FROM PALMETTO RECOVERED THE BODY OF MR ISSAAC BURNS YESTERDAY. MR BURNS, WHO WAS FIRST REPORTED MISSING SEVEN WEEKS BACK WHEN HIS HORSE STRAYED HOME RIDERLESS, WAS FOUND IN A THICKET CLOSE TO THE ATCHAFALAYA RIVER BY SEARCHERS LED BY MR JOHN LAWRENCE, JR OF SWEET RIVER PLANTATION. OTHER MEMBERS OF THE SEARCH PARTY, WHICH MADE USE OF TRACKING DOGS, WERE MESSRS JARED WHITNEY, ELI HOOKER, SHELBY SIMS, CLAYTON GREEN AND JONAS MUNSON. THE BODY, WHICH WAS IN AN ADVANCED STATE OF DECAY, WAS IDENTIFIED AS MR BURNS BY THE BOOTS HE WAS WEARING, THE GOLD WEDDING-RING AT HIS FINGER, AND SUCH OF HIS CLOTHES AS HAD SURVIVED THE MOISTURE AND THE HEAT. AS FAR AS CAN BE ASCERTAINED, MR BURNS DIED OF SNAKEBITE, BUT THERE WERE TRACES FOUND NEARBY OF OTHER FOOTMARKS OF AN UNSHOD MAN. THIS, TOGETHER WITH THE FACT THAT MR BURNS WAS FOUND TO HAVE BEEN ROBBED OF HIS PISTOL—A .44 COLT DRAGOON— LEAVES FURTHER QUESTIONS TO BE ANSWERED. SHERIFF ETHAN T. WHITESIDE, WHEN QUESTIONED BY OUR REPORTER, CLAIMS THAT ALL EVIDENCE SUGGESTS AN ENCOUNTER BETWEEN MR BURNS AND THE RUNAWAY BLACK JUSTUS, FORMERLY PROPERTY OF MR LAWRENCE, WHOSE FLIGHT HAD BROUGHT MR BURNS INTO THE WILDERNESS WITH THE AIM OF RETURN-ING THE AFORESAID BLACK TO SWEET RIVER. THE FACT THAT A DANGEROUS NIGGER IS NOW LOOSE IN THE WILDER-NESS ARMED WITH A PISTOL GIVES US ALL CAUSE FOR CON-CERN. IT IS TO BE HOPED THAT THE AUTHORITIES WILL MAKE AN EARLY ARREST. MEANTIME, IT REMAINS FOR THIS PAPER TO EXTEND ITS SYMPATHY TO THE FAMILY AND FRIENDS OF THE LATE MR BURNS, AND TO HOPE THAT HIS UNTIMELY DEATH WILL SOON BE AVENGED.

DRONE OF the hovering fly brings her awake. Sound itching her in the confined space until her eyes come open. Sheba sighs, rolls over on the bed, its sheets damp from the moisture of her body. Inside the room it's sticky and hot, hard to settle for sleep. She lies unclothed, her dress and drawers flung aside to the floor in a crumpled heap, sweat pearling her yellow-brown body. Out beyond, the window mirrors the sunset in a blaze of colours: reds and purples, greens and golds.

Swats at the fly, missing as it drones and hovers in once again. Sheba breathes out slow, sinks back, her dark head lolling on the pillow. Heat got her restless so she cain't settle noway. Like she lyin' here waitin' for somethin' to happen, she don't know what. This evenin', she left pretty much to herself. Old Man Lawrence gone over to Palmetto to the auction there, an' ain't like to be home 'fore dark. And John—he was due to go out an' see Sheriff Whiteside 'bout that reward they got out for Justus. Either way she here alone with the heat an' buzz of flies. That, an' the restlessness.

John. Turns the name over in her head a while, smiling. Ain' often she git to call him that. Most times, it still Massa Lawrence. Even when they here in the bed together. Once in a while, though, he ask her to call him by his name. Come to think, it kind of a nice name. She could maybe git to like it in a while.

Different, up here, from the way it been back in the quarters. At the big house they all of them eat better'n the field hands. Sleep in soft beds, nights. Dresses he give her to wear, they pretty too. Now she his woman, she have to look high an' fine over the other wenches on Sweet River. 'Course, it ain't all good. Hagar don' take to her none, nor that little bitch Beth that she seen hangin' round Ole Massa sometimes with that dumb smile on her face. An' John himself kin be pretty mean when the mood gits into him. But he ain't always that way, not with her. . . .

Smiles again, sly, her eyes half-closed, letting her hand settle

164

over the soft mound of hair between her thighs. Somethin' else, makin' out with a white man. Like nothin' she done before. Some of the things they done in this bed still fire her up, jes' rememberin'. Truth to tell, she guesses he ain't no better'n Justus was, but the difference excites her most times. Strange taste of him—an' the sweeter smell. Not so rank an' funky as the blacks on the quarters. That, an' the way they look when they joined into one. White into golden brown. . . .

Sheba licks at her lips, her eyes fully closed. Lower down, her hand steals over the bush of hair for the moist sheath of flesh, fingers sliding over the groove until the foretaste of pleasure starts to stir in her loins. She parts the wet petals, slips her fingers into that warm moistness, stroking gently until the bud slithers up against her hand.

Whiles, she thinks of Justus. How it was between the two of them when she in the quarters. Nowadays, though, she don't think too long. He another part of the life she knowed, an' he gone from it. He a runaway now, an' she the Massa's woman. Ain't for her to think on him no more. 'Sides, he was carryin' on fine enough with them other wenches, from what she heard—Cora an' Lucy, for two. Then the time they brung him to the barn to serve them bitches from the other plantations. . . . Yeah, Justus been doin' all right, seems like. She sure as hell gonna do the same.

It pretty good, bein' the Massa's wench. This the kinda life she should always have. Sure don't aim to change it for no runaway nigger.

Whole of her insides turnin' slippy now. Juices runnin' out an' down over her workin' hand. Droplets gatherin' in the hair and on her thighs. Lifts her hips, the rhythm taking her as her fingers move faster. Colours blazing on her shut eyelids. Feel of the pleasure sweet and sticky, throbbing back at her own touch. Head back, she thrusts in a frenzy, starting to moan. . . .

Crash of the door hits her like the end of the world. Sheba shakes her head, eyes half-opening at the sound. From lower down, the building pleasure beckons her. Drawing her fingers deeper, she works on, unable to stay herself now. Back in the next room a chair crashes over to the ground, and she hears a smothered curse. Ain't John's voice, she knows. Recognition comes to her as the wave breaks at last, lifting her on over the edge of the world. Sheba rears up at the joyous torment of her hand. Shrills out, coming in a lather of moist juices that spill over her fingers and thighs.

She's still lyin' there loose as the bedroom door thuds back on its hinges. Ole Man Lawrence standin' there. Hung to the door like he daren't let go. Studyin' at her from half-shut eyes. Sheba lies there. Gasping. Spent. Hand to her loins as her own eyes meet him.

'Beth?' His voice comes slurred, uncertain. 'That you, Beth?'

Reek of the whiskey fumes fans across the room, reaching her where she lies. Sheba's face puckers a little at the stink, but she don't move. By now, she guesses, she oughta be scared. But she ain't. Nothin' to fear from this worn-out old goat. Anyhow, she done had her pleasure a minute back, an' ain't nothin' he kin do 'bout that. Still gazing at the figure by the door, Sheba smiles.

'This Sheba, Massa,' she says. 'Reckon you found the wrong door, ain't that so?'

'Sheba?' For a while the yellowing face registers disbelief. He been lookin' for Beth, all right. Sheba got a good idea what for, too. Old Lawrence eases from the door unsteadily. Sways a moment, licking his lips as he eyes the naked body on the bed.

'Sure, it's Sheba. Cain't see too good in here, honey....'

Staggers, all but falling. Breath coming from him with a thunderous belch. 'Jes' hold on there, child. I be right with you....'

Sheba lies, watching as he goes down on his hands and knees, crawling with painful slowness towards the bed. Smiles again, sly as a cat, still watching as the white head rears up slow over the edge of the bed. And with it, the bleared, wicked glitter of those black sunken eyes.

'Sure look mighty pretty from here, Sheba,' Old Lawrence says.

Reaches over as he speaks. A twisted, leathery hand moving to touch the warm, smooth flesh of her inner thigh. At the touch Sheba draws away. Hand covering herself as she looks down on him, an expression of mock horror on her face.

'Mercy, Massa Lawrence!' She cain't quite keep the laughter from her voice. 'What you tryin' to do to me?'

Beth use to say that, too, the old man thinks. He smiles lopsidedly, raising himself up by his hands at the edge of the bed, feeling the numbing pull of pain that hauls across his chest.

'You a fine-lookin' gal, Sheba,' Old Lawrence tells her. Leers, the movement twisting the side of his face to leathery crevasses. Startin' to haul hisself up towards her. 'Figger you an' me oughta git to know each other better. . . .'

Dirty ole sonofabitch, all the same Sheba smiles.

'Don' know 'bout that.' Tries to sound more scared than she feels. 'I ain't yo' wench, Massa. Young Massa John, he done bed me. I don't reckon it right, somehow.'

'Don't you trouble none over that,' the oldster tells her. 'It's gonna be all right, you hear?'

Reaches again for her, overbalancing as she rolls aside. Old Lawrence sprawls across the bed facedown, noise of his unsteady breathing rasping harsh in his throat. For a moment, hearing his struggle to breathe, Sheba wonders if he gonna die on her. . . .

'Don' reckon that a good idea, Massa Lawrence,' she tells him. 'Ain't much you could do for me, fixed as you is right now.'

The white head lifts with an effort. Black, uneven stare of those eyes, fixed full upon her. Sheba meets the look, feeling the onset of something else, different from before. Kind of a mingled excitement and revulsion. He drunk as a fish, an' he sure ain't nothin' to look at—yellow, pouched face, lined like a tree, an' them twisted hands with the swelled knuckles. . . . Thought of him touchin' her anyplace enough to send the shivers down along her back. But all the same. . . .

He a white man. A Massa. It somethin' different, sure 'nough.

'God damn,' Old Lawrence mutters. Runs his tongue around his lips at sight of her, fighting the queasy lurching of his belly. She sure is one hell of a wench. 'Jes' let me git on up to you, child,' the old man tells her. 'I aim to show you what this old feller kin do.'

Sheba chuckles in her throat, soft and low as a sated cat. She lies, watching him struggle and heave his body over the bed until

167

he lies beside her. Waits for the first leathery touch of his fingers at her breasts, and reaches to put his hand from her. 'Let's see how you feelin' first, Massa Lawrence,' she tells him.

She lies quiet, her hand searching for the buttons of his pants. Deft fingers unfasten them one by one. Sheba reaches inside and lifts him out. For a moment her face grimaces at the feel of his slack, shrunken flesh.

He lies there, too. Grunting and gasping as her hand works on him, fondling, sliding, trying to rouse him up. Not a chance. Lawrence's wrinkled member lies unresponsive in her grasp. The effort and the drink too much for him. Abruptly the naked girl turns away, letting go her hold on him.

'Nothin' much here, seems like,' Sheba says. 'Better see what I kin do.'

She goes down on him, sucking the slack organ into her mouth, teasing at it with lips and tongue. Taste of him is sour and sweaty—old man's smell, too, hinting of death and decay. He grunts and heaves about some as she works at him, but his pecker don't grow no bigger. After a while Sheba moves away, taking her mouth from him.

'Don' reckon you good for much a-tall,' Sheba says, turning from him, hunching over on the bed. 'Me, I figure you better be goin', 'fore Massa John come back. He ain't gonna like it. . . .'

'Aw, c'mon now, honey,' his voice hoarse, thick and slurred even as he pleads with her. 'He ain't gonna be back, not yet awhile. We got time. . . .'

'Time for what? You cain't do nothin' for me!'

Old Lawrence slides off the bed, buttoning up his pants with clumsy fingers. The white-haired oldster stands a moment, swaying, drunken tears in his eyes.

'Don't be that way, Sheba child. . . .' Bites on a foul taste as the vomit swims up in his throat. Reels, off balance, with one hand on the bed, stink of his whiskey-loaded breath fanning in her face 'you so sweet an' purty an' all . . . man cain't jes' up an' leave.'

'So what you aim to do, Massa Lawrence?' Sheba makes no effort to hide the mockery in her voice.

Poised unsteadily over her, Lawrence swallows. Licks at his

lips. 'Jes' a taste of that sweet little pussy of yours—that's all I'm askin'....'

Warning slash of pain sears through his chest the moment he speaks. Lawrence shudders, gasps for breath. Somewhere back of his mind a dark thought grows, shadowing: *this got to be wrong. She his own child, though it was by a nigger wench, an' he don't care to own it.* Flesh is flesh, an' cain't be denied. Was bad enough his own son takin' his sister to bed unknowin'. But with him this a way worse. He knows everythin', an' he her own father....

All the same he holds there, wheezing to keep the breath within him, begging her with his eyes.

Lookin' on him, Sheba don't feel nothin' much. Disgust, maybe. An' kind of a slow, curlin', wicked pleasure that comes coilin' through her body like a snake.

Why not? At least she might git herself some comfort from it. 'If that what you lookin' for, Massa Lawrence,' the yellow wench says.

Easing for the edge of the bed, he slides down to his knees before her. She stands over him, spreading her sleek thighs, the scented woman of her close against his face.

'This how you an' Beth git to it, huh?' she asks.

Sees his startled look as he glances up, and holds back on her laughter.

'Guess so, honey.' The old man's voice rushes, pathetic in its eagerness. 'Don't talk about Beth now, child, jes' let me to you now....'

Dirty ole bastard, Sheba thinks.

She holds above him, straddle-legged, watching as his white-haired head sinks forward for the place between her thighs. At the first leathery touch of his skin she grimaces, shutting her eyes. But last time has left her hot, an' now any woman's son will do. After a while the pleasure-snake slithers through her loins and she feels herself go wet.

Lets the slow, building rhythm take her, rising. Sheba sharpens her breath, starts to move her hips against him, slowly at first, then with a fiercer, more urgent thrusting. Out of sight beneath her, Lawrence responds, licking and lapping at her in a frenzy, the breath sawing in his throat. She hears it, but from a distance, her senses already hazed by the onset of her coming. Sheba purrs softly, reaching to touch the swollen knob of flesh. Feels the first shivering waves of orgasm threaten as her heart thuds like a tight-stretched drum. . . .

Jerks against him, calling on his name. . . .

Lawrence feels her weight press on him sudden, driving down on his open mouth. Same time he senses somethin's wrong. Fiery pain in the pit of his belly forks up in a rush. Evil taste of vomit pulsing up in his throat, choking him as the pain rips vicious talons through his chest. . . .

God damn it! He cain't breathe!

Struggles to throw her off, but she too far gone. Sheba plunges harder on him, bucking as she nears her climax, her eyes closed, unknowing, uncaring of what happens below. Beyond the blinding, smothering darkness, the old man hears her moan. Long-drawn out, shivering sound that minds him of some critter in pain. His own pain strikes at him the same instant, harsh claws of fire and steel tearing him apart from the inside as he gags and splutters on his rising vomit. By now it a way too hard for him to bear. Had he strength, he'd scream out loud. . . .

It's a judgment, Old Lawrence thinks, as the fierce pain tears through him and her thrusting weight drives him backward to the floor. Man sins with his own flesh an' blood, the Lord strike him, sure enough. . . .

No time for him to think again. That terrible agony inside him splays its claws. He screams through the suffocating filth, his last sound muffled by Sheba's ecstatic loins. The world exploding in his face, turning black. . . .

Kneeling over him, straddling his face where he lies on the floor beneath her, Sheba hears that choking sound. It comes to her from a world away, unheeded. Her own fingers inside herself, she heaves out the last spasms atop him. After a while, the red haze thins, the room settles back around her. Sheba stays there a while listening to the harsh sound of her own breathing. . . .

There is no other sound.

Gets up hurriedly from the sprawled figure on the rug, hand

170

clasped over her mouth now as she looks down on him, not wanting to believe. Old Man Lawrence don't move a-tall. Black eyes wide, turned back in his head, staring at the open door. From his slack mouth a trickle of vomit slithers over the carpet. The stiff arms flung outward, fingers curled as if clutching at the air.

From somewhere above her the fly sets up to droning again.

'Oh, ma Lawd,' Sheba says.

Her voice sounds like a child's whimper. She sinks on the bed, pulling the sheet around her, like she tryin' to shield herself from those dead eyes of his.

Why she do that thing with him? What in hell she gonna tell John when he comes back?

Questions hammer in her head, unanswered. Sheba sits as if frozen to the bed. Clutching the sheet, too numb, seemingly, to holler or scream.

She's still there an hour later when Lawrence gets in from his talk with Whiteside.

Sheba hears the slam as the door wings shut in the room beyond, noise of it jarring her abruptly from her paralysed state. She's still turning for the door as footsteps quicken yonder, and John Lawrence comes to sight. Halts in the doorway. For a while he just stands there, looking down at the dead old man on the floor.

'Pa?' Lawrence says. Ain't grief she hears in his voice, more like anger. An' like he cain't believe the old man lyin' there a-tall. 'Pa, you hurt bad?'

'He daid, Massa Lawrence,' Sheba says. Abruptly, the ice that holds her to stiffness breaks away, and she begins to weep noisily. 'He been daid fer a while now, I reckon. . . .'

Sound of her voice brings the dark man's head around, his black eyes hard and pitiless.

'Jes' what in the hell been goin' on here?' Lawrence asks.

'Cain't tell, Massa,' Sheba gulps, fighting for breath, her eyes welling as she looks toward him. 'He kind of drunk, I guess. Come in here while I was waitin' on you. He wanted. . . .'

Chokes, unable to finish. Sobs again, hands to her face. Across the room, the lean features of the planter harden, sober and emotionless as stone.

'So he tried that, huh. The old goat,' Lawrence says. Moves to the door, pushes it closed. Sheba watches as he takes the key from his pocket and sets it to turn in the lock.

'Looks like he's gone now, anyhow,' the dark man tells her. 'You got a new master here on Sweet River now.'

Glitter of his dark eyes warns her. Sheba shrinks back from him as he steps over the body on the floor, coming in towards her.

'Ain't nothin' he kin do I cain't do better,' Lawrence says. Grins as he peels off his coat, letting it fall. Hands already busy with the fastenings of his breeches. 'I been lookin' to find me some lovin' tonight, Sheba honey. Figure this has to be some kind of celebration.'

She shakes her head, eyes wide, horror-struck, as his hands close on her.

'Massa Lawrence—John, honey! Not this way, please . . . it ain't right . . . not with him lyin' there daid an' all. . . .'

His rough hand comes over her mouth, shutting off her cries, as he pushes her back on to the bed, his weight pinning her there beneath him.

'You heed me, wench,' Lawrence says, and his voice rings chiller than a winter frost. 'This here's your massa now. What I want, I take, an' ain't nobody gonna tell me different. Not no more. . . .'

'Massa—' A terrified wail. Sheba flinches as his hand strikes her, throwing her head sidelong against the pillow.

'I want you, wench,' Lawrence grits through his teeth as he forces her thighs open, climbing on her. 'Gonna have you now, you yaller bitch.'

Pushes into her, heedless of her cries and the sprawled body on the floor beyond as he thrusts. Mindless, striving for the peak of his pleasure.

Above them in the darkened room the hovering fly keeps up its drone.

UP IN FRONT a redwing starts from the brush, skimming across the narrow trail to perch in a thicket further off. He tenses, alert to the sudden movement, then grins, letting it pass. Funny, the way his hand closed on the pistol-butt that time. Seems like he gittin' use to handlin' that thing since the hog. Now he's sorry there are only two shells left.

He follows the faint deer-trail that runs close along the course of the river, winding south and west through the cottonwood and palmetto stands. By now he's hung about and loaded with the stuff he carries. Spear in his right hand, bow at his back, skin quiver of palmetto arrows slung at the shoulder. Other skin containers on him, too. One low by his waist, half-filled with water. Another hangs at his neck. Strips of jerked meat in there, and pecans. Few persimmons, too. Found the tree out on its own yesterday, crowning a slope above the underbrush. Shook him some of them 'simmons down while he had the chance. He grins once more, reaches inside the skin bag for one of the fruits inside. Biting into the ripe flesh, he nods. Good 'nough. Oughta carry him through for a spell.

Above the treetops the sky lowers, its belly showing dark through the boughs—kind of threatening, somehow, like somethin'· ain't quite right. He frowns, halting to mop at his brow, feeling the moist heat pressing down on him. Sweatier'n usual, too. Could be we in for a storm.

Seems like an age since he left the shelter and his snares and struck off, following the river westward. Come to him after a while that he was gittin' to be too fixed in that place, that he best be movin' on. Try for the big water, even if he don't git there. These last nights he's slept rough, the way he did before. By now, though, he's over the worst of his terror. The gnawing ache of loneliness is still with him, but he no longer fears the ghosts like he did. If they about to take him, they'd of showed up way before now. And as for the critters out here, a man has to take his chances.

All the same, the loneliness is hard. Harder than he ever thought. Nestor was right, that time. Ain't the gittin' out, the stayin' loose, that the hard part of it.

Still, he ain't gone from his mind yet. Could be it'll git better.

Above his head, the trees seem to lean suddenly, leaves whispering. Down below him, ripples curl over the surface of the Atchafalaya. Flutter of wings as birds take off from close at the waterside. He frowns, feeling the sultry gust of wind pass over him, shaking the bushes beyond. Somethin' wrong? He swings round, and the first heavy drops fall spattering on his face. Same instant the rain slams bucketing down, hitting his head and shoulders and sluicing from him to the ground. Beating the ground to mud underfoot, the spray flinging up knee-high. Overhead the sudden sizzle of lightning, the deafening whiplash boom of thunder. At the sound he flinches, glancing up as he sets for a run to cover. Suddenly, he is afraid.

Shango, Nestor told him. He the god of storms, boy. He speak in lightnins an' thunders.

Could be he right about the spirits after all.

All at once the thickets are shaking around him—dark, uncertain shapes bolting headlong past him in panic flight. Blinded as he is by the rain, he sees them: squirrels there, and coons, and rabbits. Lower to the ground, the bugs and spiders and the slithering outline of a snake. All of them going by him in a stream, rushing downhill to where the trees by the waterside offer some kind of shelter.

Over his head the birds with their squalling cries. He ducks as a feathering wingbeat brushes low by his left shoulder. The night-owl swoops on by him, hooting as it makes for the trees at the river's edge. Night-owl? Somethin' wrong here, all right.

Looking back, hearing the gathering sound of the wind, he sees the thing that made them run. Towering column of darkness that spins on itself, binding earth and sky together. A strange howling sound comes from it as it moves, like to a ghost callin' out loud. He sees it mow into the distant trees, sees the woods shaken and splintered, trunks thrown like matchwood in the air. Bits of busted trees caught up in the whirling pillar as

174

it advances, moaning still as the treetops bend and scatter.

Twister!

Now he runs with the beasts, heedless of the thrashing rain, all thought of guns and persimmons and loneliness forgotten. Aware this moment only of the trapped hammer of the heart beneath his ribs, the sudden, dry parching of his mouth that owes nothing to thirst. He heard 'bout tornadoes, seen what they kin do, but he ain't never before been in the midst of one. Now he knows a fear that chills him through, stripping his mind and senses bare of all but itself. What comin' after him ain't about to turn back.

Ahead of him wind tugs in the branches, leaves scattering across his path. He plunges through them, sliding in rain-slicked mud as he stumbles for the cypress clump nearest the water's edge. About him the stream of woodland creatures flows on into the brush, uncaring now whether or not he sees, knowing him helpless as themselves before the wind.

Away to one side another larger figure goes shambling through the rain and the strewn leaves: black bear, blinded, shaking its head and roaring as it goes. Another time he would have feared those long claws, stronger than steel, that can rake a man open at a blow. Now, with the howl at his back gathering every moment in strength, dragged this way and that in the pull of the wind, he has no time for any other fear.

In front the river shows up, the water boiling and churning, foaming at the onset of the spiralling tower of wind. A fresh gust hits him and he slips sidelong, losing his footing as the rain spears into his eyes. Ploughing down the muddy bank, his feet hit water and he sinks to the hips in the dark shallows of the Atchafalaya. Hurriedly he drags the heavy pistol loose, wedging it under the cypress roots. Makes his belt fast to a warped growth at the tree's base that juts above the water, anchoring his body to the wood. He tries not to think of gators along the bank.

A moment more, and the tornado strikes.

Splintering crack and boom of trees bent over or ripped from the ground. Screech of beast and bird all about him, the mass of sounds rumbling on as if heard from a distance, drowned in the banshee scream of the wind as it mows a path through the wilder-

175

ness. He sees the black column breast the slope, whirling dark and huge, cutting off all sight of the world beyond. In its path a live-oak shudders, flies upward, torn from its roots. The air is thick with leaves and flying fragments. Twigs, branches, hunks of trees, bodies. He glimpses a black furred shape flung in the air at treetop height. Hears it strike his own cypress with a sickly thump, then fall away. The fearsome shriek of the wind is like a soul in torment, threatening to burst his eardrums. He covers his ears, crying out in terror, bedding his face to the wood. Beyond him, a cottonwood stand bends and snaps jagged as a row of stalks before the force of the wind, torn trunks spinning skyward as the din goes on. Seems like it never goin' to end.

Blackness in his head, the earth swinging crazy under him. Water flying up across his back as the world tilts sideways. Against his body the wood vibrates, the huge cypress shuddering as the pillar of darkness passes. Roots lift, tearing from the ground, writhing like tentacles as the wind bears them to the eerie light. He feels the sudden shock as one of them snaps at the far side, the tall tree leaning by a shade.

Shango, he prays, out of his head now in fear. *Shango*!

Huge shadow crossing the water, sucking up everything in its path. Caught in the twister's grip, the river yields, funnelling upward into the eye of the storm. Water, mud, fishes, reeds, egrets and herons—a scatter of broken shapes, all drawn up into a roaring spiral that beats against the woods across the water. The wind of its backwash passes, water spraying the ruined land. The smashed shapes flung, scattering to break against the tree-stumps along the bank. Showers of fish falling, floating belly-up in the churned water. On the far bank a cypress upended, dragged from its roots, rammed into the riverbed like a gigantic spear. A broken branch, flying, thuds to embed itself in the trunk above his head. About him the terrible howl goes on, and the cracking boom of woods giving way at a blow.

Against his belt the growth breaks, pitching him over his head in the water. Floundering up for air, spitting muddy spray, he comes up to the top. About him an uneasy stillness comes down, broken only by the steady hiss of rain. The twister is gone, passing him by inches, the tug of its wake alone enough to drag his own tottering cypress from its roots. Now it howls on in the distance, shattering out its trail through the wild. Behind it, only death and silence.

His gaze travels along the river, following the path the wind took before him, seeing it all: the white fish-bellies and crumpled heron feathers afloat on the frothing water, the trees with their shredded tops, corpses of coon and rabbit hanging from the splintery trunks, impaled on the jagged wood. Justus shudders, his bush of hair standing on end, prickling at the scalp. He reaches the gun from where the torn roots left it, wipes it clean of mud. As in a daze he hauls up for the bank, shaking still in every muscle, eyes wide in fear of the thing he has seen.

How in the hell did it miss him?

Overhead a livid light glares for an instant and is gone, followed by the distant growl of thunder. Sagging against the mud of the bank, he nods weakly. Musta been Shango, like Nestor tole him. Musta heard him prayin' back there in the cypress shade, when the wind come in.

Away behind him a sudden creaking groan. He turns to see the cypress lean slowly down towards the water as the last roots rip out from the mud, its smashed boughs hanging loose. The shattered crown is full of snakes, their curling bodies clinging grimly to the wood as the tree gives way. He watches, fascinated and horrified in one, hearing them hiss as the cypress slams down in a sheet of spray and flounders up on the bank, rolling in the water.

Looks like Shango heard him all right. Tree or snakes, either one would have killed him for sure.

The spear he lost at the water's edge floats on the surface, the hoop-iron still lashed in place. He bends, reaching it from the river, breathing more easy now. Looks like he got everything, at that.

He's already turned to move up the slope when the noise halts him in his tracks—heavy, hissing noise, too deep-throated to come from a snake. Even as he looks around for it, the shape he took for a smashed tree bole heaves itself up from the mud in front of him, and starts slowly forward, waddling on its short legs, belly low to the ground.

Gator.

Down in the water he'd feared them, but figgered the danger was past. Now, in the aftermath of the storm, he's met by one on the land itself. Thrown clear, maybe? Watching the glint of those eyes above the broad snout, the thrusting bulk of the armour-plated back, he stands rooted, biting his teeth together, the hair standing stiff as a wire brush upward from his head, clasping his muddy spearshaft as the rain scythes down. Waiting.

Closer in. The strange hissing noise gathering force as the great jaws slant open. He looks into that yawning maw, feeling his own gut lurch as he takes in the rows of ugly yellow teeth. At this distance the stench of breath fans him, hitting warm and foul against his naked body. The gator halts, heaves, then comes on again, long tail scattering twigs as it slithers in readiness for a blow. Sunken eyes fixed on him, glittering.

Spear hefted, he clenches his teeth in terror. Not a hope of piercing that armoured back. Has to be the mouth, or under it, into the gut. And he needs to keep clear of the jaws and the tail. Justus' eyes narrow, mad for the moment as those of the brute he faces. Along his back the hairs prickle upward, itching against the skin.

He leans, striking quick as a cat for the throat beneath the open mouth.

The hiss cuts off short, jaws half-shutting as he moves. Gator sees him coming, rolls sidelong in mud from the blow. Justus drags his arm halfway back, leaping up the bank as the tail whacks in, slamming a fallen bough and snapping it across with a crack that goes whiplashing on among the broken trees beyond. It scutters round on its undersized legs, floundering awkwardly on the treacherous ground. Finds the huge black man above it, higher up the bank, still there with his long spear poised, thick hair bristling in a bush from his head, eyes glaring mad in the darkness of his face, teeth bared, savage as a dog.

Gator sets where he is, studying. Not venturing to move. For once, he's in trouble. Should he try for higher up the bank, that spear could pierce his throat long before his own teeth and tail got to work. Had he been above that far, a mud-slide would have taken the man into the water, and the huge jaws pulled him down. Not any more. Gator hisses, swinging his head from side to side. Still the standing man doesn't move.

Something wrong about this man, too. Not like the rest. Something in his eyes, the mad stare. Gator knows he's backed his enemy into a corner where the man will fight viciously, beyond his normal strength. Eyes and bristling hair are signs enough. That, and the long spear lifted for sight of his throat.

One way out. Gator edges down the muddy bank slowly, inch by inch, hissing as he goes, keeping his head low, offering no easy mark. Eyes on the tall, standing figure as he moves. After a long age, he slides backwards into the water, strikes away along the riverbank.

Blood in his ears, thundering. Harsh, sawing sound of his own breath coming loose. He watches the low, plated shape swim out of range before he moves, scrambling hurriedly through the mess of smashed boughs and bodies to the lip of the slope. Falls to the ground, letting the shaking moment of fear take him over. Lying quiet until the hammer of his heart stills, and the world comes into focus about him.

The world that meets his eyes shows ugly still, stricken by death: a desolate landscape of shattered trees bare of their branches and leafy crowns, spiked ruins that here and there hold the luckless corpse of some creatures flung there by the wind. Leaves and splintered boughs thick on the ground, other wretched corpses tangled in among them. Justus grimaces, swallowing. Like a bad dream, all of it—the wind, the gator, everything. Like somehow it never happened. Yet the hanging corpses of coons and rabbits blood trickling down the stripped boles, are proof enough it was no dream.

After a while he hurries away again, stepping careful looking out for bodies in the wreckage. Eager to be gone from this place of death.

Following the path of the tornado, deeper into the wilderness along the Atchafalaya.

'LAFAYETTE HERALD', JUNE 15th, 1865

IT IS WITH THE DEEPEST REGRET THAT THIS PAPER REPORTS THE DEATH OF MR JOHN LAWRENCE, SR., AT HIS HOME ON THE FAMILY PLANTATION OF SWEET RIVER. ACCORDING TO A STATEMENT MADE BY HIS SON, MR LAWRENCE DIED SUDDENLY AT HOME SOME THREE DAYS AGO FOLLOWING A VISIT TO PALMETTO TO NEGOTIATE POSSIBLE SALES FROM HIS WORKFORCE ON THE PLANTATION. THE CAUSE OF DEATH WAS GIVEN AS HEART FAILURE. MR LAWRENCE WAS SEVENTY-FIVE YEARS OF AGE.

AS ONE OF THE MOST PROMINENT AND RESPECTED CITIZENS OF THIS COUNTY, MR LAWRENCE WAS HELD IN HIGH REGARD BY ALL WHO KNEW HIM. HIS PASSING WILL BE DOUBLY MOURNED AT A TIME THAT HAS SEEN THE FINEST OF THIS COUNTY'S GENERATION DECIMATED, AND THE IDEALS FOR WHICH THEY FOUGHT TRODDEN UNDERFOOT.

OWNERSHIP OF THE CONSIDERABLE LAWRENCE ESTATE REVERTS AUTOMATICALLY TO THE DEAD MAN'S ONLY SON AND HEIR, MR JOHN LAWRENCE JR. AWARE AS WE ALL MUST BE OF THE PROBLEMS SUCH OWNERSHIP IMPOSES IN THESE TROUBLED TIMES, WITH ALL SLAVE PROPERTY PRO-NOUNCED 'FREE' BY OUR YANKEE CONQUERORS AND NO MENTION AS YET OF COMPENSATION TO THOSE WHO HAVE FED AND CLOTHED THEM THROUGH THE YEARS OF WAR AND PEACE ALIKE, WE EXTEND OUR GOOD WISHES TO MR LAWRENCE, TOGETHER WITH OUR CONDOLENCES ON HIS GRIEVOUS LOSS.

WE TOO KNOW THE BEST OF OUR AGE IS PASSED. IT REMAINS FOR MR LAWRENCE, AS FOR US ALL, TO GRAPPLE WITH ADVERSITY AND NOT TO YIELD.

COME EVENING, he reaches what was once a clearing in the woods.

Lonely, his path through the wilderness that day, like walking a graveyard. The twister itself is long gone, but its track shows plain, smashing a littered gap four hundred yards wide through the brush and woodland above the riverline. On as far as the eye can see, like some great claw ripped the wilderness open from one end to the other, scooping out every bush and tree from the earth. He walks in silence among splintered trunks and branches, some of them hung still with the bodies of bird and beast, wincing when an unseen corpse yields softly underfoot, looking in vain for sight of a living thing.

One time a cottonmouth wriggles across his path and he halts, standing quiet like Nestor tole him. Though well within striking distance, the snake doesn't spare him a look, sliding on over a felled sycamore bole and away into the brush. Not long after, he sees a lone deer standing in the open, in plain sight among the shattered forest trees. When Justus approaches, the animal makes no move, those dark eyes staring back at him like he ain't there at all. Reading that look, he trembles. Ain't only men go outa their heads, he figgers. Kin happen to wild critters, too.

Dark all but fallen by the time he comes in sight of the clearing. The air is already cooler than before. Leaned to a shivered birch trunk he stands, looking. Leastways, from the look of it, was once a clearing there. Not any more. Scattered with ripped tree limbs, busted trunks sticking up sideways and upside down from the ground where the wind thrust them like blades in the earth. He grimaces, brushing the sweat from his face. Pauses to check the two remaining loads in the pistol at his belt. Took him a while to git the mud cleaned outa there. Ain't no knowin' iffen it gonna shoot again, come to think. Good thing he still has the spear and the bow.

He has pushed from the tree-bole, starting forward, when he first hears the noise.

First off the sound is kind of distant. He frowns, listening harder. Then it comes again and he knows he hears it right enough. Kind of a low moaning sound coming from that clump of standing trees away to the right. Even as he finds the direction, the noise comes once more. Howling, crying sound, like to a woman hollering out. Listening again, he pales to a greyish, sickly hue, licking at his lips. Don't have to be smart to tell that ain't no beast calling there. An' this far into the wilderness, didn't ought to be no woman, neither.

His glance makes the silent trees, the last echoes dying. Nothin' here in this place. Leastways, nothin' alive.

It have to be some kind of ghost.

The crying sound goes on, lifting and falling over the distance, hanging a while in the crowns of the standing trees, echoes coming hollow and strange in stillness. Justus scowls, teeth baring behind the bloodless lips. Clenching both hands on the grip of the spear-shaft, he turns aside from the path he's been following. Treading cautious and slow over the uncertain wreckage that strews the ground beyond, he moves in towards that stand of timber, and the source of that sound that raises the hair at his neck.

In among the mass of live-oaks, he pauses, drawing breath. The hickory shaft gone slippery in his palms. On every side the looming trunks close in, vast, knotted boles whose upper boughs are hung with streamers of Spanish moss and covered by leafy crowns. His dark outline blurs, becoming one with the shadows. Only here and there, where the wind flung down a stray trunk in passing, does the light fall in upon him as it dies. And all the time he moves, he hears that howling and crying, going on and on.

By now he knows it surely for a woman's voice.

Last of the blood-tinged light falls in from the cleared space on the left, and he sees.

Use to be a cabin here once, walled from timber logs, sod-roofed. Looks like they had a stiffened deerhide for a door. Not now. Reason he kin see so good is the gap in the trees, that been stove in by a falling live-oak the wind must of took down. Come down clean on the cabin. Roof smashed in like a furrow to the plough, log walls caved and scattered loose. Hide door twisted and swinging by splinters from the frame. Base of the live-oak has its bared roots towards him. Someplace near the smashed cabin wall, under the branches, he figures he sees somethin' else lyin' pinned to the ground.

Ain't from there the sound comin'. That the woman.

She stood closer to him than the cabin. Pressed up agin a tree ten paces off, her face hid by the trunk, hollering and hitting out at the wood, long hair shook about her face, tangled and mussed up with twigs and leaves. Dress looks like it torn, too, all but offen the shoulder. At sight of the grimed white flesh his own eyes narrow, hardening. He clasps the spear uncertainly, looking about for signs of a fallen weapon. Not a thing. Even as he looks she hauls back off the tree, head flung up as she yells out again.

'Caleb! Caleb! Oh, my God!'

He watches as she whirls round, away from the tree, stumbling back towards the wrecked cabin. There by the smashed wall she drags among the thick overhanging branches, wrestling helplessly for a hold on the wood, all the time howling and calling out like a beast in torment. Settled into the soft ground, the tree shows no sign of giving. Branches thudding back into place the minute she leaves go. After a while she gives up and sinks on to her knees, covering her face with her hands.

'Oh, God! God!' The sound muffled, choking into inarticulate sobs. 'Caleb! What in hell am I gonna do!'

Sight of her helplessness decides him. One hand comes clear of its grip on the shaft, letting the weapon trail to the ground. Ain't much this one kin do 'gainst him, he figgers. All the same, he best look out for sign of any white man. That be a killin', for sure.

He comes out from the shadow of the trees, making towards her over the open ground.

Set as she is with her back to him, she doesn't hear him till he all but stood behind her. Then she senses the unmistakable change in the stillness about her and swings round, making as if to get to her feet. Seeing in that moment the huge bush-haired black man who towers head and shoulders above her, his wide shoulders blocking out the light, her eyes go wide and scared and a scream chokes off, dying in her throat.

183

'Who — who are you?' The voice faltering, unsure even of speech for the moment.

He doesn't answer. Jes' watches her from where he stands, silent, holding to the spear with its ugly hoop-iron point, taking in the pale, terror-stricken face, smudged by dirt and tears and blood where a stray twig tore a gash in the cheek. Tangle of white ash-blond hair about the face, dirty and straggled with leaves. The hands with their upturned palms raw and bloody from hauling on the wood.

Ain't no plantation miss, that for sure. Dress is a calico print like he seen Sheba or a dozen others wear, back on Sweet River. Tore off the shoulder, and stained with the live-oak bark and moss, leaving a dark bruise-mark on the white flesh. Close to, he sees she's tall—taller than Sheba, and full-bosomed. Powerful build, for a woman.

Her eyes on him still, wide open in surprise and fear. Pale blue eyes in a white face. Almost the colour Burns' eyes had. Not quite the same, though. Cain't find the same meanness there.

From her, his own look strikes on, downward among the heavy branches. Under the felled tree a man lying, flat to the ground, his head toward him. The figure doesn't move.

White man. That much he could of told already. From here he cain't be seen too plain, but it don't look good. His head fallen back and he ain't makin' a sound. Justus eyes the prone shape a while. Slowly his glance comes back to rest on the woman.

'Please—'. Seeing the uncertain look of his eyes, some of the fear ebbs from her face. Now eyes and voice alike begging him as her hand reaches helpless for the still shape under the tree. 'Please help me . . . cain't move it off him . . .'

Still he doesn't speak, studying them both. White woman. White man. Right now, he don't owe them nothin'. Then again, they ain't done him no hurt—not yet.

'He your man, lady?' The question ungentle, spoken harshly out of a frowning face. At the sound of it she stiffens, clenching her own bloody hands, pulling herself up to a full height, about the level of his shoulder.

'My husband!' For an instant the pale eyes lock with him. Then the moment passes and she turns, fighting to control the shuddering of her body. The look of her eyes when they come to him again is fearful as before. 'Will you—will you help us?'

Justus frowns deeper. Shrugs at last, laying down the spear. Don't look like it kin do no harm. Leastways, the man ain't gonna be in no shape to beat his head in, should the fancy take him. An' he can't see no gun.

'No other men hereabouts?' he asks, and she shakes her head, starting again to sob as she wrings her hands together, tears spilling afresh from her eyes.

'No-one!' The word breaks as though torn from her, racking the body. Her wild look rakes the desolate stand of trees around them in despair, almost in hatred. 'We're alone out here in this terrible place, and now . . .' The voice falters, begging. '*Please help . . .*'

He grunts in answer, pushing by her to kneel by the fallen man. One look serves him. The upper trunk and the boughs were what took him, burying him waist-deep in a sprawl of busted branches. Hands to the heavy wood, he spares a glance for the upturned face. Thin features, gone to an ugly grey-white colour. Reddish hair and beard, streaked thick with grey. Good bit older'n her from the look of him, but that don't signify. What holds him is the fixed stare of the eyes, glaring past him now into the treetops beyond. The lips too drawn back, baring the long yellow teeth, Cain't see what's under the tree lower down, but he kin guess. Justus sucks in his breath, sighing. He turns, looking back over his shoulder to where the woman stands trembling behind him.

'He long daid, lady,' he says.

For a moment her eyes stare back at him, angered, refusing to believe. Then her look goes again to the prone shape under the boughs, and her face convulses. She shrieks aloud, covering her face with her hands.

'Get it off him, for the love of God!' she yells.

Facing her, hearing that scream, Justus knows himself angry for an instant. Who in hell she think she is? White woman out here alone—he could do what he like with her. Wouldn't no one be the wiser. Ain't cut out here to take no shit from no white miss! With the thought comes fresh awareness of his own unquenched need.

After days and nights alone in the wilderness the look of her is good to him. She young and healthy, he reckons. Good as Sheba for what been keepin' him awake nights. Hunger at the sight of her vies with his rage. At once he's conscious of a quickening in his pulse, slow heat of the swelling at his groin. . . .

Silent, he turns from her. Grips with both hands under the nearest bough. Sets himself to heave upward from the ground.

The weight of the tree fights him. He feels its strength dragging at his arms, wrenching the great muscles of his back and shoulders. Justus snarls, teeth bared as at an enemy, anger surging in him until he's all but blind to the redness before his eyes. He pushes in under the boughs, lifting and sliding, wedging his bare feet to the ground. Beyond him, a slow, sucking noise as a bough pulls out of the earth. His shoulder is under the trunk, pain of the bark biting into his flesh as it shudders and turns. Justus gasps, heaving to the limit of his strength. Part of the heavy bole gives back, one bough cracking underneath as the huge weight lifts and slides sideways, thundering against the ground. Justus jumps clear as the tree falls, breath hissing harsh through his teeth, sinking on hands and knees as the pounding of his heart settles again.

One glance at the body shows that his first guess was good. Below the waist there's nothing to be seen but a mess of crushed flesh and splintered bone. Thick blood fouls the trunk, sticking to his hands. He wipes them against the ground, grimacing.

'Oh, my God! Caleb!' The wailing shout at his back tells him that she, too, has seen.

About him the world comes clear again, his own breath settling. Justus grunts, looking to his scarred hands, feeling the dull ache of strained muscles and the slow trickle of blood, where the live-oak cut into his shoulder. Slowly, he gets to his feet.

'You got a shovel someplace?' he asks.

She turns from him with an ugly choking sound, her body shuddering from head to foot.

For a while he stands, eyeing her turned back. Then he nods, shrugging his broad shoulders.

Guess he ain't too good to look at, at that.

Climbing inside the wrecked cabin, clambering over the broken boughs of the tree, he looks round him carefully. Ain't too much left, he reckons. Shards of busted dishes everywhere. Table torn loose and rammed into the log wall, three of its legs smashed. Up on the leaning wall itself, furs are nailed, spread and tattered from the wind. Musta been some kinda trapper, he guesses. Over in the corner lies a long-barrelled gun, throwed clean 'cross the cabin like as not. Leastways, the stock is smashed, and the metal buckled hopelessly out of shape. He throws it from him, scowling. Not a sign of a goddamn shovel.

Coming out by a gap in the far wall of the cabin, he finds a long-handled woodman's axe fixed in the trunk of a nearby tree. Levers it from the wood. Not much use for diggin', but handy in other ways. Climbing back through the ruined place, he hacks himself one of the lower boughs clear of the trunk. Leans over it to slash off the twigs, chopping the narrow end to a rough point. He lets fall the axe. Grips the bough two-handed, then jabs it into the earth near the body, where flies have already begun to gather at the nostrils and the eyes. Justus grimaces, digging harder. Don't do to think on death too long. Man wouldn't take the trouble gittin' born.

Crude though the digging-stick is, the soft ground yields. Pretty soon he's worked up a sweat and stands looking down into a man-sized hole, the dirt heaped up to one side. Justus jabs the stick to earth, breathing hard. He turns to where the white man lies, still staring up at the treetops as the buzzing cloud settles over his eyes.

The woman has long since turned again, squatting on her heels to watch him. When he looks toward her, the face that meets him is empty, bare and numbed of all feeling, pale eyes wide in a tear-stained face, like to the eyes of the deer he met, comin' in. Justus scowls, uneasy in this place of death. He bends, the woman watching still as he lifts the smashed body in his arms and lowers it into the fresh-dug hole, gritting his teeth a little as the splintered legs hang loose and the mess of blood catches on his hands. Stepping back, he wipes his palms on his breeches, slapping at the gathering flies.

From down in the pit those staring eyes accuse him. Justus licks his lips, tasting the salt of his sweat. By now it's fully dark, the trees around them blurred black outlines against the night. Time for the ghosts to come a-hauntin' now. Cursing under his breath, he grabs the stick, shoving the heap of earth hurriedly over that upturned face.

In time, it's done. He hits down the earth, firming it with the flat of the axe. Stands back, sweating, to thrust his rough-hewn stick into the ground. Should serve for some kind of marker, like in a real graveyard. Man oughta have a mark of some kind. Letting the axehead drop to the earth, he brushes with his free arm at the sweat that slicks his brow.

Back of him, her sobbing breath is the one answering sound in the stillness. He turns, glancing to her. The woman hasn't moved, still squatted there on her heels, watching him. Pain, grief, whatever—something has brought the feeling back into her, and she has begun to weep again, making no move to halt the tears. They fall, streaking down her dirt-smudged face, dripping on to the stained calico dress, sliding to make a shiny trail down over the swell of her bosom. All the time her eyes, watching him, searching him. At once uncertain and afraid. The way the deer looked when his first arrow hit. By now she knows the way things are, and what he might do should the fancy take him.

Justus frowns, looking again to the level mound of earth. Oughta say somethin', he knows. Man shouldn't be took without a word. This was a white man and no friend of his, but maybe that ain't all that matters. He come a long ways from Sweet River. Since he slipped Lawrence, he seen death and dyin' plenty times. The gator in the bayou was close enough. Then the dog he killed in the water. Burns and the snake. The critters he hunted, the deer and the wild hog. Then the twister, an' that gator on the bank. Now this one, crushed under a falling tree.

Plenty ways of goin', but it every time the same. He oughta say somethin', with her lookin' on an' all.

He rests one hand on the planted stick, looking towards the far stand of trees. Dark already. Any spirits hereabouts, they be listening, that for sure.

'Lord pity this poor white man,' Justus says to the silent mass of live-oaks. ''Cause he sure as hell died hard.'

188

He turns from the fresh-dug grave, hefting up the woodman's axe, hearing her weeping break out once more as he slips the handle into his belt. Picks up the fallen spear from the ground.

Time to go. He sure ain't fixin' to stay here with the ghosts in this place.

His look takes in the woman before him, sobbing yet, her muddied face wet with tears, the pale blond hair tangled about her face and bosom, her blue searching eyes still on him. For a while he stands there, spear in hand, looking her over. Not speaking. The silent dark grows more oppressive around them.

Ain't no way of changin' it. She white, an' he black. It don't fit a-tall. He got himself any sense, he leave her now. Take off fer hisself like before. That way, he safe from a hangin' when the next white folks turn up an' she hollers out rape. That way it goes, most times.

You *hate* white folks, Justus. Remember?

Sure as hell do. Lawrence first. Twist his haid clear offen his body, git the chance. Then Jacob. Figger I'd cut that son's pecker off him first, then kill him good.

But Jacob ain't white, man. He black, like you.

He near as white as he kin git, I reckon. After Lawrence, he be next.

Jacob black, Justus. You ain't thinkin' straight. You gonna kill Jacob an' let this white women be? No sense in that as I kin see.

Aw, to hell with thinkin'! Never got me noplace. One thing sure: cain't leave her out here alone. She goin' be daid 'fore many days are out.

'You best come with me, lady,' he says.

At that she starts, shaken for the moment from her pain. Shock in the stare of the wide eyes. The mouth that opens, robbed of words.

'Ain't noplace else fer you to go, I reckon.' His eyes scan the wreck of the cabin, the marked grave under the trees, in another part of his mind, cussing himself to be so dumb. She gonna drag him down, slow him. Maybe he never git to the big water now. 'You come with me, now, we kin set up camp somewhere outa this place. . . .'

Pity in him as he speaks, pity at her helplessness. Not pity only. The need still there, teasing in his loins. Making the blood hot, tripping the words at his tongue.

'It was the gun that did it,' the woman says, her pale eyes looking through him at some other place, the white face, stricken yet with the thing it saw. 'Both of us out of the cabin when it come, and he turned back for it. I called out to him, but he wouldn't listen.... And then, the tree falling....' Her voice shakes, sobs racking her afresh as her eyes fill at the memory. 'And him underneath ... Oh, Caleb!'

She lifts a hand to cover her face, head sunk forward, weeping. Justus frowns, awkward for the moment. With his left hand he reaches to take her own.

'Come with me now, you hear?' he says.

She shakes her head. Strikes at the black hand, pushing it away. He stands back from her, watching as the weeping goes on. The first spurt of anger dying again to pity.

'Have it your way,' Justus says. Then, more gently, 'Reckon I be goin', now....'

He turns from her silently. Huge black figure looming against the line of trees, hung about with his food containers and his weapons: the bow and palmetto arrows, the pistol, the hickory spear, the woodman's axe. Slowly moving away through the shattered space towards the next stand of timber that crowns the slope along the Atchafalaya.

Behind him the woman looks up to darkness. Suddenly alone in the cleared stretch, with only the dead for company. At the far side, where the shadow falls thickest, a tall shape moves. Darker against the dark, vanishing among the trees. She leaps up, stifling a cry, glancing about her for a miracle.

None comes. Her face sets, hardening in sudden determination.

She follows the dark figure at a run, heading for the shadow of the trees.

'HE WAS gonna give it up, this time,' the woman says.

She sits across from him on the far side of the fire, looking to him through the dying flames. He has watched her as she wolfed down the meat and the pecans he gave her. Handed her a long drink from the skin water-flask. By now her voice is calmer, void of grief. She has done crying, her face showing weary and drained in the wavering light of the flame that touches on the dark circle of trees beyond.

'Told me, after the first year we had out here. If it didn't get no better, we were goin' to leave—head back home for Texas. . . .' She pauses, feeling his silence across the distance between them. 'Me, I knew it. Couldn't have stood another year like that. And it didn't get no better, never would. We was all ready to go. Once we had things fixed up, we'd have been out of here, for sure. . . .'

The talk runs out suddenly. The look of her eyes on him is mute, piteous as a wounded critter in a snare. Justus says nothing. Figgers it better she say what she have to, than keep it bottled in. After a while he makes to offer her the water-flask again, but she shakes her head, smiling weakly at last.

'You been good to me, you hear. I thank you for it.'

Shrugging. Not answering. His eyes still on her. Thinking. That trouble you storin' up there, boy. You hear me?

'He a trapper, your husband?' he asks.

'You figger he was, huh?' Sadness now in her smile, pale almost as her eyes and hair. She gazes a while into the trembling flame, and sighs. 'No, he was a schoolmaster when I met him. Come from some little place along the Brazos I ain't never heard before. Always reckoned he could be his own boss, make it rich trappin' furs in the wilderness. Guess he never was too handy with that gun . . . that damned gun. . . .'

Abruptly, her eyes well, brimming over. She swallows, looking away from him.

'Sure am sorry 'bout that,' he says.

All the while feeling the hot tides of the blood that pulse beneath the skin. Seeing her white body, wanting her, torn by the raw hunger of his need. Yet at the same time knowing the distance between them. And the white man's answer. The knife first, then the rope.

'Reckon you best git some sleep, lady,' he says.

He could force her if he wanted—wouldn't be too hard. But that ain't never been his way. He figger if a woman want him, he don't need to push. 'Sides, this one got other matters on her mind.

He scowls, turning aside to sleep, the fire beyond him already burning down. Eyes shut, he hears the sound as she rises, crossing a couple of feet away to lay herself down. The sound of the calico brushing the ground like a touch along his nerves, turning the blood to fire. He scowls fiercer, angry at himself now, bites the clenched knuckles of his hand.

You brung yourself enough grief here, boy. Stayin' loose hard enough as it is, without a woman to tend. An' a *white* woman— that one hell of a difference.

Against his face the ground is soft, soothing after the hours of daylight: the battle with the live-oak, the burying. He sighs, feeling the darkness spread through him, letting himself drift on a tide of weariness, slowly breathing out as he goes under. . . .

The sound of her voice brings him awake, suddenly.

'I'm cold,' the woman says.

Something in her tone makes him wary. He turns over on his side, facing her.

She's still lying there like before, watching him. Now, in the flickering light, her face is changed: those blue eyes studying his own half-naked body, as if seeing it for the first time. Meeting that look, he senses his need returning, heat in his groin as his penis lifts and swells, pushing tight at the cloth of his breeches. The altered expression of her face tells him that she too sees, and knows.

'I'm cold,' she says again. Then, her voice grown husky, 'Warm me.'

Sound of her voice catches him two ways. Knowing her whiteness as a warning, something forbidden him to touch. And warring with it, the force of his body's hunger. Seeing now that she is looking at him the same way, for an instant he don't know which way to jump. Then the overpowering call of the blood in his veins decides him. At once, he feels his throat thicken against speech.

'Come here,' he says, his own voice hoarse in stillness. 'Come here to me.'

Her eyes still upon him, searching. Seems like they goin' to stay forever like this, each studying the other. At last she nods. In a sudden motion she kneels upright, pulling the dress off over her head.

Thunder of his pulse comin' hard enough to bust him open. Seems like he kin hardly breathe. He lies where he is, watching her as she shucks off her drawers and stands naked in firelight before him. Wavering orange light shows her unclothed body, its sudden, startling whiteness. Seen close, out of the loose-fitting dress, she is lithe and slim as a deer. Full-bosomed, but tapering to narrowness at the flanks. His eyes going down her, slowly, to the firming swell of hips and thighs. The low mound of her belly, that vanishes into a bush of tawny gold. From where she stands she looks at him. In the uncertain light her eyes are bright, expectant. Justus sets his teeth, feeling his heart begin to flutter at his ribs.

'Come here,' more urgent now than before.

Barefoot, she crosses the space between. Lies down beside him.

Her face close to his, now. Warmth of her breath upon him, stirring the flesh. Blinded by her whiteness, for a moment he doesn't move. Her woman-scent in his nostrils, overpowering him. Dare he touch her his way? A white woman? He got to, now. Ain't no goin' back.

His hand reaches, stretching uncertainly, as if afraid of being burned. Falls soft as a shadow at the nape of her neck. At the first touch of her flesh he feels her shiver, her blue eyes widening as they look into his own. His touch sliding on, following the smooth narrow curve of her back, cupping the fullness of the buttocks beyond. Seems like she can't stop herself from shaking. When his hand closes at her breast she moans out, her eyes closing.

Frowning as the realization dawns. She as hot for this as he is. How come, he wonders. That man he buried back there—what he been doin' all this time? He shakes the thought from him, letting go to the swooning touch of the senses. Across from him, her eyes open.

'What your name, lady? he asks.

'Mary.' She too reaching, almost warily, her hand flattening on the breadth of his naked chest. Both hands ghosting on him now, stroking pale spirit-lines down the blackness of his flanks. Crossing to his belly. 'Mary Kimball. And you?'

'Justus.' His hand slipping downward for the darkness between her thighs. Abruptly she shudders, gasping. He finding her already moist, eager for him. Her hands frantic now at his belt, tugging at the fastenings of his breeches.

'Hurry, Justus,' she says.

Heat of his straining flesh as the breeches give at last. His manhood swells, throbbing urgently against her palm. After long denial, the cool touch of her on him is almost more than he can bear. Justus grits his teeth together, eyes closing, breath escaping in a harsh whistling sound.

Jee-sus! He gonna be shootin' off before they even started!

'Easy now,' he murmurs.

Her hand leaves him suddenly and she rolls away from him, her back to him now as she crouches on hands and knees, drawing him hurriedly after.

Kneeling behind her, he knows a momentary flare of anger. Don't she want to look him in the face? Wantin' a man, but not to see he black—that it? Sure's hell show you, you white bitch! Lays hold on her buttocks as she rears against him.

Black of his hands on her smooth white rump. Oh, my Lord!

No time for anger now. The thunder of blood in his root is beating pulses in his head, his breath sawing harsh. Ain't gonna be time for nothin', if he ain't quick. Her hand comes out, guiding him. Soft, unbelievably sweet touch of his flesh. God! Closing his eyes, fighting to hold off the explosion.

'Give it to me!' she moans.

She lifts to him, and his manhood enters her.

No resistance as he goes in. Softness. Moisture and enclosing warmth. Sinking himself into her, he feels an uncontrollable shudder against him, a sudden trickle of wet heat along his swollen shaft. Mary cries out under him, trembling as the force of the orgasm takes her, her face laid against the ground. Her sudden coming sets him off. He grasps at her flanks, thrusting himself furiously into those dark, unseen depths, groaning himself, now, feeling the onset of his own climax as it approaches. Before him the hollow curve of her back, the strewn blond hair that hides her face. Her buttocks, working against him in a frantic rhythm. He reaches upward, grasping for her breasts. His eyes widening as his powerful thrusting grows faster yet, taking him to the edge. Beneath him he can hear her moaning.

'Yes! Yes! Again... Oh, Yes!'

Deep inside her, the dam bursts at last. Justus yells out harshly as the sap pours from him, flooding her, filling her as the spasm takes them both, black and white, clasping and shuddering together. In front of his eyes a bright pinpoint of light spreads to a fearsome size, blinding him utterly, lifting him for a moment out of life itself. ...

Sinking to the ground, slowly. Their sweat mingling, running between them as she turns to him. Their bodies close, the black and the white entwined. Each with arms about the other.

Her eyes full of tears. This time, though, she smiles. Leaning to kiss him on the lips.

He lying quiet. Returning her kiss gently, his passion spent, his dark hand touching her tenderly. Fingers tracing the dried blood over the cut in her cheek, softly, as at some kind of sacrament, fondling the thick, pale tresses of her hair.

Stillness, and the fire beyond them burning down to embers.

'RECKON YOU don't think too much of me, do you?' she asks.

Almost daylight now, the fire burned away. Birds already setting up to sing in the far trees as the night greys out and the shadows shrink. The two of them still lying close and naked, each holding to the other, the drawers and the crumpled calico dress flung in a heap beyond them. On the other side, his shucked breeches, thrown across the pile of his weapons and skin flasks.

Justus meets her questioning look, not answering. Right now he don't think too much a-tall, still dazed from what has been. Contentment possesses him, the remembered ecstasy of joined flesh. Touching her shoulders and the supple curve of her back, his hands recall the sweetness of their bodies fusing together, the scalding instant of fulfilment. Afterwards, the sated peacefulness, the gentle sexless touches, the clasped sleep in each other's arms. Might have thought about it once. Not any more.

Seeing his puzzled expression, she frowns, looking uncertainly at the black gleaming arms about her waist.

'Woman just buried her husband, beds her down with....' Watching his altered face, she checks herself, hurriedly, '... with another man same night. Don't look too good, huh?'

'You want to tell me about it?' he says.

'Ain't never done nothin' like it before.' The words coming from her in a rush. For an instant she turns her head away. Turns again at last to look him in the face. Makes as if to speak, falls silent. Forces herself to speak again.

'Fact is, we didn't do this kind of thing any too often while we was married, Caleb an' me....'

'How come?' For once he wants to know the answer.

'You seen him,' Mary says. Lying against him, her lip trembles a moment, her blue eyes filming over. 'He was way older'n me when I met him first—over fifty, I reckon. Hadn't never married. Back then, I didn't know nothin' of those kind of things. First few months we was all right. Leastways, I thought so. But after a while, the work and the worry got to him. Didn't seem like we could make it happen no more....'

'Uhuh.' All the while eyeing her, studying as she speaks. No fakery he kin see in the open face and the look of her eyes. She talkin' straight enough, he reckons. 'Time I found you, looked like you was pretty broke up over it, all the same.'

'He was a good man, Justus.' At once the mouth firms up, the chin jutting determinedly. For an instant he reads something like defiance in those eyes. 'Always treated me kind, no matter how

196

bad things got. I had any kind of self-respect, I reckon I'd have stayed by him when you left me . . . but it's been so long. An' you been good to me, too, Justus. I know that.'

He shrugs, awkward. Not knowing what to say. Her hand lies at his chest and he reaches to lift it gently, brushing it with his lips. Her eyes well up again at the kiss.

'How come you married him?' he asks.

'You ever been in Texas, Justus?' Mary asks. At the shake of his bushy head she smiles, not without sadness, it seems to him. 'I figgered not. You ain't never been a woman neither. It's one whole different world out there, I'm askin' you to believe me. Back where I was raised, place name of Butler's Fork, was but one dirt road an' five shacks set down by a muddy stream. Pa kept the one store in town.' She sighs, brushes a moment at her wet eyes. 'Seemed to me, growin' up there, was nothin' to the place but dirt and flies an' the smell of drink on every man's breath. An' none too many men to be had. They was all somebody's husband, an' most of 'em old. Looked like I was about to end my days in that godforsaken place, stuck into a hole until they dug me under. Then Caleb Kimball came by, aimin' to set up a school there, an' we took up together.'

She pauses, looking him in the face. Questioning. He nods, not speaking.

'Caleb was tired of teachin',' she says. 'He couldn't wait to strike out into the wilderness, be his own master. When he asked me to marry him, go with him out of Butler's Fork, it seemed like a dream. He was a good man, an' I figgered I wasn't about to get no second chance.' Biting her lip now, remembering. 'You reckon you can understand that?'

His look full upon her, he nods. 'Yeah . . . yeah, Mary. I kin understand it, at that.'

'You already heard the way it went,' she tells him. 'We come upriver so far, then after in a one-ox waggon he bought at the last settlement out of the wilderness. Built us the cabin yonder, set out to trap the critters hereabouts. Caught us some, but not enough to get by on. Ox died in our first year, waggon bust an axle. He never did get around to fixin' it, an' now he never will. . . .'

She falls quiet at that. The words all unloaded. Nothing more to be said.

'Reckon you tole me how it was,' he says.

Silence a while between them, the two of them lying motionless, their bodies touching lightly one against the other. Each feeling the regular pulse of the other's heart against them. Their arms twined. White, black. Black on white.

'Best you should hear 'bout me, now, I guess,' Justus tells her at last.

She lies, not answering, looking into his eyes, her soft hands upon him. He goes on.

'They had me workin' as a field hand on a plantation in Lafayette County. Drove us hard, back there. Young master, Lawrence his name was, he a mean sonofabitch. Had me whipped, one time. . . .'

'Yeah, I seen that.' Her touch gentle on the furrowed scars. 'So you won loose, huh?'

'Uhuh—broke out one night. Been loose ever since. One man, Nestor he called, reckon if I git far enough downriver I make it to the big water . . . maybe git over to A-frica, like he come from years back.'

He breaks off suddenly, glimpsing laughter in her eyes. Mary fights to keep it down. Fails. Leans against him, spluttering.

'The big water? You talkin' about the ocean? Oh, Justus, how you think you're gonna get over there alone?'

She pauses, her laughter stilled for the moment by the anger in his look. Sighs, reaches out to run her hands through the thick bush of his hair. 'Justus honey, listen to me. They'll be out after you already as it is. You try to board a boat from any port on the coast, you gonna end up in jail. . . .' Trying to smile as her eyes plead with him. 'Think about it, Justus. Ain't that how it is?'

At her touch the sullenness leaves his features. He shakes his head, forcing a wry grin. 'One thing sure, Mary. You got yourself a runaway here.' His face sobering again as he speaks. 'They had a warrant out for me some while now, 'Fore I took off I struck Lawrence, an' killed one of the dogs they sent after me. Could even be they blame me for one of the patrollers that caught up with me. . . .'

'You mean you killed him too?' For an instant her face shows a tinge of fear.

'No, Mary. Snake bit him. That's how I come by the pistol.' He pouts a moment, reflecting. 'Had me the chance, I might've, I guess, but it didn't work out that way. All the same, he daid by now. . . .'

'Good enough for them to hang you, huh?'

'That, an' what we done already,' he says.

At the sudden words she flinches, the truth of it striking home, her own features grown more sombre in a moment.

'Yeah,' Mary says. 'I've seen lynchin's in my time, even at Butler's Fork . . . an' what I seen wasn't any too good.'

She reaches over then, her arms at his neck. Covers his mouth with her own. After a while she draws away.

'You can trust me, Justus,' Mary says. 'Sure would hate for you to be taken from me now.' Her voice falters a little, the eyes uncertain still as she looks to him. 'In a way, it's bad that it worked out like this, but right now, I wouldn't want to change it. How about you?'

He smiles then, drawing her to him with his powerful arms, feeling the long warmth of her against him. Sweet scent of her hair against his nostrils as they kiss again.

'Mary honey,' he tells her. 'Seems to me you almost worth a hangin', right now!'

They laugh then, embracing, heedless of the spreading light that spears through the trees around. For a time there are no more words.

Presently they move apart, dressing at last as the new day breaks in the east.

'YOU STILL aimin' for this big water of yours?' Mary asks.

At first he doesn't answer, busy as he is at the string of his bow. Last few days some of the fibres have begun to fray loose, and he's had to work fresh strands in. Now he draws the thickened rope

199

over his lap, tensing it against the pull of finger and thumb. Uhuh. Nodding as it answers to the hand.

'Ain't thought about it much.' Laying hold on the wood of the bow, he hauls the looped end of the string over the hickory tip. Half-draws on the finished weapon. It answers, all right. Now he sets it down. Glances up, frowning. 'You figger I ain't gonna make it, that right?'

It's her turn not to answer. Sitting back of him in the entrace of the shelter he's made them. Same turf, leaves and moss as before, over a frame of willow saplings. The lighter bow he made for her a coupla days back from hickory switch rests up beside her at the wall. Best she should learn to use a weapon while they out here, he reckons. Now she draws her knees up to her chin, watching him warily.

'I been thinkin' on it,' Mary says, hugging her knees as she speaks, her blue eyes peering through the pale strands of hair overhanging her face. 'Ain't too many ways you can jump. Canada's a way too far, that's for sure. Me, I'd say the ocean is as bad, or like to be. . . .'

'You kin tell me somethin' better?' Anger crackling sudden in his voice as he speaks. He senses already that she's right—that the big water is a ways too far off, that if he ever reaches it, he won't make it past the coast patrols on to any boat. Still, the knowing does nothing for his own smouldering temper this morning. Like he lost, an' cain't find his way back without her help. 'Jes' let me know it, huh?'

'Could try Mexico, I guess.' The spasm of annoyance crossing her face in turn as she answers. Being in the one place is beginning to wear on her nerves, too. Mary has been long enough in the wilderness. 'Has to be your best bet, I'd say. Either that, or the Big Thicket. . . .'

'Come agin?' His hand leaving the bow as his head turns, questioning. 'Where this—thicket?'

She smiles a moment at that. Chin rested on her raised knees as she stares him in the eye.

'South a ways.' Shaking back her hair in a gesture that includes the trees beyond them. 'Couldn't rightly say how far. Never did see the place, but I heard. Like to a jungle, they reckon. Plants growin' so thick together you can't hardly wriggle by. Has to be someplace further out from this wilderness here.' She pauses, studying the ground a while before she speaks again. 'They do tell that men hid out there safe for years—men like you. . . .'

'Black men? That your meanin'?' Bristling up again as the words rub at him the wrong way. For an instant he glares into those pale eyes, feels the hardness of his look return.

'That's it, black men.' Mary meets him with a steely gaze. 'You mighty touchy this mornin', seems to me. Sure you ain't sickenin' for somethin', Justus?'

'Reckon not.' Turning from her, glowering still as he lifts the bow, gets to his feet. The rage still in him, seething like to hot coals. 'I best be goin' now, anyhow. . . .' He halts, looking back to her, and for a moment his resolution falters. Though the dress covers her, his mind etches out the contours of her body beneath, recalling the good memories of these past days and nights. She one hell of a woman, sweet or mean, he thinks.

'You wanna come along?' he asks. This time, though, she frowns, shaking her head.

'Reckon I'll sit here,' Mary says. 'Somebody best look after the house.'

She bends over from him, plucking at the grass by her feet. He stands a while watching, waiting, hoping she gonna look up, maybe change her mind. She don't look up. Just goes right on pecking at the grass clumps with her finger. Meanness in the set of her back, and the bowed head that refuses to look his way. Abruptly he feels his own anger rise, and bites hard, gritting his teeth together.

'Be back 'fore night,' he offers at last.

Mary makes no answer.

The harsh black face of Justus twists in a spasm of fury. He swings about on his heel, fitting the bow across his back, and sets off for the nearest stand of trees. He avoids looking back, knowing as he does that she won't lift her head until he's gone.

Walking the open land, his thoughts keep pulling him back to the place he has just left. To Mary, and that shelter among the timber. Somethin' eatin' both of 'em today. Looks like they caught in some kind of snare, and ain't no way out of it. The bright day presses on him with its light and heat. Hot glare of the sun hitting the string of bayous yonder, setting them to shimmer between their cypresses and cottonwoods like threaded glass on a wire. Steam fanning up off the water, shrouding the low-lying thickets, where the last deer of the morning graze in safety, knowin' there ain't a man in miles. Since he met her, they come away from the line of the river, following the marshy spread of bayous further south. Out here the wilderness begins to take on a different look, the thick stands of trees thinning out slowly as the land flattens and sinks lower, timber and shrubs hugging the gentle, shouldering lifts in the ground that pass for hills hereabouts. For the rest, one vast spread of tall grassland studded with bayous and inlets that heads outward to the farthest limit of the eye. And below the grass, thick mud quivering underfoot, sometimes plunging a man over his chest in water. Over these past few days he's learned the few tried paths through this wet, uncertain landscape, knowing that the tall grasses all too often hide gators and cottonmouths. . . .

Looking on it now he scowls, anger in the breath that hisses from his clenched teeth. His mind ain't in this place. Right now, it ain't even with Mary at the camp. He thinkin' back to Sweet River. Standing quiet in the swaying grassland, the dark mud at his ankles as he stares out across the empty land. Remembering the night in the nigger graveyard. Nestor, and Mede, comin' out there to tell him goodbye. Bringin' him food for the journey. Nor them only. Cato, too, an' Glory an' William. Every last one. All of 'em in there rootin' for him, willin' him to git free, like somehow they was all of 'em clear of Sweet River should he break out. . . .

They should see him now. Trapped in this godforsook wilderness where he ain't never gonna git loose. Settin' down roots agin. Fixin' shelters. Layin' his snares.

His white woman, too, fixin' to turn him into some kind of slave.

Bitterness in him, rising at the thought. His hands at his sides, clenching.

That right, boy! She out to make a slave of you, you hear?

202

Breath low in his chest, rasping. He grates his teeth together, the veins cording in the thickness of his neck. She ain't about to git away with this!

He turns, following the quaking path through the mud, going back the way he came.

She's still there when he gets back, squatted by the entrance of the shelter with her knees up to her chin, hugging them with her arms. At his sudden appearance she glances up, frowning. He glares back at her, bitterness like poison in him, running thick and venomous in the blood. For a long time neither one of them speaks.

'Figgered you might bring somethin' back,' Mary says at last.

'Yeah, that right? Looks like you figgered wrong.' He slumps heavily to the ground, dragging the bow from his back, laying the quiver by him. Eyeing her over his shoulder.

'We gonna have us a talk, I reckon,' Justus says.

'Ain't much to be said, is there?' Mary's voice takes on an unaccustomed shrillness. She gets to her feet, dusting stray flecks of grass from the torn calico dress, anger and despair struggling together in her speech and in her pale eyes. 'Ain't moved from this place in days. Ain't got no mind to move a-tall, you ask me....'

'Now listen here—' he begins, rage already choking him as he speaks. She cuts him off, her face in its anger taking on an ugly, mocking look.

'I thought we were gonna get *out* from this wilderness sometime!' Her voice rings through the sheltering trees, accusing him, the echoes drifting back all around. 'Looks like I was wrong there, too, don't it? We gonna be stuck here forever ... ain't never gonna get out....'

'I tole you—' Protesting now, holding vainly to the rising fury within. 'I aim to try for the big water....'

'The hell with your big water!' Her voice hits back at him, shrieking now, her blue eyes ablaze. 'What you know about anythin', anyhow? You just a dumb nigra, Justus, you hear? You don't know nothin'....'

He's on his feet, lungeing fast towards her with his great hands open. All hope of words lost as the rage consumes him utterly.

Wanting to hurt her, to humiliate her the way she hurt him with those pitiless, wounding words. Right now the sting of them is keener than Lawrence's whip, putting an edge to his anger.

'You gonna find out who boss here, woman. You hear me?'

Faced by the advancing black shape, Mary turns pale for an instant, but her own anger holds her fast. Tight-lipped, she grabs the bow from the wall. Hurls it toward him as he comes in. He ducks the flying weapon, feeling the tip sting his shoulder in the moment before he swats it aside to the ground. Going for her as she stands to meet him, striking out with bunched fists for his face. Justus wards off the blows with his arm. He grabs hold of her flailing arms, forcing them down.

That first instant or so she fights against him with all her strength. He feels the despairing rage inside her, giving a steely power to her wrists. He snarls, teeth bared in effort as his own huge muscles exert themselves. Across from him the blue-eyed stare wavers, the face flinching in sudden paid. Abruptly her arms go down.

'You listen to me now, you hear?' Breath coming harsh as he stares her in the eye, his hands heavy on her shoulders, forcing her down before him.

The last of her strength gives out with a pent-up sobbing sound and Mary sinks under his hands, sliding slowly down against his legs until she kneels in front of him.

Same instant, looking down on that bent head, he feels the meanness go from him like a boil bursting, venom seeping from the wound. On her shoulders his hands go gentle, touching light at the bruises on her flesh. The long, shuddering sound of their breathing the one sound in the stillness.

'Mary,' his voice trembling. 'Mary, honey . . . I'm sorry. . . .'

'Me too.' Her voice answering, almost inaudible, her face at his loins as she speaks. Her warm breath, fanning him through his breeches. 'Don't hardly know what come over me. Guess I'm just a bitch, an' that's all there is to it. . . .'

'You quit that, you hear?' His throat tightening of a sudden, eyes filling up the same moment so he looks down at her through a wellin mist. 'Ain't no-one for me but you, Mary. You know that. . . .'

He reaches to her, making as if to draw her up with him, but she stays there, kneeling, her hot face against him still. When she glances up at last, she smiles.

'Gonna take the sting from you, you big black son,' Mary says.

He watches her, only half believing what he sees as she lays her fingers on the growing bulge in his breeches, works slowly at the buttons until they open, one by one.

'You don't have to do that, honey,' he says, but the thick tautness of the speech betrays him. Mary smiles, reaches her hand in at the unbuttoned space.

'Don't talk,' she tells him.

Feeling her hand close on him, he swallows, his eyes closing. At once his manhood grown huge, swollen, a thick throbbing, ebony staff that fights her enclosing fingers. Her breath on his bare flesh, shivering. Mary leans forward slowly, brings her mouth to him.

Sudden leaping sensation as she takes him, holding him gently between her lips, enfolding him utterly. Sight goes to a blaze of black and gold. Every feeling in his body drawn down into that pulsing root that swells like it about to burst any time now.

'Oh, Mary. . . .' Melting now, leaning against her as the fierce pleasure takes over. His hand at her hair, fondling as she works on him. 'Mary honey, that so sweet . . . so sweet. . . .'

Pleasure spirals upward, searing at every fibre of his nerves. Groans aloud, his head falling back, reaches down inside her dress to fondle her breasts, the warm nipples coming up hard against his palms. Ain't never been nothin' like this before, not with any woman he ever known. Feeling her rear against him now as her mouth takes him all the way in. The bright flare of light explodes suddenly. He gasps, shuddering against her, Mary taking his jissom as it spurts from him in fierce, jetting spasms, the moment of orgasm overwhelming him, blotting out the world. . . .

Afterwards, it like a world ending. Spent, he sags to earth, to lie beside her now in stillness, his manhood drained. Neither one speaking as he holds her to him, as if to will away the distance that has been.

'What in hell we been fightin' over?' he asks at last.

Mary doesn't answer. Reaches instead to lay a finger to his lips.

Her own eyes are still closed, her breathing hard and rapid, the taut breasts straining against the cloth that covers them. Sated as he is, he sees her own unquenched need. She too roused, unsatisfied.

Yeah, Justus thinks. He owe her that, at least. After what she done.

He leans over, touching her gently, fondling her breasts until she shivers, murmuring, ready for him. Justus reaches under the dress, fingers hooked into the waistband of her drawers, easing them down, away from her. Mary grasps his hand, guides it home between her thighs, her eyes opening, looking up to him. Each smiles on the other. They do not speak.

One bee gonna seek out the honey, Justus thinks.

He lifts the dress back over her breast, feeling her slim body tremble, and goes down, burying his face in the soft bush of hair, her hands in his own thick fleece as she opens to him, her voice above him, calling his name. . . .

THAT NIGHT, lying beside her in the moist dark, he speaks again.

'We gonna move, girl,' Justus tells her, 'strike out south through the bayous, far as we kin go. Sooner or later we git loose from this wilderness. . . .'

'You reckon?' Mary turning in his arms, snuggling close to him in the warm gloom of the shelter. No mockery to her question now. Smiling as she asks it of him, half-asleep.

Justus swallows, remembering. Lays his hand gently on the thick blond tresses of her hair.

'That a promise, honey,' he says. 'I git you from here if it the last thing I do.'

Afterwards when she sleeps at last, he lies awake, staring up to the black roof of the shelter, sweat breaking out on his brow, even at this late hour. He brushes at it angrily, thinking of the promise he has made.

No way back, boy. It what you tole her, ain't it? It gonna have to be.

He got the feelin', though, it ain't gonna be too easy.

NEL BESTSELLERS

T037061	BLOOD AND MONEY	*Thomas Thompson*	£1.50
T045692	THE BLACK HOLE	*Alan Dean Foster*	95p
T049817	MEMORIES OF ANOTHER DAY	*Harold Robbins*	£1.95
T049701	THE DARK	*James Herbert*	£1.50
T045528	THE STAND	*Stephen King*	£1.75
T065475	I BOUGHT A MOUNTAIN	*Thomas Firbank*	£1.50
T050203	IN THE TEETH OF THE EVIDENCE	*Dorothy L. Sayers*	£1.25
T050777	STRANGER IN A STRANGE LAND	*Robert Heinlein*	£1.75
T050807	79 PARK AVENUE	*Harold Robbins*	£1.75
T042308	DUNE	*Frank Herbert*	£1.50
T045137	THE MOON IS A HARSH MISTRESS	*Robert Heinlein*	£1.25
T050149	THE INHERITORS	*Harold Robbins*	£1.75
T049620	RICH MAN, POOR MAN	*Irwin Shaw*	£1.60
T046710	EDGE 36: TOWN ON TRIAL	*George G. Gilman*	£1.00
T037541	DEVIL'S GUARD	*Robert Elford*	£1.25
T050629	THE RATS	*James Herbert*	£1.25
T050874	CARRIE	*Stephen King*	£1.50
T050610	THE FOG	*James Herbert*	£1.25
T041867	THE MIXED BLESSING	*Helen Van Slyke*	£1.50
T038629	THIN AIR	*Simpson & Burger*	95p
T038602	THE APOCALYPSE	*Jeffrey Konvitz*	95p
T046850	WEB OF EVERYWHERE	*John Brunner*	85p

NEL P.O. BOX 11, FALMOUTH TR10 9EN, CORNWALL

Postage charge:

U.K. Customers. Please allow 40p for the first book, 18p for the second book, 13p for each additional book ordered, to a maximum charge of £1.49, in addition to cover price.

B.F.P.O. & Eire. Please allow 40p for the first book, 18p for the second book, 13p per copy for the next 7 books, thereafter 7p per book, in addition to cover price.

Overseas Customers. Please allow 60p for the first book plus 18p per copy for each additional book, in addition to cover price.

Please send cheque or postal order (no currency).

Name ....

Address ....

....

Title ....

While every effort is made to keep prices steady, it is sometimes necessary to increase prices at short notice. New English Library reserve the right to show on covers and charge new retail prices which may differ from those advertised in the text or elsewhere.(5)